ByProduct presents a **DARK TRAILS** adventure:

DARK WATERS

THE VOYAGE OF THE *BAR JACK*

BY MARK MURPHY HARMS

Also by Mark Murphy Harms

Delivered to the Ground

Dark Waters is a work of fiction.

A ByProduct Imprint

ByProduct Publishing

2608 York Ave. N

Robbinsdale, MN 55422

ISBN 978-1-7340726-2-4

Cover design by Charles Ross

Copy editing by Janie Barnell

Title page drawing by Chris Beck

Note appended to document:

This is a faithful reproduction of a manuscript written by Sir James Henry Ker LeRoque. It is a private work not intended for publication and should be respected as such.

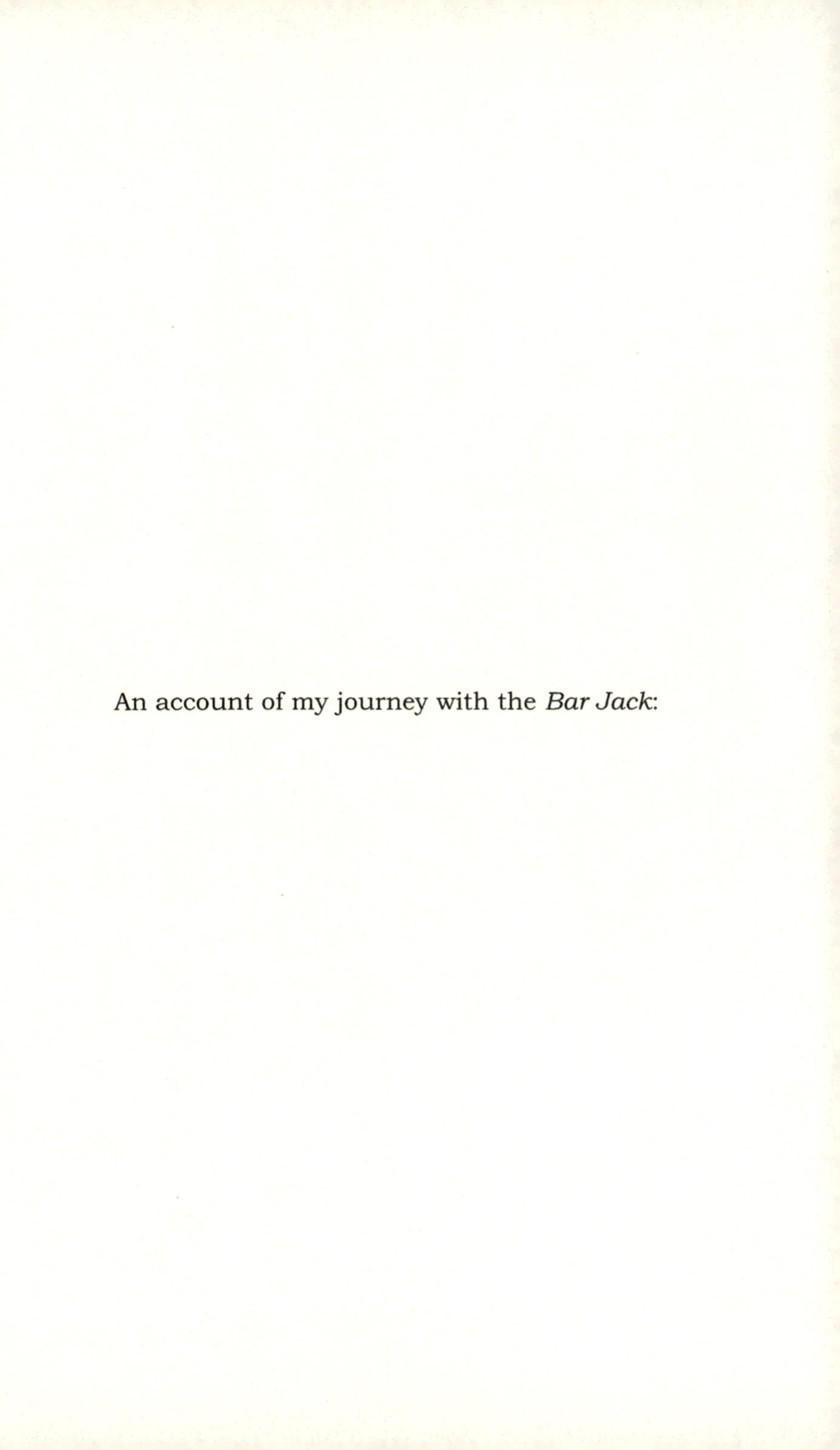

An account of my journey with the *Bar Jack*:

United States
Texas
New Orleans
Galveston Island
Seminole Confederacy
Angola
Gulf of Mexico
Mexico
N
W
E
S
0
300
Miles
El Radio
Havana
Cuba
Isle of Youth
Bay of Pigs
Volcan Rojo
Yucatan Straight
Merida
Chichen Itza
Campeche
Yucatan
Veracruz
Isla Lanza
Villa Hermosa
Tabasco
Palenque
Cayman Islands
Jamaica
Barbados
Kingston

Chapter 1: A Fool's Errand

17 February, 1819, London

With a degree of nervousness, I stepped out of the carriage and beheld the imposing edifice of Newgate Prison, made more ominous by the chilly winter drizzle. The gloomy interior of gray stone, heavy banded doors and iron gates did little to lighten my mood, nor did the stench. The Keeper ushered me down a corridor and into a small visiting room.

"Wait here, sir, if you please," he said. "We'll bring the prisoner shortly."

The door clanged shut. I removed my gloves and top hat, put them on the rough-hewn wooden table, sat down and checked my pocket watch – ten o'clock. As I idled the minutes, my nervousness verged on trepidation. I was about to meet a pirate.

The pirate had been the sailing master of the notorious *Vipere*, a French-built corvette that had dared to prowl the waters off England's coast, plundering many valuable cargoes. Its crew even once brazenly pillaged a seaside village, murdering two of its men and raping several women. Despite the war and the threat of invasion, the Admiralty had to act. Piracy in the remote corners of the world could be overlooked pending other priorities, but piracy so close to home could not be suffered.

A squadron was dispatched but the *Vipere* kept eluding its grasp. Eventually a timely bit of information led the squadron to the West Indies and, after a lively chase, it cornered the *Vipere* and battered it into submission. The surviving crew members were hauled back to London, tried and sentenced to hang. However, after last year's colossal naval battle at Guernsey, the King suspended the hanging of pirates, such was the need for men to refill the depleted ranks of the Royal Navy.

The door opposite me opened and a guard escorted the shackled prisoner into the room. Though I am loathe to admit it, my nervousness edged toward fear when the prisoner sat in the chair across the table. There was a disturbing fierceness in the eyes of the pirate before me, the eyes of Ann Rackham.

"Sir, is there anything else you require?" The guard asked.

"No, thank you, you may leave us," I replied.

I had assumed she would be an imposing woman but she was actually rather small, and younger than I expected, or appeared so. The plain brown gown she wore did little to highlight her figure. Her dark hair was cropped short, only hanging to her shoulders. Her skin, while fine, had a ruddiness to it that suggested mixed breeding, as did her thick eyebrows, which made for an unsettling contrast with her blue eyes. She might have been called pretty, especially if dressed and made up properly, but for the deep scar that angled from the outside of her left eye down to the corner of her mouth.

"Miss Ann Rackham, I presume," I said.

She nodded.

"Pleased to make your acquaintance," I continued. "My name is Sir James LeRoque."

"How may I be of service, Sir James LeRoque?"

I had expected a grittier voice, like the gruff speech heard in the criminal rookeries of the East End, but hers had a song-like quality, sweet even, which made the undertone of contempt all the more unnerving.

"I'll get straight to the point," I said. "I purchased a small ship and need a sailing master. You may have the post if you wish it, though the voyage could turn very dangerous."

She squinted the slightest of smiles.

"Scraping the bottom of the barrel aren't we, sir, trying to pluck me out of this rat hole."

Her accent was American, though which region, I wasn't sure, southern states perhaps. Her bluntness was off-putting but I had to remind myself she was a pirate and accustomed to working alongside coarse men.

"The availability of sailing masters is, I admit, rather limited at this time," I replied. "But, beyond scarcity, there are other things that recommend you. For one you are familiar with the waters of the West Indies and the Gulf of Mexico."

"Where do you plan to go?"

"I intend to follow the route of a scientific expedition launched nearly two years ago and now presumed lost. A friend, a good friend, Dr. Paul Seymour, was the lead naturalist of the expedition. I want to find him or learn what fate befell him. He was going to the shores of the Yucatan peninsula."

"Volcan Rojo?"

"Yes."

"It was a suicide mission, then," Miss Rackham said.

"The ship, the H.M.S. *Squirrel*, was well armed, a 22-gun sloop of war. Little but a French frigate or a hurricane would pose a threat."

"I doubt a 100-gun ship-of-the-line would be safe plunging into the heart of El Radio."

El Radio, or The Radius, is what sailors were calling the area around the newly formed volcano that erupted in 1815 off the coast of southern Mexico.

"You believe, then," I said, "the stories of sea monsters."

"The stories are lies," she said, "because no one who goes deep into El Radio returns to tell a story."

"I will go where I must."

"And you think I'm fool enough to take you."

"A fool's errand it may be," I said. "But wouldn't you rather die at the helm at sea than rot here until you are eventually hanged? It is true the navy has pressed many of your colleagues into service with promises of amnesty, but the navy will not take a woman. I'm likely the only one fool enough to seek your services."

Her look hardened, then, slowly, the fierceness retreated from her eyes. An expression of anguish crossed her face, reflecting, I surmised, a deeper anguish.

"Can you offer me amnesty?" She asked.

"Yes," I said. "My brother, Archibald LeRoque, is the Earl of Kirkaldy in Scotland, a member of the House of Lords, and serves as liaison to the prime minister. He was able to secure a parole for you and a full pardon pending my safe return. Mind you, we have the Admiralty's blessing but little else. This is a private endeavor that I'm financing with what fortune I have."

"What sort of ship?"

"A two-masted schooner called the *Bar Jack*. She was a prize taken by a privateer but her disposition was tied up in the courts. She's been docked at Bristol for two years. I was able to obtain her for a discounted price. She took a bit of a beating during her capture so she'll need refurbishing."

"Is she armed?"

"No, but she's modern and Bermuda rigged. Should be quite fast, I am told, once we get her up to par. I assume you are familiar with Bermuda rigging."

"Yes," Miss Rackham said. "Who's the captain?"

"I'll be the captain," I said.

"What ships have you commanded?"

"None, save my family's yacht."

She shook her head. "Do you have a crew?"

"Ah, not just yet," I said. "Crews are no easier to find than sailing masters, but that brings me to another reason that recommends your services: I intend to crew the *Bar Jack* with women."

"You must be joking."

"I'm afraid not. My cousin suggested it. She tells me the McIntyres back home have crewed a whaler with mostly women, so desperate they were for hands after the navy came through and nabbed every able-bodied seaman they could find."

Miss Rackham rubbed her face with her shackled hands. I thought perhaps she was going to sob, then she looked at me with a weary expression.

"You want me to be master of a ship of fools," she said.

I gave her my best smile, suddenly feeling better about the interview.

"Indeed," I said. "Will you take the post?"

It was her turn to smile and I detected a spark in her eyes that revived my nervousness.

"What choice do I have, Captain LeRoque? Yes, I'm your man," she said.

* * *

I told Miss Rackham that her release would be secured in three days' time and I would arrive in the morning with a coach to take her to Bristol. On my way out, it occurred to me that traveling in a prison gown would not do, so I took a carriage to a ladies' clothier in Piccadilly.

"Nothing fancy," I told the clerk. "Something respectable for traveling. A bonnet, I suppose, too, and suitable undergarments and shoes."

I regretted I had to approximate Miss Rackham's size. I scribbled a note to the Keeper and instructed the clerk to have the package delivered to Newgate Prison. From the shop I went to meet a dear friend for lunch at Boodle's Gentlemen's Club.

* * *

"Good God, James, you've gone off your chump," Major Elliot Darnsby said when I told him of the venture I was organizing. Darnsby was on leave from the Royal Horse Artillery. He had been among the few who escaped the debacle at Waterloo.

"Yes, I quite possibly have gone mad," I said. "But no one is lifting a finger for Paul, or for the brave men of the *Squirrel.* I feel honor bound to try."

After eating we had retired to the lounge. Darnsby waved the waiter over to pour another glass of port.

"Poor Paul, the lad was brilliant." Darnsby gestured broadly with his cigar. "If anyone could have found the answers to the mess the world's in, it was Paul."

"He may yet live," I said. "We don't know. If there's a chance of saving him, we should at least make the attempt."

"The attempt could endanger your life, and the lives of your crew. It's an awful risk, James."

"I intend to be as circumspect as possible. I shall call on Bridgetown, Kingston, possibly Veracruz and other ports. If I learn the *Squirrel* was destroyed and all hands lost, I will consider the quest fulfilled. As to my crew, I will make it plain to them the dangers we may face."

"You might have trouble filling your ranks," Darnsby said.

"Perhaps, but I already have one volunteer – the wife of the *Squirrel*'s carpenter. She seems at least as determined as myself. And, of course, there's Miss Rackham."

"Can you trust her, old boy? She is a pirate."

"Time will tell," I said. "I know how to read a chart and know the basics of navigation. I don't think she could hoodwink me in that way."

"You know, of course, the name, 'Ann Rackham,' is fiction. Remember our school days reading Charles Johnson, his account of Jack Rackham and Anne Bonny, the notorious pirate couple?"

I shrugged. "Perhaps she's a descendant."

"Ha!"

Darnsby sat back, puffed his cigar and stared up at the silver chandelier. Though I am not short, he was taller than me and blond haired. We had been friends since childhood and shared a room for a time at Cambridge. I leaned over and clutched his wrist.

"Come with me, Elliot," I said. "It's a grand adventure, with purpose to it, like we dreamt of as boys."

Darnsby put his hand on mine.

"My heart yearns to go, old friend, make no mistake, but I am duty-bound to the service. You know old Bonaparte is biding his time before he has another go at our island. The peace talks just go round and round."

I sat back, taking my turn to contemplate the chandelier. I knew the threat of invasion was real. We barely fended off Napoleon's fleet at Guernsey. Times were dark – England's holdings in the Mediterranean lost, India beset by rebellions, the colonies in the West Indies struggling. Louisa, my cousin, had insisted these events were not supposed to have happened, something had gone terribly wrong and it was tied to the Aurora and the eruption off Mexico. She was not alone in her thinking, though I was skeptical. Paul thought he had found the key, anitite, he called it, a peculiar alloy of iron and nickel. Gathering a substantial sample for study was the primary purpose of the *Squirrel* expedition.

"You know, old man," Darnsby said, breaking my reverie. "You could use someone who knows how to fight on your little venture, some muscle as the rogues say."

"I intend to avoid violence," I said. "But, if assailed, I know how to defend myself. While I could never best you at boxing, I had the upper hand when it came to fencing."

"You'll need more than skill with a small sword."

"I'm a fair hand with a pistol and a rifle."

"No, I mean real combat. When it comes, if it comes, it will be like nothing you've experienced - fast and brutal, an overwhelming chaos where the finer points of fencing rarely apply."

"I cannot doubt what you say, given what you've been through. I'll have to hope I can rise to the occasion."

"There's no rising to the occasion, James, just sinking to your bloodiest instincts. It can make all the difference if you have someone with experience. I have someone in mind who just might be persuaded to go with you."

* * *

That night, in my rooms at the hotel, I fetched my small sword and withdrew it from its scabbard. It was an elegant little weapon, a nimble thruster, light and convenient to carry, but, after what Darnsby had said, it seemed inadequate. I thought about the broadsword hanging on the wall at our family manor in Kirkaldy, its formidable double-edged blade and basket hilt from which hung a colorful tassel. I remembered surreptitiously playing with it as a boy, dreaming of my ancestor on the rough side of the family, the Ker side, who fought with the Highlanders at Culloden.

I appended my letter to Louisa, instructing her to send the sword forthwith to Bristol.

* * *

The next afternoon Darnsby introduced me to Leopold von Sydow at a tavern on Boswell Street. Sydow was a lean man, tall, dark-haired, who, contrary to fashion, wore a beard. He was courteous but his gray eyes were not welcoming.

Darnsby had said that he and Sydow met during the chaos that reigned after the defeat at Waterloo. Sydow was a son of a minor baron and had been a cavalry officer in the Prussian army. He and Darnsby and the remnants of their respective units, through several scrapes and close calls, made it to the coast and escaped on an English warship. Sydow had studied natural history and indulged a hobby of taxidermy. After arriving in England, not wanting to return to a Napoleon-ruled Prussia, Sydow found work at the British Museum.

While I talked about my plans, Sydow's stern expression never changed except the slight raising of an eyebrow when I mentioned crewing my ship with women. After I finished, he remained silent a moment.

"What is a good English word? Ah, yes – preposterous," Sydow said with all the weight of his German accent.

"That's what I told the lad," Darnsby said. "Mad as a tricorn hatter, but he's determined to tilt this windmill. What do you say, Leo, my man? It's more exciting than stuffing birds at Montagu, a chance for some action, see the world, and all that."

I was gratified that Darnsby was playing the advocate. A soldier like Sydow would be a comfort to have to hand. It was obvious to me, however, that he would decline.

"Herr LeRoque," the Prussian officer replied. "You may add one more fool to your crew."

Chapter 2: The Road to Bristol

Letter dated 3 April, 1815:

Dearest James,

I know you deplore superstition and you'll probably find the following to be the ravings of lunatic but I feel I must confide in you. Four nights ago I was entertaining a few friends, it was getting late and we perhaps imbibed a bit too much wine, when young Juliet McIntyre suggested I conduct a tarot reading. I agreed and she wheeled me over to the whist table where I fetched my deck from the drawer.

"What question," I asked Juliet, "would you like answered?"

She thought for a moment then proclaimed: "The question shall be, 'What is the fate of mankind?'"

Ever philosophical, Juliet didn't dilly with questions like, "What kind of man will I marry?"

"So be it," I said.

I closed my eyes while shuffling the cards and endeavored to open my mind to the inscrutable powers of the world. I felt an odd tingling at the back of my neck. Must be the wine, I supposed. Satisfied with the shuffling, I opened my eyes and set the deck on the table.

"Cut," I commanded.

Juliet did so with an exaggerated gesture while the other ladies laughed. We were quite beside ourselves. Slowly I laid out the cards using Sforza's hexagonal three-in-six spread, which I found to be manageable and always seemed to suggest the best stories. Such an array of major arcana! You wouldn't have believed it – the Fool, the Magus, the Empress, the Devil and the Moon made up five of the spokes and the last was the troubling Two of Disks. I grew worried, though I knew not why, and hesitated to continue.

"Is anything the matter, Louisa?" Juliet asked.

"I don't know," I replied.

I forged ahead and drew the inner triad: The Hanged Man, Death and the Wheel of Fortune. The last set to motion a spinning in my head, images and scenes flashed in my mind – a colossal pillar of smoke with a ball of flame billowing at the top; savages performing ecstatic rites; images of creatures too alien or demonic to describe; and scenes of a great battle where blue-coated soldiers slaughtered those in red. I felt a presence undergirding it all, a malign intelligence, a vast rage, enduring from untold depths of time and now set loose. I heard screaming. The screaming, I was later told, was my own.

The episode ended quickly and soon I recovered my senses. Needless to say, the ladies were quite put out, except Juliet, of course.

"I gather the fate of mankind is not what we'd hope," she said.

I know you must think it was just a case of feverish nerves but there was realness to the vision that I cannot set aside as mere delirium. And, as you must know, the next night the sky blazed with an aurora of unheard of intensity. I feel it in my bones, James, the world has changed and in a way that should not have happened. I find that it excites my interest as much as it terrifies me.

I do so hope you are well. Please come visit when your studies allow. I miss our conversations and our arguments.

Your loving cousin and obedient servant,

Louisa Henrietta Ker LeRoque

* * *

20 February, 1819, London

Mr. Leopold von Sydow met me very early in the hotel lobby, a single trunk and a leather satchel his only luggage. He wore a top hat and a gray frock coat of high quality but considerable wear. We were served coffee while we waited for the coach I'd hired.

I told Sydow that I would consider him my second in command, though we would have to defer to Miss Rackham regarding matters of sailing. Sydow told me his employer, far from being put out by his abrupt departure, had given him a list of animals and plants and said he would be paid well for any specimens of which he could bring back. His employer, the British Museum's chief naturalist, also asked him to keep detailed notes of his journey. These could prove useful to subsequent research. Upon reflection this did not surprise me. The ranks of the scientific community, I knew, were eager for reliable information about the region to which we were headed, a region now cast in shadow.

* * *

I must admit to how comely Miss Rackham looked when she emerged from the doors of Newgate Prison. The gown I'd purchased fit admirably well. Yet she moved awkwardly in it and, as she approached, her deep frown, framed by the bonnet and accentuated by the scar, implied she was not happy wearing it.

I introduced her to Sydow and the three of us boarded the coach bound for Bristol. Miss Rackham had no luggage. She and Sydow regarded each other warily and my taciturn companions said little as we got underway.

I fell to thinking about that letter I'd received from Louisa four years prior, how worried it had made me, not for the fate of the world, but for Louisa's health. I had been anxious to return to Kirkaldy but, as I was standing soon for my doctorate, I couldn't get away. The disaster at Waterloo followed two months later and I found it difficult to dismiss the notion that Louisa had somehow foreseen it.

I did manage to return to Kirkaldy that July and was cheered to find Louisa in good health and good spirits, though I was a little alarmed that she and her friend, Juliet McIntyre, had embarked on a deep study of the occult.

"You're right, James, it's mostly rubbish," Louisa had said. "But we're trying to sort what might be useful."

I didn't press the matter. She was always one to follow her enthusiasms. Anything that could keep her spirits up had to be counted for the good. My cousin had been paralyzed from the waist down, the result of a riding accident when she was fifteen. Most assumed she would die, which was usually the case with such injuries. But a young doctor named Charles Bell had new ideas for treatment which included regular massaging and moving of her legs. While Louisa cannot walk, the rest of her bodily functions have remained healthy, or reasonably so. She was, however, prone to bouts of melancholia.

* * *

At the town of Maidenhead, we exchanged our city horses for a country team. Miss Rackham availed herself of the ladies' facility.

"I don't know what to make of that mädchen," Sydow said as the driver saw to hitching the new team. "Do you fear she might run off?"

"I have given the matter some thought," I said. "I don't think she would abandon us while we're in England. She's a foreigner here with no means of support. She might do so later, I suppose, at a distant port of call, but I've decided to trust her come what may. My cousin urged that I do so. She has an intuition for these things."

"Your cousin knows Miss Rackham?"

"No, but she has a foresight I've come to respect."

Sydow responded with a look of amusement, whether at my credulousness or the general nature of our nervous times, I couldn't say.

Soon we were on our way. The sun made an appearance which eased the winter chill and made the landscape less dreary.

"So you're a pirate," Sydow said to Miss Rackham as we jostled along a rough stretch of road.

"I was a pirate," she replied.

"What are you now?" He asked.

"Sailing master of the *Bar Jack* in the employ of the honorable Sir James LeRoque. What are you, Mr. von Sydow?"

Sydow grunted, then said: "Much the same. I was a soldier. I assumed I would be again but who can say... in diesen schwarzen tagen."

"Tell us about your experience at Waterloo," I said.

"I only saw the battle at a distance," Sydow said.

I urged him on and he explained that he was second in command of a Prussian cavalry detachment sent ahead to make contact with the British. It was then that an extraordinary storm hit the main body of the Prussians. Sydow's detachment was on the fringes of the storm but still had to take shelter. When the storm subsided, they pressed on and when they reached the battlefield, they found the British army in rout. Sydow and his men tried to return to their own force but were cut off by French cavalry. The detachment turned north, hoping to circle around, and that is when they joined forces with Darnsby's unit fleeing the battlefield. The French pursued vigorously as they ran for the coast, battling their way through skirmish lines to get there. A fortunate encounter with a British ship-of-the-line enabled their escape, its guns holding the French at bay.

What Sydow couldn't know at the time was that the British army had fallen into disarray because an aide, on the eve of battle, had shot and killed its commander, the Duke of Wellington, before turning a pistol on himself.

Black days indeed.

* * *

Several miles beyond Reading we stopped at a country inn. Sydow and I shared a room while Miss Rackham took one of her own. I remained uneasy about her; she had been so quiet. However, she met us promptly for breakfast then we were on our way. She did not wear the bonnet. We trundled along the North Wessex downs on a chalky road under low, thick clouds.

"Perhaps you could tell us something interesting about your travels, Miss Rackham," I said, hoping to coax a few words from her.

"I don't want to talk about my past," she said.

"What do you want to talk about?"

"How long is the *Bar Jack*?"

"Eighty-eight feet," I answered.

"Beam?"

"Nineteen and half feet, I believe."

"Where was she built?"

"Bermuda, in 1804. She was sold to an American merchant; his name escapes me. I understand she was originally gaff rigged and later converted to Bermudian."

"What's the look of her lines?"

"I can't rightly say, I've never seen her. I'm told she resembles the H.M.S. *Pickle* except longer and a higher aft deck. I'm wondering how many hands we'll need ..."

The coach skidded to a halt; the horses whinnied and jostled in their tackle.

"Was ist das?" Sydow exclaimed.

Through the window to my right, I saw a man with a scarf over his face holding a blunderbuss.

"Stop there!" Came a shout from the left side.

Through the other window I could see two more masked men, each with a pistol in his hand and another holstered.

"Hands in the air, driver," one of the men on the left said. "This is a robbery in case you need to be told. You folks in the coach, come on out now, nice and slow if you please."

Sydow withdrew a small pistol he kept under his coat.

"Put that away," I said. "You'll get us killed."

"Right," Miss Rackham said while tying on her bonnet. "We should play it calm for now."

She and Sydow eyed each other for a moment, then he put the pistol back in his coat.

"Come along, folks, or this will get ugly real quick like," the man outside said.

Sydow pushed open the door, showed his hands and we all stepped out to find ourselves in a wooded area. The coach had rounded a bend and stopped because of a blockade of wooden spikes on the road. One of the robbers wore a woolen cap and had a full growth of beard under his scarf. The other was taller and thinner and wore a shabby top hat.

"What have we here, two gentlemen and a lass?" The man with the top hat said. "I do apologize for the inconvenience but we'll be needing your money and valuables. Keep your hands in the air, now."

The man with the blunderbuss came through the coach's cabin and out to our side.

"Nothing else in there," he said.

The robber with the top hat padded down Sydow and me, extracting our wallets, coin purses, watches and Sydow's pistol.

"You know, loaded guns can be dangerous," he said, putting the pistol in his own coat. He then sorted through our purses and wallets.

The bearded man, the stoutest of the three, eyed Miss Rackham menacingly. My heart pumped wildly. I hoped this would end soon.

"Well, a tidy little haul," the man with the top hat said.

I wasn't sure how much Sydow carried but I had 20 guineas or so in spending money.

"We'd love to have a look at your luggage but I'm afraid we're a little pressed for time," top hat continued.

It was a well-used road. Another coach or wagon was bound to be along soon.

"I want the girl," the bearded man said in a grinding voice. As well as a second pistol, he had a long dirk hanging on his belt.

"Not practical, old man," top hat said. "You know the routine, take the cash and coin and be off. Like as not we'll just be a line on a magistrate's report. We take the girl, every bloke for miles around will be hunting us. No, no, we got enough here to keep us in pretty wenches and rum for months."

"I'm takin' the girl," the bearded man insisted.

He grabbed Miss Rackham with his free hand and pulled her close. She didn't make a sound.

"Take your hands off her!" I shouted.

The bearded man leveled his pistol at my face: "Another word and I'll put a hole in ya."

The man with the top hat reached out for Miss Rackham. "Be sensible. Let her go. We'll swing for sure if you keep on like this."

The bearded man turned his pistol on top hat. "Shove it up your arse. She's mine."

At that point Miss Rackham stuck her finger into the trigger guard of the bearded man's pistol. It went off with a crack. Blood and brains spewed from the back of top hat's head and he crumpled to the ground. The bearded man, surprised, staggered back and released Miss Rackham. Quickly, very quickly, she drew the man's dirk and thrust it into his solar plexus.

Sydow scooped a handful of gravel into the face of the man with the blunderbuss. Sydow charged him but the man deflected the rush and Sydow hurtled by. The man brought the blunderbuss to bear on Sydow.

Another crack, but it wasn't the blunderbuss. Miss Rackham had shot the last robber with the bearded man's second pistol. She stood there, a smoking gun in one hand, a bloody dirk in the other, and three men dead at her feet.

"Heiliger fick," Sydow said.

* * *

Elliot Darnsby was correct: battle was bloody and fast. I was not prepared for it and felt nauseous and light-headed. I watched Rackham wipe blood off the dirk with a dead man's scarf then reload the two pistols. She took the bearded man's belt, holstered the guns, sheathed the blade and tossed the rig into the coach.

"Spoils of war," she said.

I could articulate no objection.

"We should get the bodies off the road and clear the blockade," I said when my senses recovered sufficiently.

The driver was visibly shaken and I gave him my flask of whiskey to help his nerves but not before I took a pull of my own. The blockade looked more formidable than it was and soon we were ready to proceed, but the driver was in no condition to drive the team. Sydow took the reins and I sat beside him on the bench with the blunderbuss on my lap. He shook the reins and whistled the horses forward.

"She's a killer, that one is," Sydow said after a few miles.

"Indeed," I said. "Do you think it was a mistake engaging her services?"

"Mistake? Nein, kapitan, she is a kriegerin, a warrior."

Sydow produced his own flask, took a pull and handed it to me. It was awful English liquid but I drank it nonetheless.

"You did your part, Mr. von Sydow, but I was useless. I suppose I'm not a warrior."

"Ach! Don't worry yourself. I remember my first combat. All confusion and fear. I shouted senseless orders my men rightly ignored. You'll find your feet, kapitan."

* * *

We arrived in Swindon, found the magistrate, and explained what happened. He was unbelieving that a woman could do all that until I divulged that she was Ann Rackham. At that the magistrate was nonplussed and I had to produce the letter of release with the prime minister's seal and explain we were on urgent Admiralty business.

Too late to push on to Bristol, we found an inn. Lying in bed I wondered if I had what it took to see this quest through. I didn't know. I supposed that was what adventures were for, to find out what one was made of. I hoped it would be sterner stuff than so far revealed.

The next day we arrived in Bristol.

Chapter 3: The *Bar Jack*

23 February, 1819, Bristol

The three of us stood on one of the quays of Bristol's enormous harbor looking at the ship meant to carry us to far destinations. I was crestfallen and near despair. I had been told she had some damage but was not prepared for the mess of holes and splintered wood that was her deck. The *Bar Jack* was a shambles. Good God, the money I'd paid for her.

"We're going to sail in that?" Sydow said. "It's a wreck."

Rackham scrutinized the vessel, her reaction unreadable. I felt I had been hoodwinked. Perhaps I could sell it, take what I could get, then book passage to Bridgetown and hope to find something there. Rackham smiled, amused, I supposed, by the irony of the situation and my embarrassment.

"I'm sorry, Miss Rackham. I was assured the *Bar Jack* was seaworthy. Clearly I was misled."

She looked at me, still smiling, her eyes as bright and merry as a child's.

"The *Bar Jack* is a fine ship," she said. "Rakish even, I'll lay to that. We need a carpenter."

* * *

I was buoyed by Rackham's enthusiasm but remained dismayed with the condition of the *Bar Jack*'s deck. We boarded and closer inspection did not help – shattered windows, doors torn from their hinges, numerous holes, splintered wood, tangled rigging – it all seemed an impossible mess.

"This boom needs replacing but the masts are in good shape," Rackham said. "Let's see below."

The below deck, while musty, was in better shape. Rackham took the lantern I had brought, opened a hatch to the lower hold and poked her head in. She did the same with the other hatches.

"Looks sound, not much seepage. We'll want some ballast," she reported.

"The bottom was supposed to have been scraped and painted so that much should be done," I said.

The bill for the service had been extraordinary, twice what it would have normally cost. Rackham handed the lantern back to me and put her hands on her hips.

"I can't get to work in this damn gown," she said. "I'll need suitable clothes, tools and such."

"Of course," I said.

* * *

I advanced Rackham two months' salary so she could obtain clothing and other personal effects. I also gave her a fund she could draw on for ship's expenses and told her she must keep accounts. She went to do her shopping and Sydow accompanied her. I went to pay a call on Mrs. Brenda Kedward, wife of Thomas Kedward, the *Squirrel*'s carpenter.

Mrs. Kedward lived in a small but tidy cottage in Portishead, a nearby fishing village. She answered the door and I took off my top hat.

"Mrs. Kedward, if I may," I said. "Sir James LeRoque at your service."

She was a lean woman and strong, gripping my hand firmly. She had dark eyes and long, black hair woven into a braid and tinted with strands of gray. She had the serious bearing and determined countenance common to those of Welsh stock. She served tea.

"Are you certain you want to go?" I asked. "I intend to exercise the utmost caution; nevertheless we likely will face grave dangers."

"I'm as sure as a woman can be, sir," she said. "When I received the letter from your cousin, I knew immediately this was my opportunity to do something for Thomas. I must go. I would not want to live with myself if I declined."

The weight of what I was doing had been growing on me. Now it grew a little more.

"I'm pleased to have you along, ma'am," I said. "The state of our vessel is, at the moment, rather beleaguered. We are in need of a carpenter."

"Yes, I know, I went to look at the ship a few days ago," Mrs. Kedward said. "I can handle a hammer and saw – I grew up on a farm – but I don't know much about repairing ships. My father-in-law does. Rhys is a cripple, lost a foot in the service and has bad rheumatism, but I think I could persuade him to direct the repairs. He needs something to do other than sit in his chair and drink rum all day. He can't go with us, of course, but perhaps by the time we're done with repairs, I'll know enough."

"Mrs. Kedward, your words are music to my ears. Can you start tomorrow?"

"Rhys and I will be there if I have to carry the old toad myself."

* * *

On my way back to the quay, I stopped at a print shop to have hiring notices made up:

Wanted
Able-bodied women willing to serve
on long voyage aboard schooner Bar Jack.
Work will be hard and journey dangerous.
Will train.
Standard wage for starting sea hands.
Pay increase as merit determines.
Apply in person morning of 3 March at
Gull Quay, slip 9.
Proprietor and captain:
Sir James Henry Ker LeRoque

I was not optimistic the notice would attract suitable hands but it had to be tried.

I met Rackham and Sydow for supper at the Three Goats Inn where I had secured rooms. It was a rough-hewn place but its tavern had a congenial atmosphere with a mixed crowd of sailors and businessmen.

Rackham was now clad in brown trousers and a plain black pea coat which had the effect of hiding her female figure. After the meal she smoked a pipe with us and worked on her third pint of bitter.

"The sails are in bad shape," she said. "Even if we patch them, they won't hold up long. We asked around. It's going to be hard to find decent sailcloth."

"Well, my dear," I said, feeling a little smug after a second glass of port. "I actually anticipated that would be the case. My family's business, among other things, is textiles. Our mill in Kirkaldy specializes in sailcloth. I expect a shipment within two or three weeks, enough, I should think, for two sets."

"Uncut?"

"Yes, uncut. I wasn't sure of the proportions."

"That's good," Rackham said. "For the best, actually."

"You see, then, I'm not entirely useless."

"No, not entirely."

Sydow guffawed then said: "We need lumber and there isn't much around."

"I suppose that will be my next priority," I said.

I dreaded paying extortionist prices. My fortune, such as it was, was shrinking fast enough already.

* * *

On board the *Bar Jack* the next morning, I followed Rackham around with a ledger making a list of things we would need, a list that grew appallingly long – fittings, hinges, cookware, cordage, tools, etc. Fortunately the ship came with charts, a chronometer, barometer, compass and sextant which were held in a bank's vault.

Around 11 o'clock a wagon driven by Mrs. Kedward came down the quay. Next to her was an old man wearing an old-fashioned tricorn hat. The wagon was loaded with planks and beams.

"Ahoy," Mrs. Kedward said. "Sorry we're late. It occurred to me you'd need lumber. We were going to use it to add a room to the cottage when Thomas returned but I thought it could be put to better use here."

I was delighted with the unexpected boon and told Mrs. Kedward I would compensate her for the materials. She introduced Mr. Kedward and I introduced Rackham as Miss Ann Smith, an alias we had agreed to use.

We set to work and soon I was in shirtsleeves and sweating. Sydow and I mostly sawed away at splintered wood to be replaced with patching. Mr. Kedward hobbled around on a crutch directing the efforts. He and Rackham talked frequently about how the repairs should proceed. Mrs. Kedward applied herself to the finer work of shaping the new wood as needed.

The days following proceeded in similar fashion. I considered myself a fit man – I had regularly spent time at the Cambridge athletic club – but I was not accustomed to such labor. Sydow seemed to relish it. Calluses formed on my hands.

Rackham spent her mornings on board, taking measurements and devising a sail plan. Often, in the afternoons, she would wander off to scrounge in the city, usually returning with a couple of useful items like pulleys or cleats. Sydow occasionally went with her. They seemed to have developed a rapport.

One afternoon I was holding the door to the main cabin while Mrs. Kedward screwed in the hinges.

"I know Miss Smith is Ann Rackham," she said. "Louisa told me in her last letter you intended to hire her."

"I suppose I should scold Louisa in my next letter," I said.

"Miss Rackham sure knows a lot about ships and sailing," Mrs. Kedward said. "I wonder how she comes by it."

"I doubt my speculations would be any better than yours."

"This is what I think. She was an only child of a sea captain. Her mother died young so her father raised her on board a ship."

"Imaginative but possible," I said. "I do hope you don't spread around who she is. It could cause trouble."

"Mum's the word, captain, but people will wonder."

* * *

When the advertising sheets were ready, I hired two newsboys to post them on public notice boards in the vicinity. Rackham had suggested a crew of twenty. The ship could be handled with fewer but she didn't want to make the Atlantic crossing with just the minimum, particularly given the hands would be green.

Rackham was late that evening coming in from her afternoon wanderings. Sydow and I were about to retire when she appeared wearing a wide-brimmed leather hat she had picked up somewhere.

"I found two volunteers for our crew," she announced. "They seem like smart girls. I think they'll work out. I put them on board, told them they could stay there."

"Who are they? Don't they have their own places to stay?" I asked.

"Names are Jenny and Maggie. They were whores. Their pimp probably won't be too happy they left."

I was too astonished for words.

Sydow laughed. "Is that so? Perhaps I should pay a visit. Make sure they are comfortable."

"You'll do no such thing," I said. "Prostitutes? I won't have the *Bar Jack* become a brothel."

"They only whore because they have to," Rackham said. "They're tough girls and we need tough girls on this cruise. They won't be whoring anymore, I'll lay to that, so keep your wick in your breeches, Mr. von Sydow."

"I only have love for you, mein fraulein."

* * *

Maggie Wilson was a stout woman with an ample bosom while her friend, Jenny Cooper, was wiry thin with pretty eyes but a beak of a nose. Mrs. Kedward seemed put out by them at first but the pair showed they were ready workers and their help was welcome. The *Bar Jack* was beginning to look less of a wreck. She needed paint but that, too, was in short supply.

On the morning of 3 March, I put on a clean coat and top hat in the hope that the hiring notice would have attracted at least a few applicants. I was not prepared for the mass of women that had assembled on the quay.

"Heilige scheisse!" Sydow exclaimed.

Sydow, Rackham and I waded through the crowd to the gangway where Mrs. Kedward, her father-in-law, Jenny and Maggie held back the ladies.

"Make way for the captain!" Sydow bellowed.

There were several dozen applicants, some with children, all making their pleas to be hired. Most were young, some far too young. Was it the desperation of our times? I remembered Louisa's words when she suggested employing women: "Men go to sea seeking adventure. Many women have the same yearnings yet are deprived of opportunities. I think more than you suspect will answer the call." I didn't believe her until now.

I climbed up to the deck and turned to the crowd.

"Ladies! Ladies! May I have your attention. I am Captain James LeRoque. We were not expecting so many of you. Please be patient and we will interview you in due time."

I retreated to the cabin with Sydow, Rackham and Mrs. Kedward.

"What are we going to do?" I asked. "It will take a week to interview them all."

"Sailors need some strength to do their jobs," Rackham said. "I could devise a test to weed out the weaklings."

I agreed and Rackham made her preparations. I addressed the crowd again and instructed those with children, or who were pregnant, to go home.

Later I directed their attention to Rackham (whom I called "Miss Smith") She stood on the upper aft deck and picked up a crate loaded with tools, cleats and other weighty objects. She carried the crate down the steps and across the main deck where she set it down at the bow. She then pulled a halyard and raised a jib attached to the foremast and bowsprit. She lowered it again, picked up the crate and carried it back to the upper deck.

One by one the applicants attempted the same task. Some performed it easily, others couldn't lift the crate, many struggled to carry it down the steps. Several, knowing they would not be able to do it, went home. The women encouraged each other or jeered each other by turns.

The last in line, a tiny lass they called Kitten, gamely gave it go, though I had little hope for her success. She could hardly lift the crate so she put it down and dragged it to the steps, then, going backwards, she slid the crate down one step at a time, then over to the bow. She lacked the arm strength to pull the sail up so she used her legs, walking the halyard back, shimming up the line and repeating until the sail was hoisted. Dragging the crate back to the steps, she hauled it up, again, one step at a time, grunting and squeaking the whole way. When the crate was returned to its starting spot, she lay back, respiring heavily.

Cheers erupted. Sydow clapped. Kitten sat up and looked at me with questioning eyes. Technically she hadn't performed the task as demonstrated. I looked to Rackham, she gave me a nod, and I motioned Kitten to stand with the others who had succeeded, twenty-six in all. Now we had to winnow that number down to fourteen.

* * *

None of the women had any sailing skills to speak of. Rackham and Mrs. Kedward inquired about other skills – woodworking, writing, drawing, cooking and, especially, sewing. Sewing was useful in itself and it indicated capacity to learn knots, rigging and other complications of sailing. We took those that seemed to have the most knowledge. Kitten had few skills of these types. She was an orphan and, I surmised, survived by beggary and thievery.

"She's got spirit," Sydow said when the four of us discussed who to accept. "She can think under pressure. Good soldier material if she was a man."

We agreed to take her and our complement was filled. We assembled the recruits below decks where I addressed them:

"Thank you all for coming and for your eagerness to join the *Bar Jack*. Now it is my duty to attempt to persuade you not to join. A year and ten months ago, His Majesty's ship, the *Squirrel*, a 22-gun sloop-of-war, set sail for the West Indies on a scientific expedition. She has not returned nor has there been any word of her disposition. Our mission is to find her or discover what fate befell her. The journey will take us to what are arguably the most dangerous places on earth. Piracy is on the rise and Britain's relations with France, Spain and the United States are precarious. While I intend to avoid danger and confrontation, we may be compelled to journey into the area known as El Radio. You have likely heard stories ..."

The women murmured. I waited for it to subside.

"Yes, the peril could be great, perhaps insurmountable, but I believe we owe it to the brave men of the *Squirrel* to try. You may not, however, feel the same way and I would not argue against such feelings. It is quite possible that if you embark on this voyage, you will not return. Likely the most sensible thing for you to do now is go home. However, if you choose to stay ..."

I went on to explain that they would have to sign a contract and would be subject to maritime law and discipline. However, until we left port, they were free to leave with whatever pay was due them. All the women signed on. The moment was gratifying but added to that dread weight of responsibility.

"Don't be sentimental," Louisa had told me. "Women have as much right to risk their lives as men."

In any case, the *Bar Jack* had its crew.

Chapter 4: The Seer and the Savant

2 July, 1816, Kirkaldy, Scotland

A mild breeze blew in from the North Sea across the links pockmarked with white, sandy blowouts. The mist had receded under the morning sun and dew glistened on the verdant gorse. It was an unusually warm day in what had been, so far, an unusually cold summer. I rode with my cousin on the back of an old draft horse named Sadie who was large, plodding and very gentle.

"It's so lovely to get out into the air," Louisa said. "Thank you, James, for obliging me."

Her arms hugged my waist tightly and her useless legs dangled over Sadie's flanks.

"I have a notion of who's behind Napoleon's rising fortunes," she said.

"Is that so?" I replied.

"Yes, and I'll thank you not to be dismissive."

"I'm listening."

"Giselle LaFoy, Napoleon's consort."

"I've heard the name, the emperor's new dalliance."

"Do you know when she arrived at his court?"

"I suppose a few months ago when I'd heard talk of her."

"Earlier than that. Madame LaFoy arrived in April of last year, just after the Aurora, but that is not well known."

"Women come and go from the courts of kings and emperors," I said. "I don't see the coincidence as remarkable."

"Ah, but Juliet has learned more; she has relatives in France. Giselle was married to a French officer, Colonel Jacques LaFoy. They spent time in Spain during the French invasion. The colonel has since died."

"So now the widow seeks bigger fish," I said.

"The point is where the colonel died," Louisa said. "He died in the jungles of Mexico and Giselle was with him at the time. It happened shortly before the eruption of Volcan Rojo. They departed France on a frigate called the *Méduse* in 1814 just before Napoleon was exiled to Elba."

"Interesting, but I don't see how this ties to Napoleon's resurgence."

"According to your brother, the *Méduse* is listed by the Admiralty as whereabouts unknown. The ship never returned but Giselle did."

"There are other possible explanations," I said.

"Perhaps, but it is uncanny," Louisa said. "Think of it, the storm that scatters the Prussians, the aide that kills Wellington. These things shouldn't have happened. And there's another connection: The aide, Francis Whitaker, had relatives in France. He was a cousin of Giselle's. Your brother read the transcripts of the inquest."

"Does Archy take stock in your ideas?" I asked.

"No, he's harder headed than you, but he does think Wellington's murder was a plot of espionage."

"You think there's more to it than that."

"I think Giselle has powers and she's using them to support Napoleon."

We stopped at the shore near the village of Kinghorn and dismounted. We sat on an old bench and looked across the Firth of Forth to the distant harbor of Edinburgh. I recalled fond days of sailing in the bay. My brother and I and friends would take the yacht to the Leith waterfront and ply its many taverns, acting like we were true men of the sea. The old hands indulged us, knowing we were nobility.

"I know you don't believe me," Louisa said. A lock of her hair had escaped her riding cap and fluttered alluringly in the breeze. "But I've come to realize such powers are real or have become real. I've been experimenting and I have the knack, James. I can connect with other people's minds and communicate without speech and beyond earshot. More than this is possible, I'm sure."

My heart wanted to humor her, wanted to believe. I also worried I might have to take a firm hand to prevent her eccentricity from slipping into delusion and madness. Talk of magic and spirits had become common since the Aurora. It was the duty of rational minds to stand firm against such superstition. I didn't say anything, just gently tucked the loose strands of her hair back into their proper place.

"Let's go back home," she said. "I'll show you. I've been very scientific."

"And you'll give up this line of fantasy if your demonstration fails?"

"Agreed."

* * *

I lifted Louisa off the horse and set her into a wheelchair that her maid servant, Sophia Cobrero, had brought out. She pushed the chair into the house and I followed.

Miss Cobrero was one of the newer servants but she and Louisa had grown close. I was fond of her, too, in no small part because of her brown eyes, silky black hair and petite frame that was fetching even in the plainest of dresses. We went to the gaming parlor that had become Louisa's study. The billiard table bore stacks of books and she'd had her father's giant desk moved in which now was cluttered with papers and letters. We gathered around the whist table where Louisa did most of her entertaining.

"Now, James," Louisa said, "you and Sophie will go to the kitchen or the cellar or wherever you want. You will give her a word or phrase and she will communicate those words to me through her mind. You will return here without Sophie and I will tell you the words you have given her."

"Ridiculous," I said.

Miss Cobrero took my hand, gave me a mischievous smile and led me out of the parlor to the back of the kitchen.

"What are your words for Miss LeRoque, sir?" She asked.

It's funny in moments like this how hard it can be to think of something. I pondered a while, then said, "Scipio Africanus."

Miss Cobrero smiled and closed her eyes. She concentrated, her cheek twitched a little, then she opened her eyes.

"I have communicated your words to my mistress."

When I returned to the parlor, Louisa said, "Scipio Africanus."

I felt a chill. My mind stretched for an explanation.

"Uncanny, I admit," I said. "Perhaps the test was too easy. You know I've been working on an index of all mentions of Scipio in the classical literature."

"I know," she said. "You hope to write a definitive biography. We can try again, something more challenging."

An idea occurred to me.

"Give me your pen and ink and a sheet of paper," I said.

On the dining room table, out of sight of both women, I scribbled a few lines on the paper and folded it. I fetched Miss Cobrero from the pantry and took her outside to the gardener's shed. I wanted to make sure there were no signaling devices that had perhaps been placed in the pantry. I gave Miss Cobrero the paper.

"Communicate this, if you please," I said.

She read the lines silently and again concentrated. When she was done, I took her hand and led her to the main parlor and told her to sit still on the divan. I opened the door to the gaming parlor, just a crack, and told Louisa to recite the lines while I kept an eye on Miss Cobrero.

Louisa spoke:

And now Peter is taught to feel
That man's heart is a holy thing;
And Nature, through a world of death,
Breaths into him a second breath,
More searching than the breath of spring.

The words stunned me; the edifice of what I had believed cracked. The world was not what I thought it was. I sat on a nearby ottoman to collect myself. Louisa wheeled herself into the main parlor.

"Did I recite the lines to your satisfaction?" She asked.

I nodded.
"The verse is beautiful," Louisa continued, "but I don't know the poem. The style seems familiar."
"It's Wordsworth," I said. "The poem is unpublished. My friend, Roger, reviewed the manuscript a few weeks ago and he read the verse to me. You could not have known it. My God, Louisa, what is happening?"
"The world has changed, James."

* * *

11 November, 1816, Oxford

Dr. Paul Seymour greeted me warmly and we exchanged pleasantries over tea in the lounge of Wadham Hall. I had been wanting to visit since my return to Cambridge for the autumn term but various duties kept me from making the trip to Oxford until now. These had been trying days for everyone. The summer's chilly weather and abundant rain had ruined crops in much of the country and famine threatened.
My recent experiences with Louisa had raised many questions. We agreed her abilities should be kept secret but we also agreed that we should consult Paul who could be counted on to be discreet. If anyone could shine rational light on the phenomena I'd witnessed, it was him.
I told Seymour I wanted to speak in private and he led me to his office. He was a small man, lean, almost to the point of being gaunt. He'd always had the appetite of a sparrow. His office was tidy and seemed little used. I explained to him the abilities my sister had acquired, not only her ability to communicate with receptive individuals (I was not among them, though we had tried) but also her uncanny premonitions associated with Tarot cards.
Seymour stroked his chin.
"Hum, yes, I imagine the cards are largely incidental," he said. "A ritual that prepares the mind, like a batter's routine when standing before the wicket."
"You're not incredulous, then?"

"No, hum, I might have been, even a few months ago, but things have come to light that make what you say believable. You and Louisa are right to keep close counsel, however."

"What things have come to light?" I asked.

I first met Seymour at Cambridge. He was shy to the point of absurdity. I was drawn to his keen intelligence but it was Darnsby who drew him out, egged him to come with us on our adventures. Seymour turned out to be utterly fearless when it came to physical dangers but, among people, he stammered and fidgeted. Of girls he was terrified. He did overcome his shyness – Darnsby took credit for it – to the point where he was able to secure a position at Oxford and become a member of the Royal Society. He was a chemist and, by all accounts, a brilliant one.

"I've been wanting to confide in you," Seymour said. "Understand this must be kept in the strictest confidence."

"Of course," I said.

"After the eruption in the Gulf of Mexico and, as you probably know, the eruption of Mount Tambora in Indonesia shortly thereafter, I inferred that a great quantity of ash and other matter would have been spewed high into the atmosphere and eventually would encompass the globe. I, hum, wanted to see if I could capture some of it. I organized an outing to the Lake District with a few students. On the top of Skiddaw Mountain, we raised several large sheets of cheesecloth and let the wind buffet them for several days. The air up there, I assumed, would be clear of the pollutants of the cities.

"We carefully furled the cloth and returned to Oxford where we rinsed it in distilled water and boiled the water down until it left a crusty residue which I began to analyze. I discovered traces of various elements, nothing very unexpected, except, hum, what seemed like an unusual amount of kamacite, an alloy of iron and nickel commonly found in meteorites.

"I used a solvent to separate out the kamacite and analyzed it further. It behaved normally to most of my tests but I observed it was exhibiting chirality. This is something typically only seen in organic matter. Further tests showed it was subtly catalytic with certain organic chemicals. This struck me as odd because ..."

Seymour was soon deep into the details of chemistry that were beyond me.

"I hate to interrupt, my friend, but you're talking over my head," I said.

"Ah, hum, yes, I get carried away. The point is, hum, the point is ... Come with me. I'll show you."

* * *

A long table laden with beakers, vials and tools dominated Seymour's laboratory. Shelves along the walls contained the same kinds of items plus tins of various sizes and books. An unpleasant sulfuric odor prevailed.

"I had done about all I could do with the tiny amount of the alloy that I had," Seymour went on as I followed him to the back of the room. "I wracked my brain to devise other kinds of tests but failed to think of anything, not without a larger sample."

At the corner of the laboratory, Seymour pulled back a curtain in the corner that revealed a strange apparatus.

"Then I attended a lecture where Professor Darlington demonstrated his work with optics. I don't believe, hum, his work is very groundbreaking but it gave me an idea. He was kind enough to lend me some equipment which I modified."

Mounted horizontally on a tripod was a brass tube about a foot long and about four inches in diameter. A much narrower tube protruded from its side and was connected to a hand pump. Atop the main tube was a screw cap. One end of tube was connected to a shrouded lantern. On the opposite end, about four feet away, was an easel supporting a painter's canvas primed white.

"It was a whim, really," Seymour said. "I had no, hum, serious expectation that anything interesting would come of it, but why not shine some light on the alloy and see what I could see."

He prepared a demonstration, first by unscrewing the cap and spooning a dab of white powder into the tube.

"This is mostly ammonium nitrate," he said. "The actual alloy is not visible."

He screwed on the cap, then worked the pump to create a vacuum inside the tube. After which he held a small flame under the tube for a minute or so. Satisfied that it was warm enough, he inserted the flame into the lantern which flared before he closed its hatch.

"A magnesium concoction. It burns brightly but not for long," he said.

Seymour closed the curtain and bade me to sit on a stool near the device, then he removed a cover from the front end. An image of billowing smoke appeared on the canvas.

"A projection," I said. "This is fantastic."

"There's more. Wait a moment," Seymour said.

Soon what seemed like normal smoke formed into regular patterns, circles within circles, expanding, disappearing and being replaced by others. I looked on in wonder.

"I knew this was extraordinary," Seymour said, "but I didn't know what to make of it. I drew sketches to record it. At some point, hum, it occurred to me that it was responding to my moods or thoughts. Try thinking of something unpleasant."

I obliged by thinking of that dark day when Louisa broke her back. The image on the canvas changed – in the circles of smoke, what appeared to be sharp-edged caltrops spun out the center and off the edges.

"Incredible," I said.

"Now think of something pleasant."

My mind turned to Miss Cobrero as it often did during idle moments. The smokey image turned softer and became a series of unfurling petals like an exotic orchid that blossomed unendingly. It was like a dream and soothing. Then the lantern went out and the display was over.

* * *

Seymour fetched his portfolio of drawings and we went back to his office. I was glad to get away from the fetid odor of the laboratory. He handed the portfolio to me and I slowly leafed through the sketches. The images resembled what I had seen but with considerable variety.

"I've dubbed the alloy, anitite," Seymour said. "I wrote a short monogram of my findings and sent it to the Royal Society. They were wary of publishing but highly interested. I told them that to learn more, I would need a larger quantity. We're now organizing an expedition to the West Indies and Mexico. I believe the Admiralty is set to give us a ship but the details have yet to be worked out. It is, hum, as Elliot would say, very hush hush."

"How do you know the alloy comes from Volcan Rojo as opposed to Tambora?"

"I don't know with certainty, but, hum, given the strange events in the region and reports of deformed plants and animals in the jungles, I'm confident it is the likely place to find more anitite. Anitite is, as I said, reactive with organic matter so, in enough quantity, it might cause deformations. If I had more, I could test it with ..."

"Oh, damn me, what is that?" I exclaimed, looking at a hideous drawing of a face.

"Ah, hum, yes, that one," Seymour said. "That was the second time I had seen what seems like a face in the projections. The first instance unnerved me to the extent I couldn't draw it. It may be a random pattern that happens to look like a face. I'm not sure."

The face was grotesque, a gaping ovoid mouth with a narrow, extended jaw. Bulbous brow ridges defined eyes that were otherwise black voids. The expression was horrifying but I couldn't tell if it was angry or anguished.

"You don't think it's a spirit or demon?" I asked.

"Whatever it is, I don't think it's supernatural. I'm a materialist. Everything, at some level, has a scientific explanation, though we may not always have the means to discern it."

I put the drawings back into the portfolio. I'd seen enough.

"My speculations," Seymour continued, "run along the lines that anitite is reactive to thought. Perhaps someone nearby had a vivid nightmare and we are seeing an image of it."

"It would explain how Louisa can communicate thoughts with her maid servant," I said.

"Indeed."

"What else is possible?"

"I don't know, but, hum, I believe it vital we find out."

Chapter 5: Gifts

12 March, 1819, Bristol

On board the *Bar Jack*, we established a routine of repairs in the morning and sailing instruction in the afternoon. This went fine for a couple of days, then some of the women fell to complaining and bickering. A few took umbrage with having to work alongside Jenny and Maggie because they had been prostitutes. I witnessed Rackham struggling to hold their attention as she explained the workings of the ship. It struck me as odd that Rackham was not more forceful with the women. In any case, the state of affairs had to change.

I convened a morning meeting in the still disheveled captain's cabin with Rackham, Sydow and Mrs. Kedward.

"The girls need discipline, kapitan," Sydow said.

"Yes, I know," I replied. "Miss Rackham, how would this behavior be handled on a pirate ship?"

"It wouldn't happen," she said. "Each man signs on knowing his place and duties. He knows punishment is severe if he shirks. There was rarely any problem. If there was, the quartermaster would dole out punishment, but we don't have a quartermaster."

"Mr. von Sydow, could you assume that role?" I asked.

"Sir ... they're women. If they were men, yes, I'd have them licking my boots with a wave of my hand and thanking me for the opportunity, but ..."

"I know, it's a conundrum," I said.

"For Christ's sake," Mrs. Kedward said. "The girls aren't made of porcelain. I'm sure they've all taken their licks at one time or another."

"Would you be willing to dispense corporal punishment if the need arises, Mrs. Kedward?" I asked.

"I'd be happy to."

"Very well, here's what I ask: Mr. von Sydow, you will impose Prussian discipline and Mrs. Kedward will be your enforcer."

"Javol, kapitan."

* * *

I assembled the women and addressed them from atop the aft deck:

"Ladies, you are the crew of the *Bar Jack*. As such I cannot tolerate complaining, defiance or shirking of tasks. All tasks are vital to the smooth running of the ship; our survival is at stake. Miss Smith is our ship's master. To her instructions you must pay rapt attention. To her orders you must obey immediately and to the letter. The same applies to Mr. von Sydow, and Mrs. Kedward, and to any who are chosen to fill roles of leadership.

"To that end Mr. von Sydow, a former Prussian army officer, will assume the role of establishing order. I remind you that you have agreed to the rules of maritime discipline. I also remind you that you may leave if you find this too demanding. That is all."

I turned the proceeding over to Sydow whose brooding but affable nature transformed into that of a tyrannical taskmaster.

"None of you are sailors," he bellowed. "Until you are, you are all equal, that is to say, you are all equally useless. You have to earn the right to be a sailor on the *Bar Jack*. That task begins now."

Sydow made them perform drills of synchronized exercises, then dismissed them to their morning chores. The next two days were better but murmurings and occasional sneering persisted. On the third, one of the women, Alice, a particularly vocal complainer, blurted: "I cleaned the head yesterday. Make one of the whores do it."

Sydow seized her and shouted, "Mrs. Kedward, if you please."

"Let go of me!" Alice shouted.

Mrs. Kedward marched over and wrapped a cloth around her hand. She balled it into a fist and struck Alice sharply on the mouth.

"You will follow orders or you will leave," Sydow said. "Which is it?"

The blow had been more galling then injurious. Alice's look of rage softened as she seemed to ponder the alternatives. At length, without speaking, she picked up the bucket and walked toward the head.

* * *

The mood was somber following the episode with Alice but all of the women were taking their jobs seriously. The mood lightened with time. Sydow and I were always on hand for Rackham's sailing instructions. I know a fair amount but nothing like her understanding. Sydow also wanted to know how to handle the ship if the need arose. He even participated in drills with the women – folding sails, hoisting sails, working block and tackle, tying knots, and so on.

The *Bar Jack* began to look respectable; most everything was fixed and patched. She needed paint and I still struggled to procure any quantity. She also needed sails, the current ones sufficed for training, but, rotted as they were, they looked horrible and would never weather the rigors of the sea. I often looked out on the bay, watching for the shipment from Kirkaldy.

I did receive a package from my brother. His letter wished me good fortune, hinted that he envied me and my adventure, and indicated that relations with the United States were improving so I shouldn't hesitate to seek refuge in an American port if necessary. I should be wary of the French, however, who had taken a renewed interest in the West Indies. Archy's letter concluded with the following: "Enclosed is a spyglass. It is the finest German optics from the firm of Utzschneider and Fraunhofer. May it aid you in seeing the dangers ahead."

The optics were remarkable, much sharper than the old spyglass I possessed.

One afternoon a ketch anchored off the end of the quay. With my new spyglass, I saw that it was the Marion, one of the McIntyres' cargo haulers. I hurried to meet two hands who rowed over in a dinghy.

"Looking for the *Bar Jack*, sir, told she was here," one of the hands said.

"You've found her," I replied. "I'm James LeRoque, the captain."

Thus began the process of loading many crates onto the *Bar Jack*. Sydow marshaled our crew to assist the Marion's hands, mostly old sailors who were highly amused and grateful for the women's help.

Sydow, Rackham and I inspected the contents of the crates as they were brought on board. The sailcloth was excellent and amounted to more than I expected. Other crates contained quantities of paint and varnish, which was a pleasant surprise. There were also blocks, tackle, heavy hawser and other kinds of rope. One crate contained six muskets and the women brought on kegs of powder and shot. Another box had several cutlasses and boarding axes.

"We have something to fight with now, kapitan," Sydow said.

I was astonished and somewhat bewildered. Then they hauled up a very heavy crate. I pried it open.

"What on earth?"

"A nice piece there," Rackham said. "She'll come in handy, I bet."

It was a swivel gun, one-inch caliber, of a type often used by whalers and armed merchant vessels. It came with a quantity of round shot, grape shot and four harpoons.

The captain of the Marion asked to come aboard and I welcomed him warmly.

"What is all this?" I asked. "I was only expecting sailcloth and spare rigging."

"Compliments of the McIntyres, I was told to say. They wish you Godspeed, Captain LeRoque."

I was so elated with the boon I hardly noticed the cloaked woman who came on board with the captain.

"Sir, I have a letter from Louisa for you," she said. "And this."

I knew the voice. I turned to look at Miss Cobrero who held the broadsword I'd requested.

"I hope you have room for one more on you ship, sir," she said with a smile.

* * *

Letter dated 3 March, 1819:

Dearest James,

I hope this letter finds your preparations going well. I trust you found willing volunteers for your crew. I am excited for you, and anxious, of course, but I believe we are doing the right thing no matter how absurd others think it. Sir McIntyre was among them but Juliet brought her father over for dinner one evening and we discussed your journey. He scoffed, but after a glass or two of port and a cigar, he said, "It's ludicrous for a ship to sail to the West Indies these days unarmed."

"Then send some arms to James," Juliet pleaded. "I know you have plenty hidden away."

I do believe Sir McIntyre is helpless before his daughter's wishes.

"Well, maybe I will," he grumbled. "If James won't be dissuaded from this fool's errand, then the least I can do is help him make a good start of it."

I do think, in the old man's heart, he wants to go with you. In any case I assume you are pleased with the arms and extra equipment.

And I send you my own gift – Sophie. Do not turn her away as I fear you may be tempted to do. She is a good worker and excellent cook. She also speaks Spanish and Portuguese which I assume will come in handy. But more than that, she will be a link between us. I do not think distance will prevent our minds from communicating; the bond between us has grown strong. And trust me when I say she wants to come. I tentatively floated the idea and she eagerly embraced it. She knows the peril; I would argue better than you do yourself. Her abilities are of much the same caliber as my own. You will need her, James.

I very much wish I could be with you. I am dying to meet Miss Rackham. I sense she is formidable. Do you find her so?

Best wishes and Godspeed, James.

Sincerely, your loving cousin and obedient servant,

Louisa Henrietta Ker LeRoque

P.S. Juliet is soon off on her own adventure. Ostensibly she is visiting relatives in France while the peace lasts but she intends to do her own investigating. She will travel to Spain as well. We believe Giselle LaFoy found something there that may be the key to much of what has happened.

* * *

I finished Louisa's letter and looked at Miss Cobrero sitting opposite me in my cabin. Common reasoning was telling me I should not allow the young woman to go on this perilous journey but the fact of the other eighteen women on board rendered such reasoning contradictory.

"You want to come of your own accord?" I asked.

"Yes, I believe I must come," Miss Cobrero said.

"Louisa in no way cajoled you?"

"No, sir, she and I are of one mind on this."

"I suppose I could use a steward, or stewardess, and you can help with the cooking and other chores as needed."

"Thank you, sir."

"You will have to sleep in a hammock in the hold with the other women."

"That's fine. Louisa told me as much."

* * *

The next days were spent making sails – cutting, stitching, hemming, inserting grommets and so on. The old sails served as guides but the new ones were fashioned to patterns Rackham had drawn that, she said, should improve their performance.

Miss Cobrero, or Sophie, as she asked to be called, teamed up with Jenny, the wiry former prostitute, to prepare the meals. I sensed the other women were not necessarily pleased to have a servant of an aristocratic family aboard but Sophie's cooking won them over from about the first spoonful of soup.

I spent much of my time running errands. The *Bar Jack* needed to be victualed for the Atlantic crossing and I wanted to get orders in so there would be no delay when we cast off. The prices were dismaying. I also purchased a supply of garments. The women had taken to wearing trousers which were, admittedly, more practical than skirts aboard ship, but it was a hodgepodge array. Thinking some uniformity would be good for appearances, I consulted Mrs. Kedward and she consulted others. We decided to follow the Royal Navy's standard seaman's apparel of cream-colored blouses, hemp canvas trousers about calf length, straw hats and rope belts. Instead of blue neckerchiefs we opted for red. I found a clothier able to supply the items, as well as pea coats, shoes, stockings, etc.

* * *

One evening a disturbing event happened and I wasn't sure what to make of it. After supper at the hotel, Sydow and I went for a walk along the wharf. It was a misty evening of a kind that was both enchanting and foreboding. The harbor lights glowed with an eerie aura and a muffled quietude prevailed except for ships creaking with the incoming tide and the occasional shout of stevedores. We were on our way back to the Three Goats Inn when we heard yelling along the quay.

Hurrying toward the sound, we found three men standing at the *Bar Jack*'s gangway brandishing pistols.

"C'mon, lassies, just give us the girls and there won't be no trouble," one of the men shouted. "If we have to come and take 'em ourselves, it could get bloody."

"What's the meaning of this?" I asked.

The men turned their pistols on us. They were an unkempt, unsavory lot and, unfortunately, Sydow and I had not thought to arm ourselves.

"This is no business of yours. Move along now before ya get hurt," the apparent leader said.

"This is my ship," I said. "I am Captain James LeRoque."

"I don't give a rat's arsehole who you are. Two of my whores are on board and I'll have 'em back."

"Prostitution is illegal," I said. "The women aboard this ship are my lawful employees. Now go or I'll summon the constables."

The women on board were in the hold or hunkered behind the gunwale, except for Alice, who stood defiantly at the top of the gangway. From the corner of the aft deck, I saw a small figure in shadow. She wore a dress so I knew it was Sophie. She seemed to be concentrating intently on the leader.

"I'll gun you down before you do," the leader said. "Ain't but two whores we want. I'm sure you can find a couple more for your bleedin' stupid crew of bitches."

I was thinking I had little choice but to comply when the leader jerked his head around.

"What was that? Who spoke? No one talks to me like that."

The other criminals looked as bewildered as I was myself. The leader turned toward the ship.

"Shut up, you bitch."

"Ain't no one sayin' nothin', boss," one of the other men said.

"What are you talking about? I heard it plain as day."

The leader pointed his pistol at Alice who wasn't speaking.

"Ah, you shut up, bitch, stop with that singing."

He looked around and saw no one was speaking. He looked to his men. "You hear the singing, don't ya, some foreign song?"

The men shook their heads.

"What do you mean it will stay in my head?" The leader spoke to the air. He dropped his pistol and put his hand over his ears.

"Stop the bloody singing!"

"It's witchcraft, boss, let's get the hell out of here."

The men stuffed their pistols into their coats and fled. The leader followed, hands still covering his ears. We watched them run down the quay and disappear into the night.

"That was ... gespenstisch," Sydow said.

I looked back toward the aft deck but Sophie was no longer there. Sydow picked up the pistol dropped by the leader.

"Another piece for the armory," he said.

Sydow volunteered to spend the night on board and I thanked Alice for standing her ground. On my way back to the inn, I saw Rackham who emerged from the shadows. She wore the belt with two pistols and the dirk appropriated earlier from the dead highwayman.

"They wouldn't have got by me with the girls," she said.

I put a hand on her shoulder. "I don't doubt it. Just as well it didn't come to violence."

Rackham, too, spent the night on the *Bar Jack*. I returned to the inn thinking about Sophie and Louisa and just what all they might be capable of.

Chapter 6: Setting Sail

24 April, 1819, Bristol

We completed the sails, then took to painting. The only colors we had in quantity were black, white and brown, so we painted the upper hull brown and painted a black and white checker pattern just below the gunwale. With that work done and the new sails raised, the *Bar Jack* looked reborn.

Our efforts had attracted attention and onlookers often loitered along the quay. Sometimes they made catcalls at the women who responded with jeers and the occasional obscene gesture. I supposed I should put a stop to it but I enjoyed the pride the women were taking in their work and their vessel.

Rackham had stayed curiously distant from the other women. She gravitated toward the company of men and she and Sydow had become friends. I sensed no romance, more like chums, and I couldn't recall knowing of a friendship quite like that between the sexes. Recently, however, I had noticed Rackham becoming friendlier with the women, joining their laughter and chatter while the work went on.

Kitten, the small urchin girl, had grown stronger – she was the only one who could shimmy up a mast without the aid of a ratline – and her pallor had vanished, the result, I was sure, of regular meals and honest work.

Maggie, the stout former prostitute, and Alice had become clear leaders among the women. The time drew near to decide which one would serve as bosun's mate. I awaited Rackham's recommendation.

The women looked smart in their sailor's uniforms and seemed quite happy wearing them. Mrs. Kedward looked even somewhat dashing in hers. Rackham continued to wear her pea-coat, brown trousers and leather hat and Sophie continued to wear dresses, I think, because she knew I liked seeing her in them.

* * *

The victuals arrived and we loaded them on board. We also took on a small cargo of dry goods, mostly surveying equipment, and wine and brandy to be delivered to Bridgetown, Barbados, our first port of call in the West Indies. I retrieved the ship's chronometer, compass, barometer and sextant and met with Rackham to discuss our course. Our plan was to sail at least a week in the safe confines of the Bristol Channel in order to season the crew for the Atlantic crossing. Rackham also wanted to find good ballast material as there was little to be had in harbor.

"If we do it right," she said. "I bet this boat'll make four points to the wind, a wee better maybe."

Four points to the wind was a difficult figure to believe. In order to sail upwind, a ship had to tack. It was impossible to sail directly against the wind but one could sail at an angle toward it, then zigzag to make one's course. Rackham was suggesting the *Bar Jack* might sail at a 45-degree angle toward the wind, a point of sail unheard of for a square-rigged ship. Perhaps it was possible with a Bermuda rigged vessel but I was skeptical. Rackham thought that being able to sail so close hauled would be to our advantage.

"We're not likely to outpace a fast frigate running with the wind," she said. "Upwind's a different matter. The more we can shave that angle, captain, the better we can keep your ship out of harm's way."

* * *

The next morning a large oar boat arrived, pulled the *Bar Jack* out of the slip and into the channel. A crowd of relatives and onlookers cheered us on our way. My stomach fluttered and I did my best to maintain a calm countenance.

I saw the crew was nervous, too, except Rackham who appeared amused.

"Raise the short sails forward and aft," she shouted as Maggie cast off the towline.

Alice, our newly designated bosun's mate, blew her whistle. The crew reacted and the sails went up. The day was cloudy but only a mild breeze. We could have raised full sails but kept to storm rigging and would do so until the crew gained experience. The wind caught the sails and the *Bar Jack* was underway.

Rackham maintained a steady course west by northwest. The pace was slow but the *Bar Jack* slipped through the water easily with little noise. Rackham walked the deck, inspecting the rigging and giving instructions. Our plan was to hug the north shore of the channel and stay out of the main shipping lanes.

When the channel opened to the point where we had plenty of space, Rackham ordered a turn across the wind. "Twenty to starboard." Maggie manned the helm and moved the tiller as instructed.

"Watch the booms!" Alice shouted.

When the ship crossed the wind, the long booms of the two masts swung to the other side, a movement known as jibing that everyone had to be keenly aware of or else be cracked in the head or hurled overboard. In high winds steps had to be taken to reduce the force of the jibe to prevent damage to the rigging. The turn went without incident. Rackham kept ordering turns across the wind to get the crew used to the movement of the booms.

Later she ordered the sails lowered and raised repeatedly with different shifts taking their turns. Then she ordered the storm jib flown off the bowsprit. The *Bar Jack* picked up speed and the women marveled at how fast she was going. I knew she could go much faster with the mainsails up and the main jib. By late afternoon the channel's swell increased and some folks became seasick, including Sydow. Rackham eased the *Bar Jack* into a sheltered cove near the town of Barry on the Welsh coast and ordered the last exercise of the day – lowering anchor.

* * *

The next day we practiced tacking up wind and cruising other points of sail. Efficiency improved satisfactorily. Rackham had been keeping an eye out for beaches that might supply proper ballast but saw none.

"Can't we just take on sand?" I asked.

"Nah, sand is no good," she said. "It gets into the pumps and everything else."

So on the following day, we crossed the channel to the south shore after giving way to a 76-gun ship-of-the-line that made our vessel seem tiny. Sailing back toward Bristol, Rackham spotted a rocky beach near the village of Kilve. The tide was low. We took her in as close as we dared and anchored.

We spent the afternoon and much of the next day using the dinghy to haul buckets of smooth, rounded stones. It was grueling work but I believe I was the only one who complained. When Rackham announced we had sufficient quantity, we all collapsed where we were. The afternoon was warm and sunny so I announced that we would spend the rest of the day on the beach, cook our meals there and share out extra rations of rum in the evening. I was, for the moment, a popular captain.

* * *

I sat with Sydow and Mrs. Kedward on the beach sipping whiskey from my flask. Kitten and Sophie were also there. Rackham had returned to the ship after eating. The air had grown chilly under the starlit sky but the small fire kept us warm enough. Kitten idly poked the embers with a stick. She stayed close to Sydow when she could. I supposed he had become a father figure to her, perhaps a father she never had. And Sophie stayed close to me when duties permitted.

"I think it time I turned in," Mrs. Kedward said.

She boarded the dinghy with the last of the other women.

“I hope they send the boat back for us,” Sydow remarked.

“I doubt they would leave Sophie and her cooking behind,” I said.

Sophie was not paying attention to us and looking inland. A faint glow of orange light beyond a copse of trees suggested a large fire. Villagers enjoying their own evening out, I thought.

“Something terrible is happening over there,” Sophie said.

“What do you mean?” I asked.

“Murder,” she whispered.

“I believe your imagination is ...”

A scream came from the direction of the copse, repeated bursts of agony. Maggie and Jenny had just beached the dinghy.

“What the hell is that?” Jenny exclaimed.

Sydow and I leaped to our feet.

“You girls stay here. We'll go see what's happening,” I said.

Sydow and I headed for the copse and Sophie ran with us.

“You should stay,” I said.

“I should go; you might need me.”

I didn't argue. Sydow drew his small pistol from his coat.

“Are you armed?” He asked.

“Sadly, no,” I said.

“You might think about changing your habits, kapitan.”

We slowed our pace when we saw a clearing lit by a fire. The screaming had stopped. We crept toward the edge of the trees to get a view. Sophie clutched my hand. We could do little but gawk.

A dozen robed figures encircled a large pyre, chanting low tones. Atop the pyre was a charred body, a girl or small woman, her age I could not tell. A globe of gray-black smoke hung above the flames, billowing and lingering unnaturally. I felt a kind of terror I'd not felt since childhood. I looked at Sydow. He was as stricken as I was.

A face appeared in the smoke, the same hideous kind of face I had seen in Paul's drawings – ovoid mouth, jutting chin, fathomless black eyes. Sophie squeezed my hand tightly. Then spiraling tendrils of smoke shot out from the main plume, waving and groping, until they found the heads of the robed figures, seeming to latch onto them. A deep, reverberous moaning followed.

"No, no, it mustn't find me," Sophie whimpered. Her eyes were closed.

Suddenly the moan stopped and all the robed figures turned toward us. We fled.

* * *

I nearly had to drag Sophie along with me. Sydow had dashed out ahead. He looked back, saw we were trailing, and slowed his pace. He let us get beyond him and covered our retreat with his pistol. We made the beach and ran toward the dinghy.

"What's happened?" Maggie asked.

"No time," I said. "We need to get away quickly."

Sophie collapsed in my arms and I had to lift her into the boat. Her head lolled and her eyes rolled into her head. "Louisa, help me," she pleaded.

Jenny and Kitten pushed us off and jumped in while Sydow and Maggie rowed with all their might. I held Sophie close as some kind of struggle played out in her mind.

The robed figures emerged from the copse walking in a peculiarly slow and synchronized manner, arms hanging stiffly. Voluminous hoods hid their faces in shadow but I judged some to be women. They stopped at the water's edge.

"Who are they?" Jenny asked.

"I don't know," I said. "Practitioners of pagan rites, it seems. It appears they burned a girl alive on a pyre."

"Sweet mother of Jesus. What's wrong with Sophie?"

"I don't know. A simple case of panic and nerves, I hope."

The robed figures still stood at the water's edge when we reached the *Bar Jack*. We got aboard quickly with me handing Sophie up to Sydow. The rest of the crew hauled up the dinghy.

"Miss Smith," I said to Rackham. "Can we get underway?"

"Wind ain't much but enough," she said.

"Then do it."

"Where to?"

"Away, I don't know, the other side of the channel."
"Aye, captain. Weigh anchor, ladies!"

* * *

Sydow carried Sophie into my cabin and laid her on my bed. The captain's cabin was the largest stateroom on the ship and served as the chart room and officer's mess where Sydow, Rackham, Mrs. Kedward and I took our meals. Sydow and Rackham stayed in the other staterooms that were little more than closets. Mrs. Kedward had a similar room below deck.

I fetched a canister from a cupboard and found a neckerchief which I spread flat on the table. I sprinkled a little of the contents of the canister on the cloth, rolled it up, then applied it to Sophie's forehead.

"Was ist das?"

"A mixture of crushed quartz, copper shavings and other bits of metal and minerals," I said. "It was a gift from Dr. Seymour. He said it interfered with the propagation of thoughts and might be useful as protection."

"Protection from what?" Sydow asked.

"I'm not sure but I think Sophie's mind is under attack."

I sensed the ship moving through the water, rising and ebbing on the gentle swell. Whether it was distance, the rocking motion or mineral concoction, I didn't know, but Sophie seemed to have eased into a peaceful sleep.

I found the broad belt I had packed and retrieved my sword. I pulled it from its scabbard and tested its keen edge. Louisa must have had it sharpened.

"That's a good blade," Sydow said.

"Toledo steel," I said. "Used at the Battle of Culloden by my namesake, James Ker. It's been in the family a long time."

I sheathed the sword and slipped the scabbard onto the belt. I then pulled a small case out from under the bed. In it were two dueling pistols with holsters. I put the holsters on the belt.

"Those must have cost a fortune," Sydow said.

"They were a gift from my father before he died, made by the firm of Wogdan and Barton. They have set triggers and rifled barrels."

I strapped on the belt.

"I'm taking your advice, Mr. von Sydow. At the first opportunity, I want to take the muskets out of their crate and teach the girls how to use them, and the swivel gun, too. That will be your job."

"Javol, kapitan."

* * *

I went out onto the aft deck and joined Rackham. With short sails the *Bar Jack* made slow progress yet each mile away from that beach eased my anxiety.

"I want to put in at Barry tomorrow morning and post a letter," I said.

"Aye," Rackham said.

"Then I want to head for the Atlantic. Are the girls up for it?"

"More seasoning'd be good but we'll manage."

"Very well. Something tells me we need to go now."

"I hear ya," Rackham said. "What happened at the beach?"

I told her with all the detail I could recall.

"That's the kind of thing that goes on near El Radio," she said. "It's a different world over there."

"I don't doubt you."

"One more thing, captain, I don't like being called Smith. My name is Rackham."

"Understood."

I returned to my cabin and wrote a letter to my brother, informing him of what we saw at Kilve. I thought about writing to the magistrate of Somerset County but wasn't sure if I could trust him. How could I know he wasn't part of the cult? Rumors of pagan magic, witchcraft and devil worship abounded but I had put them down to superstition accentuated by troubled times. It was clear to me now there was some reality to it all and I didn't know what it portended. My brother was in a better position to see justice served and the murderous cultists rooted out.

* * *

The crew underwent another test: Sailing into a harbor. Fortunately Barry's was small and uncrowded and the exercise, while a tad clumsy, went without incident. We anchored quite a ways from the quay. I had Maggie and another stout woman, Clair, I believe, row me to shore, drawing curious looks along the way. I posted my letter and we returned.

I met with Rackham in my cabin and told her it was time. She went to her stateroom while I had Mrs. Kedward call all hands to the deck where I addressed them:

"Ladies, I'm here to tell you we're setting sail today for the Atlantic and on to the West Indies. Last night's events were a scare for us all, but we are likely to face events even more frightful. I have confidence that you all can measure up to the challenge. However, I wanted to give you a final chance to take the sensible step of staying behind. I will provide you funds to return to Bristol and think none the worse of you. This may indeed be a ship of fools on a fool's errand."

The women murmured and looked at one another. Alice shouted: "We're your fools, captain!"

"One more thing before you decide," I said. "I need to properly introduce you to our ship's master. Miss Smith!"

Rackham emerged from the cabin clad in a leather frock coat tapered at the waist to display her figure. Her broad hat was tilted at an angle and she wore her pistols and dirk on her belt. She stepped up beside me and there were more murmurs.

"Our ship's master is, in actuality, none other than Ann Rackham, former pirate and sailing master of the *Vipere.* This fact may be off-putting and understandably so. Again, I encourage you to leave if you are apprehensive about her presence here."

The women didn't seem as taken aback as I anticipated.

"Sir," Kitten spoke up. "We already knew."

A chorus of laughter erupted. I was nonplussed.

* * *

Rackham got us underway, raising short sails again. A brisk westerly blew up choppy waters and we sailed close reach on a course south by southwest. Seeing everything was in hand, I went to my cabin to speak with Sophie. She was sitting on the bed, looking out the stern windows.

"You should be resting," I said.

"I'm fine, sir," she said.

"What happened to you last night? Can you say?"

"I'm not really sure, sir, or rather I don't know if I have the words. The people of the pyre conjured a kind of spirit. Louisa calls them daemons. She, I and Juliet were able to sense them sometimes. Louisa says they are like floating minds."

"Are they ghosts?" I asked.

"No, not souls of dead people. Louisa, even now, doesn't believe in ghosts. The minds, the daemons, are not human. We've tried to communicate with them but failed. They are very weak. They seem adrift and out of their element, sad in a way. Louisa says there are a few, at least, that are potent and might, at times, affect people and things."

"Like last night."

"Yes, I had never felt anything like it, such malice. I think it was feeding on the horror and pain of the poor girl. The daemon became aware of me and tried to invade my mind."

"Like you did with the pimp the other night on the quay," I said.

"A little, I suppose. The pimp had the ability, like Louisa and me; he just didn't know it. It gave me an opening to send him thoughts. That was a harmless trick compared to what the daemon was trying to do. I was overwhelmed but Louisa sent her thoughts to me. I'm not sure what happened. I think Louisa's presence was enough to confuse the daemon and it stopped its attack."

"Thank God for that," I said and put my hand on her shoulder. She put her hand on mine.

Someone knocked on the door.
"What is it?"
"Sir, Master Rackham wants to speak with you," Jenny said.
"Be right there."

* * *

"I want to raise the mains and sail close hauled for a bit, see what she can do," Rackham said.
"Is it a good idea in this wind?" I asked.
"I think we'll be all right," she said, then smiled. "Better to swamp her here than out in the Atlantic."
Her logic was sound. "Do it," I said.
"Raise the mains, Alice," Rackham said.
Alice blew her whistle and shouted the orders. Rackham took the helm. The main sheets were hauled up and the great white triangles reached the tips of the masts fore and aft. The wind caught them hard and the *Bar Jack* leaned to port and picked up speed. Rackham eased the tiller and turned the ship more toward the west, then shouted instructions to trim the booms.
Catching the waves head-on, the *Bar Jack* bucked and blew spray onto the deck. The booms set where she wanted them, Rackham turned the ship a little more.
"All hands to starboard side," she yelled as the ship turned even further into the wind. It seemed the port gunwale was going to touch water. I stifled an urge to order Rackham to stop.
"Four points to the wind, captain, and holding steady," she said. "She could do more but we'll try that another day."
We passed the stern of a sloop sailing inland. I could see its crew gawking as we went by. Bermuda rigged vessels were rare in these waters and to see one sailing so close hauled must have been a spectacle. I would have enjoyed it more if I hadn't been so worried we'd founder. I could see my crew was worried, too, clutching whatever they could hang on to. Sydow looked terrified. Rackham was beaming.

At last, Rackham eased the ship back to a close reach course. The women cheered, whether for their lives, Rackham, or the seaworthiness of the *Bar Jack*, I wasn't sure. When things settled, I was elated. The ship I'd thought was little more than scrap was turning out to be something special. I patted Rackham on the back.

"Well done, Master Rackham," I said. "We may yet see this through."

"We may."

I handed her my spyglass.

"My brother gave me this as a parting gift – German optics, the finest in the world – but I think it ought to be yours. My compliments."

"Thank you, captain, much obliged."

Chapter 7: The Crossing

4 May, 1819, Atlantic Ocean

We left Bristol Channel sailing a southerly course, keeping the Cornish coast in sight until, at last, Lizard Peninsula sunk below the horizon. I wondered if I would see Britain again. Rains came shortly thereafter and for three days it was blustery, wet and cold. The horror of Kilve Beach had not daunted the women's spirits but the weather did. How many now wished they had stayed home? I longed to be sitting by the fire at the club smoking a pipe.

I had to order Rackham to get some sleep. She had rested little since our departure. She went back and forth on the deck, showing the women what to do when the wind shifted which was often. The crew was green and clumsy but necessity compelled them to get better. Other than bruises and scrapes, we had so far avoided serious injury or mishap. I took my turns at the helm. Sydow did his best but struggled with seasickness.

The weather finally cleared and the wind steadied; the warm rays of the sun were heaven sent. Sydow's color returned and he strolled onto the deck where I was manning the helm for the forenoon watch.

"Feeling better, I presume," I said.

"Ja, maybe I am not much of a seaman."

"You'll find your legs eventually."

"Where are we now?" Sydow asked.

"Close to 41 degrees latitude. The coast of Spain should be about 100 miles to port. We're sailing near due south hoping to pick up the trade winds that will carry us across."

"See any other ships?"

"A sloop ahead of us this morning but it pulled away."

We had the mains up in the mild wind but Rackham didn't trust me with the jibs yet, otherwise we'd make better speed.

"I think it's a good time to show the ladies the muskets," Sydow said.

"By all means," I said. "Though I'd hate to disturb Master Rackham's sleep."

"Just instruction today. We'll shoot live tomorrow if the weather's fair."

So began the drilling of the crew in the use of firearms. They took to it eagerly. Mrs. Kedward worked up a small raft to put targets on. The next day we towed it behind us and the women blasted away. The smooth-bore muskets weren't very accurate and neither were the women. I brought out my long sporting rifle and Sydow his short carbine rifle and we were able to impress the crew with some decent shooting.

Sydow kept drilling them in shifts as the days went on. He wanted all the crew to be competent with the muskets but he chose six to be the *Bar Jack*'s "musketeers" with Maggie as their leader. Kitten, to our astonishment, proved a natural shooter. With Sydow's carbine (my rifle was too long for her), she could hit the bullseye with nearly every shot, even when the target was moving.

"The girl just doesn't flinch; never seen the like of it," Sydow said.

Even with a pistol, Kitten was accurate, so Sydow designated her the ship's sharpshooter.

Days later we pried open the crate with the cutlasses and I instructed the women in basic swordsmanship. Sydow practiced with his long cavalry saber and I with my broadsword. We sparred some with wooden dowels as practice swords. Sydow's technique was wanting, tending toward a lunging Italian style, but I surmised he would be ferocious in battle.

On the day we reached 30 degrees latitude, Rackham changed course to west by southwest. Sydow and I hauled up the swivel gun. The *Bar Jack* already had four mounts on the deck, two near the bow and two astern. Sir McIntyre had thought to put a sheet of instructions in the crate but we puzzled over its mystifying terms.

"I'm not an artillery man," Sydow said, scratching his head. "But I didn't think it would be so complicated."

"I'm ashamed to say, but it has me baffled," I said. "Who wrote these instructions?"

"For crying out loud," Rackham said, appearing behind us. "It ain't that hard."

Under Rackham's tutelage we assembled the gun and secured it to the port side stern mount. She put together the flintlock firing mechanism and proceeded to charge the weapon with a pre-measured cartridge of powder and a one-inch ball.

"When it's wet and weathery, it's better to use a match than the flint," she said.

She aimed at nothing in particular and fired. The sound was colossal, much louder than the muskets or rifles. We saw a tiny splash several hundred yards distant.

"That should discourage any prospective assailants," I said.

Sydow and I took turns loading and firing. We lowered the target and loaded the swivel gun with grapeshot. Sydow took the honor and the blast obliterated the target.

"Ja, discouraging," he said.

Over the following days, Sydow trained a three-woman swivel gun crew and a backup crew. They practiced assembling, firing and hauling it from mount to mount. He then organized battle drills. He would shout, "Beat to quarters," and, though we had no drum, the women would take up battle stations as if to repel boarders – Maggie and her musketeers, the swivel gun team, Kitten with Sydow's carbine rifle, and the rest not on steerage duty with cutlasses.

"Look lively now, girls," Sydow would shout. He liked to use phrases he must have read in sensationalized accounts of naval battles.

I wondered how effective the women would be if it actually came to a fight. They seemed eager and determined enough but battle was a man's game, and not all men were fit for it, perhaps myself included. I resolved to abide by my intention of avoiding conflict if at all possible.

* * *

One day we found ourselves in the midst of a school of porpoises. A cool northeast wind was hurrying us along. Rackham had put out a full press of canvas, raising the main jib and the outer jib, and we were making ten knots or even better. The porpoises played in our wake, raced across our bow, and leaped into the air, spinning as they did so. The women clapped and cheered and the animals seemed quite aware they had an audience.

"I believe porpoises are creatures that have entirely too much fun," I said to Sydow.

"Ja, I think they know something we don't."

As abruptly as they came, the porpoises were gone, perhaps drawn by a school of fish. They were, however, only the second most wondrous spectacle we saw that day. A whale, about a hundred yards to starboard, blew a great plume from its spout. The behemoth was angling toward us.

"Mein Gott," Sydow said.

As it drew closer, the size of it was bewildering, nearly as long as the ship. Even Rackham appeared astonished.

"What kind of whale is it?" I asked her.

"A cachalot, a sperm whale," she said. "I've never seen one this big."

The leviathan steadily drew nearer. Sophie came running up on deck and went to the gunwale.

"Have you ever seen one this close?" I asked Rackham.

She shook her head.

"Is it a danger? Should we fetch the swivel gun?"

"No, sir, he's just curious," Sophie said.

The whale swam parallel to us, not ten yards out, matching our speed.

"There's another one up ahead," Sophie said. "His mate."

"How do you know?"

"Spout ahead!" Kitten shouted.

Another whale appeared off the port bow. The one beside us pressed ahead, easily outpacing our ship, and crossed our bow, presumably going to join its mate. We watched as the pair angled off. Sophie went to the bow and placed her hands on the railing, her skirt fluttering in the wind. Two spouts went up simultaneously, then the whales were gone. Sophie held her position for a long while afterward.

"Makes one feel rather small," I said.

"Ja, unbedeutend," Sydow said.

* * *

The westerly returned the next day and we tacked to keep our course. We passed a British frigate, the H.M.S. *Pyramus*, which had to tack on a shallow angle. We flew our British colors and all the women came on deck to wave. The sailors waved back and cheered as we went by. Through my spyglass I saw the officer of the watch looking at us with stony disapproval. Nevertheless I was glad to have a friendly 36-gun warship in the vicinity. It remained in sight the rest of the day but was gone the following morning.

A week later I was in my cabin when Rackham, via Kitten, summoned me to the deck. I had been calculating our position, trying to follow Rackham's process. In a few days we should make Barbados. My eyes ached for the sight of land, my feet for the feel of solid ground. I was sure the rest of the crew did, too – the generally good spirits were flagging with the tedium of the crossing – except, perhaps, for Rackham, who seemed to belong to the sea like one of its creatures.

On deck Rackham was peering through her spyglass at a set of distant sails off the port bow. We were sailing close reach against a southwest wind.

"What is it?" I asked.

"A big sloop, flying Spanish colors."

"We're not presently at war with Spain," I said.

"No, but she turned," Rackham said. "She was headed east by northeast then made a full swing west by northwest. She means to intercept us."

"Why would a Spanish warship want to intercept us?"

"She may not be Spanish."

"Pirates?"

"I think it likely, captain."

"We're a bit of a small prize, wouldn't you say?"

"A pretty boat like ours flying a British flag this far out to sea might be worth a look."

"Christ almighty, can we outrun her?"

"I'm near sure that we can."

"Near sure?"

"As sure as I can be, if the wind holds, and I think it will."

"Could we turn around and head for the *Pyramus*?" I asked.

"She might catch us on that course."

"What do you recommend?"

"Hold course until she's closer."

Sydow came up on deck looking groggy from his afternoon "siesta."

"Was ist das?"

"A sloop, possibly pirates, trying to catch us," I said.

"Ah, shall I beat to quarters, kapitan?"

Rackham laughed. "She'll have twenty guns and a hundred and fifty men on board," she said.

"Not much point, Leo," I said. "Though I know you've been dying to do it. Ann says we can outrun her."

We waited and watched, as the alleged Spanish ship drew closer, her three masts full of sail. We could see the gun ports were open and that her bow chasers had been rolled out. Whatever she wanted, she meant business.

"Hold her steady, Maggie," Rackham said.

"She's bearing down on us pretty fast," I said.

"We'll make our turn soon, captain," she said. "We probably should have all hands on deck."

"All right, Mr. von Sydow, go ahead, beat to quarters."

With a gleeful roar, he shouted: "Battle stations! All hands to battle stations!"

Soon the deck was a flurry of activity. Maggie gave the tiller over to Rackham to join the musketeers. Sydow helped place the swivel gun on the port side stern mount. The women seemed eager but I think their enthusiasm waned when they saw the ship and the number of its guns. And I'm sure they shared the same fear I did when the sloop lowered its Spanish flag and flew a black one in its stead.

"No doubt about it now," I said.

"She raised the black too soon," Rackham said. "Her captain is hoping we'll heave-to rather than run. Her fore course and tops'ls are fluttering or she'd make better speed."

I gathered Rackham wasn't impressed with our pursuer's seamanship. The ship was about a half mile out and we were nearing the point where we would cross her bow.

Rackham shouted orders and turned the *Bar Jack* thirty degrees into the wind.

"Spare hands to the port side!" She shouted. "Tighten that jib!"

"We're turning toward her," I said, astonished.

"Yes," Rackham said. "Take the helm and hold her steady on this course."

We were sailing close hauled now, nearly four points to the wind. The pirate vessel was closing fast. Rackham went around the deck, massaging the trim of the sails so they were just so, bulging tautly and not a ripple to be seen.

"Two points to starboard," she shouted back at me.

I eased the till to starboard and the ship turned slightly to port, now even closer to the wind. The *Bar Jack* leaned and the sails stayed firm. Soon Rackham was beside me again, looking out at our pursuer.

"Now we'll see how this captain handles his ship," she said.

We crossed the pirate vessel's bow, now about a quarter mile out, and she turned to stay with us. The turn proceeded poorly. The wind spilled from her sails and she rocked clumsily in the swell as her hull rotated.

I saw flashes from the two bow chasers and, a moment later, heard a double boom. Both balls splashed short of us. From then on we rapidly increased the distance. The women cheered then started making catcalls and obscene gestures at the pirates. I believe it was Jenny who pulled down her trousers and wiggled her hindquarters at them.

“Well done, Master Rackham,” I said. “You knew the sloop would handle the turn badly.”

“I had a hunch.”

* * *

Three days later we caught sight of Barbados. After weeks of sailing on open ocean with a green crew and spending much of the time tacking, Rackham had guided us to a near perfect landfall. It was seamanship of the highest order.

Chapter 8: The New World

17 June, 1819, Bridgetown, Barbados

I ate lunch with the Royal Navy's ranking officer in Bridgetown, Commodore James White., at a rough but pleasant establishment called the Pelican Inn. Commodore White commanded the H.M.S. *Spey*, a 26-gun sloop. Joining us were Captain Amos Westropp of the brig, H.M.S. *Childers*, and Mr. Samuel Fetterman, the harbor master.

I had come ashore alone, wanting to get the lay of things before giving the crew shore leave. Despite the news of trouble in the West Indies, Bridgetown seemed prosperous. The harbor was so crowded the *Bar Jack* had to anchor in a nearby bay that had a broad beach of white sand. The town – with its fine stone buildings near the center and shacks roofed with palm fronds dotting the outer areas – bustled with activity. I had expected a prevailing atmosphere of doom but sensed none. Even the negroes seemed happy.

"I do have a letter of introduction from the Admiralty if you would like to see it, commodore," I said.

"Does it contain orders for me?" White asked.

"No, sir."

"Bah, then keep it in your pocket. I'm at your service, Captain LeRoque."

White was a walrus of a man with suitable whiskers. He went at the mutton roast and chipped potatoes with vigor. Captain Westropp was considerably younger, lean and fair-haired. Mr. Fetterman was considerably older, bald and gray.

"My errand," I said, "is to find the whereabouts of the *Squirrel* expedition, or at least learn what happened to it. The Admiralty has no resources to spare for the project so

I'm funding it myself. If you know anything of use, I would be greatly obliged."

"Sad business," White said. "A good ship, the *Squirrel.* Shame to lose her."

"So, you know she was destroyed?"

"No, not as such, it's just, what else could have happened? She wasn't bested by the French or Spanish or we'd've known."

"The last word we had," Fetterman said, "she sailed from Kingston, heading west to follow the Mexican shore to the Yucatan. I only spoke briefly with the captain when the *Squirrel* was here. She put in some stores and was on her way."

"Then Kingston is where I need to go next," I said. "I must say, with all the bad news from this part of the world, I'm surprised to see Bridgetown thriving as it seems to be."

"We've been fortunate," Fetterman said. "The corruption has not reached us here. Sugar crops have been good and prices are high."

"Wasn't there a slave rebellion not long ago?" I asked.

"Near three years now, no trouble since," Fetterman said.

"The good governor," White said, "wanted to avoid the kind of trouble happening in Jamaica, so he rounded up the planters and compelled them to ease up on the slaves - a day off a week, no flogging of women or children, agreements to keep families together, even a small wage. The planters howled at first but soon they were producing more than they ever had."

"What is the situation in Jamaica," I asked.

Westropp spoke: "Dire. I just came from there."

The young captain had a gritty voice that belied his youthful appearance.

"Port Royale is in shambles," he continued. "Kingston is hanging on but barely, only a few plantations remain under British control."

"A slave rebellion?"

"Yes, sir, two competing factions, each led by its own brujo. We'd be doomed if they didn't spend most of their time fighting each other."

"Brujo?"

"Spanish for warlock or sorcerer," White interjected. "They're like priests or witch doctors. The maroons follow them fanatically. It's that damned Seminole Confederacy in Florida. It's got all the darkies stirred up."

The Seminole Confederacy, I knew, was a powerful group of Indian tribes and escaped slaves who had declared themselves an independent country on the peninsula of Florida. Its capital was called Angola near the Bay of Tampa. The United States violently opposed them. Slaves were fleeing southern plantations in significant numbers, seeking refuge in Florida. The Americans sent an army under General Andrew Jackson to break up the confederacy but it was defeated in the swamps and forced to retreat. The French, seeing an opportunity, recognized the Seminoles as an independent nation and sent supplies and a few troops to assist them. Many people in Britain, particularly antislavery advocates, were sympathetic toward the Seminoles, but the Crown was courting the United States as an ally and, so far, had not recognized the Seminole nation.

Our conversation was interrupted when a young naval officer walked in, saluted and sat beside Captain Westropp.

"What news, lieutenant?" Westropp asked.

"Nothing important to report, captain," the lieutenant said. "It might be worth noting that a schooner called the *Bar Jack* has anchored near the *Childers*. Funny thing is the crew seems to be entirely women."

"Is that right?"

"Saw it myself, the girls all clad in sailor's tunics and trousers. Damnedest thing. A tidy little ship, though, just come from Bristol. Can you imagine crossing the Atlantic with a crew of women?"

"I can more than imagine it," I said. "I did it. The *Bar Jack* is my ship."

Commodore White guffawed. "By Jove, leave it to Scotsman to crew his ship with women. What drove you to that?"

"Practicalities, sir," I said. "There's a manpower shortage as you must know."

"You found them willing?"

"More than willing, eager," I said. "We had many more volunteers than we could take on. You might say we got the cream of the crop, all strong, healthy and capable."

"They're able to perform adequately?" White asked.

"We made it here without incident," I said. "My sailing master says they're still a titch green but coming along."

"We shouldn't be surprised," Fetterman said. "I know of a number of merchant ships that have taken on women as hands. Sign of the times."

"Your entire crew is female?" Westropp asked.

"All except my first mate, Leopold von Sydow, a former Prussian cavalry officer who keeps, let us say, Germanic discipline on board."

"A Scotsman, a Hessian and a gaggle of girls headed for the heart of the world's troubles," White said. "Astounding!"

He roared with laughter along with the rest of the table.

"Who is your sailing master," Westropp asked, "if not a man?"

"Ann Rackham," I said before I could think better of it.

The table fell quiet.

* * *

"Ann Rackham of the *Vipere*?" Westropp said in a low voice.

"Yes," I said. "I have a letter of parole signed by the prime minister."

"She's a murdering pirate," Westropp said.

"Now, now, captain," the commodore said. "We all have a few pirates pressed into our crews."

"But not as sailing masters," Westropp said.

White turned to me: "You must realize, Sir LeRogue, Captain Westropp squared off against the *Vipere* before she was taken. Lost some good men."

"I understand," I said.

"How can you trust her?" Fetterman asked.

"I don't entirely," I said. "But she so far has served faithfully. She is exceedingly competent. Saved our lives, as a matter of fact. Steered us clear of a pirate ship a few days ago and got us clean away. I've come to believe she's taking her second chance at life to heart. She's a natural seafarer. It's occurred to me that she became a pirate because it was the only way she could do what she was born to do – sail ships. I take precautions, of course, follow all her navigational steps and Mr. von Sydow's main charge is keeping an eye on her."

After a moment of quiet, the commodore spoke.

"A pirate ship, you say? Whereabouts? What's the name of her?"

I remembered the coordinates and gave them to him.

"As to the name, we didn't see one," I said. "A Spanish sloop, we think, twenty guns but poorly handled. We passed the *Pyramus* some days prior. I'm hoping the pirates stumble upon her."

"The *Pyramus*, hmm, probably en route here with orders for me. A pirate sloop would be a nifty prize to bring in. We shall see."

* * *

I was hesitant to let the women go ashore but, after weeks at sea, I could hardly confine them to the boat. I doled out a portion of their wages and asked Mrs. Kedward to remind them the *Bar Jack* could not become a nursery. Half could go to town today and the rest the next. The ladies were giddy with excitement and exchanged their trousers for gowns.

On deck I looked over at the *Childers* swaying gently in the mild swell of the advancing tide. Captain Westropp's war brig had provided a sense of security when we anchored, but now I worried my indiscretion would create trouble. It was a warm, cloudless day and we had erected a canopy on the aft deck to provide shade. That's where I found Rackham looking over a chart and smoking her long, narrow pipe.

"You've seen that ship before," I said, motioning toward the *Childers*, "while you were aboard the *Vipere*."

"Might have."
"What happened?"
Rackham snorted smoke from her nostrils.
"The *Childers* was closing on us, eager for the kill. I out maneuvered her. We raked her bow with a couple of broadsides, put her out of action. But two frigates were bearing down hard. I thought I could give them the slip but a lucky shot sheared our mizzenmast."
"I appreciate your candor," I said. "I'll return the favor and apologize for letting your name slip at lunch today. Captain Westropp, the *Childers*' commander, seems to hold a grudge."
"Yeah."
"It might be best if you kept a low profile."
"I ain't too worried but I'll do as you ask," Rackham said. "Sydow wants to go shoot birds. I'll tag along in one of the sailor suits and call it my shore leave."
"Very well."

* * *

I spent the afternoon in town accompanied by Sophie, arranging the unloading of our small cargo - tools, surveying equipment, wine and brandy - and the re-victualing of the *Bar Jack*. I ordered extra stores thinking this may be the last port where supplies would be easy to come by. A lighter would come to the ship in the morning to deliver the stores and haul away our cargo. The profit was more than I expected.
That business concluded, Sophie and I meandered through the cobbled streets, halfheartedly looking for an apothecary to supply various ointments, etc., for "women's needs."
"I communicated with Louisa," Sophie said as we walked.
"Oh?"
"She is well and says you are always in her thoughts."
"Give her my love," I said.
"Juliet is in Spain. She has visited the house where Giselle LaFoy and her husband had stayed," Sophie said.

"Interesting."

"Juliet believes Giselle found an old tome or journal kept by a missionary. He lived with the Indians in Mexico a long time ago. The tome is gone but she's trying to learn more about the priest. His name was Diego Cossio."

"Good to know, I suppose. I wonder if Paul knew about the priest. I hope Juliet doesn't get herself into trouble."

"She's smart and quick on her feet," Sophie said.

We found a spice shop where, with my money, Sophie purchased substantial quantities.

"We want to keep the crew happy." She smiled.

The clerk told us where to find the apothecary and there Sophie bought an even larger assortment of items. The grateful clerk put them in a small crate which I was obliged to carry until I engaged the services of a negro boy who offered to help.

Atop a knoll on our way back, we saw the sun setting reddish gold on the aqua-blue of the bay, the *Bar Jack* small but proud beside the stately *Childers*. Sophie slipped her hand into mine and we walked down to the beach.

* * *

A Barbados bullfinch, a red-eyed vireo, a budgerigar and, most prized of all by Sydow, a purple gallinule were the result of the afternoon's birding expedition. The hunters – Sydow, Kitten and Rackham – sat under a canopy on the beach. Sydow was preparing the birds for taxidermy with a stubby but very sharp knife.

"The museum will be happy with these," he said.

"What about that gruesome thing?" I asked, pointing to a large head of a predatory fish, its tooth-filled jaw nearly as long as my arm.

"They will want it, yes," Sydow said. "It is a barracuda. Common fish but this one was gigantic – ten feet maybe. They don't get that big, kapitan."

"How big do they get?"

"Five feet is the largest I've ever seen," Rackham said. "We found it on a beach a couple miles from here."

"I'd hate to see the fish that killed it," I said.
"Thing is, captain, it's head wasn't bitten off. Something pulled it apart."
"What the devil could do that?"
"I don't know," Sydow said. "I don't think I want to know."
"Where we're headed," Rackham said, "we might find out first hand."

* * *

A family of negroes came from their nearby huts and offered to sell us clams and oysters. Most of the crew was on the beach and the women thought it was a good idea. I paid out of my own pocket and the negroes showed us how to dig fire pits to bake the clams in the sand. Soon the gathering became a party. Several sailors from other ships joined in and, before long, I saw a pair carrying kegs of beer to our spot.
"Our crew is popular, no?" Sydow said.
"Too popular," I said.
"Relax, have a little fun, kapitan."
I grumbled something in response as I watched a dinghy pull ashore. Three men stepped out and walked toward us. When they neared the fires, I saw they were Royal Navy officers, one was Captain Westropp, and they wore pistols and sabers on their belts. The fun, I thought, may soon end. I stood to greet them and Rackham and Sydow stood beside me. I was unarmed, so was Sydow, but Rackham had her usual brace of pistols and dirk. Behind us, on the table Sydow used to clean his birds, lay the blunderbuss and the carbine rifle.
Westropp and his men stopped a few feet away, the fire casting flickering shadows on their faces.
"Captain LeRoque," Westropp said.
"Captain Westropp," I replied.
His stern gaze fell on Rackham and they eyed each other.
"You must be Ann Rackham," Westropp said.
"I am."

"I had to see for myself the woman who laid my ship low. Three of my men were killed that day, several wounded."

"It was a fair fight."

"If not for the wind change, you wouldn't have had the weather gauge."

"Your mistake was not seeing it coming."

"I'm still standing," Westropp said with a snarl.

"So am I." Rackham's voice was clear and sweet with challenge.

Silence radiated out from the point between them like a ripple in a pond and the festivities fell quiet.

"Come now," I interjected. "We don't want any violence here. It would do no one any good."

Westropp turned to me.

"I ask your pardon, LeRoque, I do not intend violence. My purpose here is not to confront Miss Rackham but to speak with you. I have some information you may find useful. My nephew was a midshipman on the *Squirrel* so I very much hope you're successful in your quest."

"Then by all means, sit and we'll talk," I said.

Westropp smiled.

"You might want to call off your girl first."

"Pardon?"

Westropp pointed behind me. I turned and saw Kitten standing in shadow with the carbine leveled at the officers.

"Good God, Kitten, put that down," I snapped.

* * *

Rackham excused herself and had Maggie row her back to the *Bar Jack*. Westropp watched her disappear into the night.

"Taking a shine to her, captain," one of the officers quipped.

"Don't know if I want kill her or bed her," Westropp replied.

"You'd be playing with fire either way," Sydow said.

"Aye, no doubt, I wonder what bedtime stories Captain Radan could tell."

"Captain Radan of the *Vipere*?" I said.

"The only Radan I know of," Westropp said. "Word is Rackham was his woman."

Captain Radan had perished during the *Vipere*'s capture, swept overboard when the ship's mast went down, though his body was never recovered. I had a hard time imagining Rackham being anybody's woman.

"What else do you know about Rackham?" I asked.

"I figured you'd know more than me," Westropp said. "No one heard of her before the *Vipere* made a name for itself."

"What about Radan? Do you know anything about him?"

"I think he was part of Jean Laffite's outfit years ago, commanded an old brig called the *Bulldog*. I hear he got caught in a storm, wrecked his ship and he was marooned somewhere in El Radio. Next anybody knows he's in Havana, commandeering a privateer, calling it the *Vipere* and making a woman his sailing master. That's what I know."

A few of the women served us beer in wooden goblets. They hovered around, clearly flirting with the officers who were inclined to return the attention.

"I suppose Miss Rackham will remain an enigma," I said. "What was it you wanted to tell me, Captain Westropp?"

"I don't know any more than you about what happened to the *Squirrel*, but my uncle lives near Kingston. When I last saw him, he told me he was visited by one of the naturalists on the *Squirrel*."

"Dr. Seymour?"

"Aye, I think that's right. They talked about the expedition. My uncle's a bit of a strange bird, collects Indian artifacts and such. Can't say for sure, but he might know something useful to you."

"What's his name?"

"Charles Morgan, owns a small plantation near Kingston, assuming it isn't overrun yet. I told him he should move to England but he's stubborn."

"Thank you, captain, I'll try to pay a call when we arrive in Kingston."

* * *

Several days out from Barbados, I took a stint at the helm for the middle watch, the midnight sky clear and moonless. The breeze was southwesterly and pushed us along nicely on a close reach course. I saw the jib fluttering a bit. Before I could say anything, Alice ordered Wanda, a short Welsh girl, to adjust it. Soon the jib was flying tautly.

My anxiety had been mounting since we left Bridgetown. The responsibility for the crew and ship weighed on me. I wondered how men like Westropp and White could manage it for so long, so many lives depending on their decisions. Death would come; it seemed inevitable. Even if we avoided conflict, it was unlikely the whole crew would avoid the tropical diseases that struck down so many. Some would die and I would have to carry that burden, that is if I survived. But more than all that, a malaise grew in my mind as we drew closer to El Radio, a faint echo of an ungraspable horror. The face in the smoke at Kilve Beach loomed in my mind.

Rackham coming up to relieve me for the morning watch also relieved me of my gloomy thoughts. She commented that the trim of the sails looked good. I found myself proud to have her approval. I gave her the tiller and went to my cabin to find Sophie sitting on my bed.

"Hello, James," she said. "It's good to see you."

* * *

Sophie's smile was different but familiar. Her voice was different, too. The sweet pitch was the same but the accent was not Spanish; it was the accent of an educated Scotswoman.

"It is I, James, Louisa," she said.

"You must be joking," I said.

"No, James, I'm really here. This is something we've tried to do – to have my mind fully enter Sophie's. Tonight it happened."

Not only the cadence of her voice but her mannerisms, the movement of her eyebrows, the knowing gaze of her eyes were Louisa's. She got up and twirled around, then clutched my hands.

"To walk again, to be light on my feet. I can even dance if you'd like," she said.

She was beautiful in her flowered patterned dress with puffed shoulders and cut to reveal her lovely collar bones.

"Louisa," I said. "But how?"

"The connection between Sophie and I grows stronger as the ship nears El Radio, her ability in particular. She was able to let me in. It's the best way I can put it."

I sat on the bed, unable to believe, but also knowing Louisa was truly here. She sat close, still holding my hands, looking at me longingly.

"Um, any news from Juliet?" I asked.

"She's in Vigo, scouring old records, trying to learn about Friar Cossio. All she knows so far is that Cossio went to Mexico in 1540 but never returned."

"Someone else must have brought back the journal," I said.

"Yes, she's trying to find out who."

"Wish her luck for me."

"I will. Kiss me, James."

I did and we embraced.

"I've dreamed of this for so long," Louisa said.

"What about Sophie? I mean ... does she ..."

"More than anything. She's here, too. Don't worry, she could expel me in an instant."

Confusion reigned in my mind which had become powerless to stop my rising passion. I kissed her again and ran my fingers through her silky locks.

* * *

I awoke to see Sophie putting on her clothes, dawn's twilight dimly illuminating her form.

"The girls will be wanting their breakfast," she said.

Her Spanish accent had returned. She bent down, kissed my cheek and left. I sighed, knowing our having slept together would not be a secret. The vicissitudes of love had always left me befuddled. This was beyond reckoning.

Chapter 9: Jamaica

30 June, 1819, Kingston, Jamaica

A lackluster wind nudged us into Kingston's harbor channel. On the south side was Port Royale, an island connected to the mainland by a string of islands. The port was now a burnt-out husk of crumbled walls and charred docks. To the north was the city itself. Said to be the bustling jewel of the British West Indies, it now appeared half deserted. Low dark clouds threatened rain and added to the gloom. Fort Augusta, situated on a narrow peninsula, remained intact. The mainland quays were still in operation, protected by the fort's 80 big guns.

Having no cargo to unload, we anchored well away from shore near a war brig flying an American flag and bearing the name, *Enterprise.* Longer and wider than the *Bar Jack*, the ship was square-rigged, had two masts, and carried 14 guns. Its crew appeared busy making repairs which suggested recent action. Rackham studied the *Enterprise* through her German optics.

"Not another victim of the *Vipere*, I hope," I said.

"Nah, first I've laid eyes on her. Heard of her, though, a pirate hunter, a good one."

I noticed other ships in the vicinity had armed men pacing their decks.

"Dangerous place, I gather," I said.

"Aye," Rackham said.

* * *

I went ashore alone, Maggie and Clair rowing me to the docks. I told them to return for me in three hours' time.

My meeting with the harbor master was brief and perfunctory. All he could say of the *Squirrel* is that it stayed in port for three days, took on stores and departed. I inquired about the Charles Morgan plantation and learned it lay north in the hills near the frontiers of territory still controlled by the British Army.

I asked what happened to Port Royale and learned that three months ago, a swarm of maroons in canoes attacked it during the night, setting fire to buildings, docks and ships before being driven off. Hundreds of men died in the battle; it was a costly attack for both sides.

I then strolled the cobbled streets, trying to get a sense of the place. Kingston's modern buildings seemed forlorn with so few people about. Many of the shops were boarded up. I wore my sword and a pistol, which, in Oxford, would have drawn stares and frowns, but here no one gave them a second glance. I found an open livery near the quays and inquired about transport to the Morgan Plantation. I was told no coaches were available for travel outside the city, so I negotiated for the use of two horses to be ready the next morning. I had to pay a hefty deposit.

* * *

"We got a signal from the *Enterprise*," Rackham said when I returned to the *Bar Jack*. "The captain wants to pay a visit. I told him he'd have to wait for you."

"Signal that he's welcome to come aboard," I said.

Lawrence Kearny, captain of the *Enterprise*, was a young man, stout, with brown hair and prominent side whiskers. He gripped my hand firmly.

"Pleased to meet you, captain," I said. "This is my first mate, Leopold von Sydow, and my sailing master ..."

"Ann Rackham," she said, reaching out her hand.

"Heard they hung you in London," Kearny said.

"They hadn't gotten round to it."

"She's on parole," I said. "Sailing expertise is in short supply in England these days."

"I suppose it is. Well, anyhow, I'm here to ask a small favor."

"I'm at your service, captain," I said.

"Excellent. You see, we couldn't help but notice that most of your hands are ladies and, well, I'm thinking, given I'm not allowing any leave because of trouble ashore, that perhaps my lads and your gals could get together this evening for a little fun. Good for morale and all that. We've got some hard months sailing ahead of us before our cruise is done. What do you say, captain? I'd be much obliged."

Sydow slapped me on the back.

"As I said, kapitan, we have a popular crew, no?"

My sense of propriety was telling me to decline the request. But my authority to raise the chastity concern was compromised by the fact Sophie now slept in my cabin. I also remembered my brother's words regarding the Americans.

"In the interests of good relations between our countries, and if my crew is willing, I will agree to your request," I said. "However, I can tolerate no rudeness and my crew must be quartered by the middle watch."

"Of course, of course, there won't be any trouble. I'll see to that," Captain Kearny said.

My crew, unsurprisingly, was quite willing. I gave Kearny a tour of the *Bar Jack* and told him about our mission.

"Some in Washington were thinking about an expedition to Volcan Rojo," he said, "but the disappearance of the *Squirrel* gave folks cold feet. I think it's a good idea but we'd want to commit a couple of frigates."

"You're not worried about sea monsters," I said.

"Sea monsters? Oh, hell, no. I think it's the French. I think they're guarding something there and they've got a squadron destroying anything that gets close."

"Plausible, I suppose," I said. "Say, captain, I've some business ashore that might take a day or two. If you're remaining in port, I'd ask the favor of keeping an eye on the *Bar Jack*."

"You bet. Least I can do."

* * *

We took the Old Hope Road east through town and on through the cane fields of the Kingston plain. The rain had stopped and the morning sun foretold a warm, sunny day to come. The road turned north toward the heavily forested Blue Mountains and twisted its way through the rugged foothills. The horses had seemed barely up to the task but were proving sturdy enough.

I rode with Sophie on one and Rackham rode the other. I reasoned that if Charles Morgan was as knowledgeable as I'd hoped, Rackham's knowledge of the region would help us decide where the *Bar Jack* should go next. And, to be honest, I still didn't entirely trust her. If I had brought Sydow instead, would she take the opportunity to sail away with the ship? It seemed unlikely, yet I sensed if she had a mind to, many of the hands would cast their lots with her.

"I'm going to borrow Kitten for the trip," I had told Sydow, "and your carbine if you don't mind."

Kitten rode with Rackham, the carbine rifle slung on her shoulder.

"I noticed you and Captain Kearny were talking last night," I said to Rackham.

The prior evening's festivities had been dowsed with rain but were nevertheless merry and mostly cordial. Only one fight broke out between the *Enterprise*'s men.

"He knows his business," Rackham said. "Told me he wished he'd been the one to lock horns with the *Vipere*."

"What did you say?"

"'Would have been a pleasure.'"

"Would Kearny have prevailed?"

"Might've. He's a sly one, I'll lay to that."

The twists of the tracks through thick woods would be ideal for ambush but I had been told the road was well patrolled. As if to confirm, when the road entered a small valley with a farmhouse, we met a dozen British cavalrymen watering their horses. Some of the men looked peaked and worn out, a reminder of the threat of tropical illness. A young lieutenant told us the turnoff to the Morgan Plantation was about two miles ahead.

A sign marked the turn and the trail narrowed. Soon we were in a dark wood of massive mahogany trees. Serpentine branches twisted overhead to form what seemed like an eldritch cathedral of a wicked god.

"Ever have the feeling you're being watched?" I asked aloud.

Rackham smiled. Kitten unslung her carbine.

"I feel something is here," Sophie said, "malicious, not human."

"One of Louisa's daemons?" I asked.

"I don't think so, it feels more substantial."

"Now I am getting spooked."

* * *

About a mile onward, we emerged from the gloom of the mahoganies into a broad valley of fields and orchards. A large house could be seen in the distance. We crossed a sturdy wooden bridge spanning a small river, then the track went through rows of tall sugarcane. As we neared the house, the crop changed to wheat and, nearer still, to vegetables on the north side of the road and lemon trees on the south.

A half dozen men, one on horseback, headed toward us from the direction of the house. The men were negroes and they were armed.

"Ah, hell," I said. "The place must have been taken. I was assured it hadn't been."

If something were to happen to the women, how would I live with myself? We'll have to flee, I thought, imagining we could outrun the footmen but would somehow have to deal with the rider if he pursued. Rackham looked through her spyglass.

"Nah," she said. "They don't look like maroons. Planter's men, I reckon. I say play it calm, see what happens."

"Slaves with guns?" I said.

"I doubt they're slaves," Rackham said.

The footmen stopped about 50 yards out keeping their muskets lowered while the man on horseback approached. He wore a wide-brimmed hat, a white shirt, a bandolier with two pistols, and a saber at his hip. Rackham whispered to Kitten who held the carbine pointed toward the ground.

"Hallo," the rider said. "I don't intend to alarm you folks but this is private property. I need to ask your business."

"I've come to visit Mr. Charles Morgan," I said. "My name is Sir James LeRoque."

"Not the best time," the man said. "Mr. Morgan's engaged just now."

"It's the only time I have," I said. "I am a friend of Dr. Paul Seymour who visited here some time ago. I am trying to find him. Captain Amos Westropp, Mr. Morgan's nephew, sent me."

"Fair enough but I'll need to check with Mr. Morgan. You can wait by the tree over there. It's got good shade."

"Thank you, and, I'm sorry, I didn't catch your name."

"Jim Hammer. I'll be back shortly."

We waited as instructed under the shade of a giant cottonwood tree. The footmen stayed nearby but kept their distance. We dismounted and stretched our legs. I told Kitten to shoulder the carbine. My watch showed half past one o'clock when Mr. Hammer returned with another rider, a man wearing a gray frock coat and a top hat.

"My apologies for keeping you waiting, Sir LeRoque," he said. "I'm Charles Morgan."

I shook his hand and introduced him to the women. If he recognized Rackham's name, he didn't show it, nor show any surprise that she and Kitten were armed.

"Caught me at a delicate time," Mr. Morgan said. He had long, gray hair and a large nose on a narrow face. "I have a delegation here and I'd like to keep that fact quiet for the time being. I do hope, sir, I can count on your discretion."

"Of course, you have my word," I said.

"Excellent, let's go to the house and I'll get you something to drink. You missed lunch but I'll have my cook make sandwiches."

* * *

The house was made of stone, two stories, and was situated near the base of a steep, rocky ridge. It resembled a small castle. A portico supported by arches surrounded the ground level and a stair ascended to the main entryway on the upper level. The manor was flanked by a barn and stable and there were several small houses in the vicinity.

A massive, broad-limbed mahogany tree dominated the front lawn. Against the trunk leaned several long rifles and sitting in the shade near them were several negro men wearing colorful headbands, some with feathers. Most wore calf-length trousers and light vests with big pockets over bare chests. Maroons, I thought, they must be. They were playing cards on a blanket spread between them.

We dismounted and Mr. Morgan instructed a hand to lead our horses to the stable. We ascended the stairs and went inside, laying our weapons on a table in the foyer. The parlor was spacious with high ceilings and partially paneled stone walls. A grand arch revealed the dining room. A large painting depicted an old-fashioned barque anchored in an aqua-green lagoon and natives trading with white sailors. Native artifacts on the walls gave the parlor an exotic air. Atop the mantel of a little-used hearth sat a carved stone, the squarish head of a god, I presumed. Fine work, I thought, but it didn't resemble antiquities from Egypt or Syria.

Two people stood to greet us. One was a very young man, fifteen or sixteen years old, perhaps, who wore a red tunic with elaborate embroidery and a headband decorated with colored beads in trapezoidal patterns. Throughout the bead work were small, uncut crystals of various colors set in apparently random locations.

The other was a woman, young but not so young as the man. She was dark-skinned and wore a kind of turban, green with a silver band to keep it on her head. Her red blouse was cut short to reveal her midsection. At her waist she wore a long skirt, green, with embroidered stripes near the hem. A star-shaped pendant hung from a string of pearls around her neck.

"May I introduce Hatchi, daughter of Chief Nashoba," Mr. Morgan said.

Nashoba, I had learned, was the war leader of the maroons who controlled much of eastern Jamaica. Why was his daughter here, and those men outside?

"And," Morgan continued, "this is Osceola, nephew of Peter McQueen, a Seminole chief."

Morgan gave the pair our names in return.

"Sir LeRoque is a Scottish nobleman."

I bowed to Hatchi and shook hands with Osceola.

"My American name is Billy Powell," the young man said in clear English. "My great-grandfather was James McQueen, so I have Scottish blood. Maybe we are relatives, hey?"

"Perhaps," I said. "I believe there are one or two McQueens in my bloodline. I would have to consult my cousin. She is the keeper of our family history."

I noticed Sophie and Hatchi holding each other's forearms, looking silently at each other.

We sat and were served lemonade. My party was served sandwiches made with savory pulled pork.

"We want only peace with the British," Osceola said to me. "We seek peace and freedom for all people."

"Noble goals," I said. "Though one often comes at the cost of the other."

Osceola seemed to mull my response for a moment.

"I mean what I say. Maybe you can tell your government."

"I shall," I said, "if I am fortunate enough to return to England. My brother is a member of the House of Lords."

A servant cleared our plates. Hatchi stood and took Sophie's hand.

"We must speak together, you and I," she said. "With your permission, Sir LeRoque."

"By all means," I said.

Hatchi and Sophie left the room to go for a walk outside. Osceola, who seemed uncomfortable in the confines of the parlor, excused himself as well.

* * *

Morgan led the rest of us to a large backroom which was his study. The ornate furnishings of the parlor gave way to simple chairs, a long table piled with books and maps, and a huge desk. He told us to take a seat while he rummaged through papers on the desk.

"You're no doubt wondering about Hatchi and Osceola," he said. "I'll relieve your curiosity so we can get to the matter at hand."

Kitten and I pulled up chairs. Rackham continued to stand, studying a map on the wall of the Gulf of Mexico. Kitten sat stiffly, eyes looking at her lap.

"I'm trying to broker a peace deal and an alliance," Morgan said. "No sense pretending things can go back to the way they were ..."

Morgan went on to say that Nashoba and his people, who now referred to themselves as the Free Jamaican Republic, wanted to come to terms with the British army and form an alliance against Kratoka, the leader of the maroons who controlled the western half of the island.

"In our enlightened age, there are few I would consider truly evil," Morgan said. "Kratoka is among them. His Leopard Men have spread a reign of terror that would make Robespierre shiver. He's bent on killing all white men on the island and beyond. They say he was a witch doctor in Africa, captured and taken as a slave. After Volcan Rojo his powers grew strong. He murdered his master and started the rebellion in the west."

"When one is enslaved, it's bound to inspire wrath," I said.

"Agreed, agreed. That's why I don't own slaves anymore. All my hands are paid and the top ones share in the profits. The writing was on the wall, so to speak. But Kratoka, there's more to his malice than vengeance. He murders blacks as freely as whites. Jamaica would be a dark place indeed if he was to prevail. And he's closer to that than you might think. Our army here is in shambles, half the men have deserted or succumbed to disease. The government in

England can't afford to send more troops because of the threat from France. The only hope is to ally with Nashoba."

"What are Nashoba's terms?" I asked.

"Generous, as I see it," Morgan said. "Britain maintains administrative control of Kingston for fifty years and property rights are respected. Slavery's a sticking point with many planters but I believe compensation can be arranged. You know, Nashoba's people have drafted a constitution, like the Americans. They're really quite civilized."

Morgan fetched a long pole from a corner of the room and used it to push open a hatch in the ceiling.

"It's getting stuffy. This lets the warm air escape."

"I wish you the best of luck with your negotiations," I said. "The idea sounds perfectly reasonable."

"I'm glad you think so," Morgan said.

I noticed Kitten fidgeting on her chair.

"Why don't you go outside and see what Sophie's up to," I said.

"Yes, sir, I think I will, sir," she said and quickly vanished from the room.

"A darling little lass," Morgan said. "I was surprised to see her carrying that fancy carbine."

"She's an excellent shot with it," I said.

"Is that so?"

* * *

Our conversation moved to Dr. Paul Seymour who had corresponded with Mr. Morgan prior to embarking on the *Squirrel.*

"Just the one letter," Morgan said. "He wanted to pay a call and talk about the Mayans and the Yucatan Peninsula. Of course I answered in the affirmative."

"Who are the Mayans?" I asked.

"They are the natives who inhabited the peninsula. There weren't many by the time of the eruption and now they're all but extinguished. Some believe, myself included, that they represented the remnants of an advanced civilization that built great cities and monuments. That stone on the mantel in the parlor is said to have come from an ancient temple torn down by the Spanish to build a church. They had a writing system, too. Inscriptions have been reported in a number of places. There are credible rumors of ruined cities deep in the jungle."

"Fascinating," I said. "But why was Paul interested? He was a chemist, not an antiquarian."

Morgan stood again, fetched a pipe and a pouch of tobacco. Raven's Mixture, he called it and offered some to Rackham and myself.

"Dr. Seymour thought the Mayans, having lived so long in the vicinity of where Volcan Rojo erupted, might have knowledge of what happened, perhaps there were clues in their myths," Morgan said. He struck a flint to a match and lit his pipe.

"Are there such clues?" I asked, taking the match, lighting my pipe and handing it to Rackham in turn.

"I only know fragments," Morgan said. "The Mayans believe there is a deep underworld, called Xilbalba, where 12 gods of death ruled a dark city. Two heroes defeated the gods and destroyed the city but a malicious spirit continued to dwell there, a spirit more ancient than the gods, a being not of this earth. An order of select priests were charged with keeping the ancient spirit confined to his underworld tomb. The order continued up to the present."

Morgan took a long pull on his pipe, blowing a puff from his nose.

"But," he continued, "they say a white witch sailed to the shores of Mexico, traveled deep into the jungle and broke the power of the priests. The witch went to the underworld and released the ancient spirit who spewed forth from Volcan Rojo to wreak havoc on the world. The Mayan's call the spirit Akabo, the darkness."

* * *

"Giselle LaFoy," I muttered, staring at the smoke rising from the bowl of my pipe. The tobacco was strong but flavorful.

"What is that you said?" Morgan asked.

"Begging your pardon. I drifted off. My cousin, Louisa, believes Giselle LaFoy, Napoleon's consort, is a kind of sorceress. Madame LaFoy traveled to the jungles of Mexico on a French frigate, the *Méduse*, and returned shortly after the eruption. Louisa thinks she's had a hand in Napoleon's changing fortunes."

"You think she may be the white witch?"

"I don't know. It seems ludicrous. But Louisa has learned more. Apparently Madame LaFoy found a book compiled by a Spanish priest who traveled to the jungle and adopted native ways. The priest's name was ..." I snapped my fingers. "I wish Sophie was here ... ah yes, Diego Cossio."

Morgan removed the pipe from his mouth.

"Diego Cossio? Do you know the fable?"

"No, sir."

"The story is he was a missionary who came to Mexico shortly after Cortez. He went into the jungle and was never heard from again. That is until 100 years later. It's said he hadn't aged at all and was leading Mayan locals against Spanish rule. The tale goes that the Pope determined Cossio was an abomination and sent an assassin disguised as a monk to kill him."

"Not long ago," I said, "I would have laughed at such ..."

The crack of a gunshot interrupted me.

"Are we attacked?" I asked, standing up.

Morgan waved his hand dismissively. "I doubt it." He went to the window and opened the shutter. "No, just the maroons having a little target practice. I see your girl is with them."

Another crack. I went to the window myself and saw Kitten reloading her carbine. One of the maroons was lining up his shot at targets placed about a hundred paces away toward the ridge. He fired and another maroon took his turn.

Morgan returned to his chair. Rackham stood by the window and watched the shooting. I went to the map on the wall.

"Did Paul talk of his route from here?" I asked.

"He said they were planning to sail to Veracruz, skirt the coast and approach as close as they dare to Volcan Rojo. They hoped to be able to make landfall to find anitite and observe the effects it had on local flora and fauna."

"Paul told you about anitite?"

"Yes, I know little of chemistry," Morgan said, "but if what he said is true, it would explain much."

I nodded and pointed at the map.

"Why cross the Gulf and approach from the west? Why not approach from the Atlantic side?"

"Storms," Rackham said. "They say they never stop raging on that coast and any ship approaching it would be smashed to bits."

"Miss Rackham is correct, from all I hear," Morgan said. "That coast was particularly devastated by the volcano's ash, down to Honduras and beyond. It's a wasteland. Perhaps the storms have abated by now but no captain I know dares approach it."

I pointed to a gap between the west end of Cuba and the Yucatan Peninsula.

"Did the *Squirrel* go through there?"

"I believe so, though it is dangerous," Morgan said. "Most ships go around and enter the Gulf between Cuba and Florida."

"Did the *Squirrel* make it through?"

"I don't know. I've heard no credible reports about the *Squirrel*'s whereabouts since she left Kingston."

"What about incredible ones?"

"I'm sorry," Morgan said, puffing thoughtfully on his pipe. The occasional crack of gunfire continued outside. "I hesitate to say this, but if anybody could tell you more about the *Squirrel*, it would be Jean Laffite."

"I've heard the name," I said, "but I don't know who he is."

"Miss Rackham likely knows more than I," Morgan said.

"Laffite is a pirate, or boss of pirates," Rackham said. "He has a stronghold on Galveston Island about 300 miles west of New Orleans."

"Why would he know anything of the *Squirrel*?"

"Pirate ships sometimes sail into El Radio to escape pursuit," Morgan said. "Some don't return, but others do and what news they get finds its way to Laffite. I imagine he knows more than anyone about what goes on in El Radio."

"Then I should like to talk to him," I said. "Would he receive me? Is he dangerous?"

"He spent time in New Orleans," Morgan said. "They called him Gentleman Jean. They say he often lets captains keep their ships once he relieves them of their cargoes. A good policy, I understand, because victims are less likely to put up a fight. But some say he's gone a little mad on his island, built a big house, painted it red and called it Maison Rouge."

I turned to Rackham.

"Ann, did you know Laffite?"

"I met him."

"Are you enemies?"

"Not that I know of."

"Would it be safe to go to Galveston?"

"Safe? I don't know. He's not a killer, least not when I was in the game, but he'll kill if it suits him."

"Would he kill us?"

"Probably not."

Hooting and cheers erupted outside. Rackham turned to the window.

"Looks like Kitten won the shooting match."

Chapter 10: The Leopard and the Rat

1 July, 1819, Morgan Plantation, Jamaica

Roast pig was served under a canopy surrounded by smoking torches that helped keep the insects away. The supper was a merry one and it struck me as interesting that Mr. Morgan, myself and my party were the only whites present. I sat next to Jim Hammer, the man who met us on the way in. He talked of his son and two young daughters, and of his hopes that a lasting peace would come one day and they could live in freedom and without fear. I wondered by what logic a rational man might not share Mr. Hammer's hope.

Kitten was all smiles and blushes, a star among the maroon embassy for her shooting prowess. Young Osceola praised her and gave her his headband of many beads and uncut gemstones which she donned as a band for her straw hat.

"You have a Seminole heart and need a Seminole name," Osceola said, raising his voice. "You are Koahkotchee and will always be welcome among my people. May the Great Spirit guide your steps."

Kitten fidgeted, tongue-tied, and folks clapped. Morgan toasted to friendship among all peoples.

Later I asked Morgan if he truly believed an alliance with Nashoba would bring the defeat of Kratoka.

"The chances are good," he said. "If the Crown gives up its claim to dominion over Jamaica, I believe many of Kratoka's people would rise against him in favor of Nashoba. Yet, while Kratoka is a murderous villain, he is also shrewd. He trades with pirates and has spies everywhere. He will try to prevent an alliance. Not long ago his men raided a plantation posing as Nashoba's followers. He knows something is brewing."

"Does he know you're trying to broker a deal?" I asked.

"I'm not sure, but he may."

"A dangerous game, it seems."

"It is."

"By the way, would you happen to know what Koahkotchee means, if anything?"

"I believe it means wildcat."

* * *

Morgan allowed my party two rooms, one for the women and one for myself. When the household had turned in, Sophie slipped into my room and, by her smile, I knew that Louisa was present.

"Hello, James," she said and took off her nightshirt.

* * *

Her head rested on my chest and I stroked her black locks.

"Sophie spent considerable time with Hatchi," I said. "What did they talk about?"

"Hatchi has the ability. Her skills are quite advanced. Sophie learned much though it is difficult to speak of it. The rites and practices of Hatchi's people are better guides, I think, than those of ours. They live closer to the world of dreams. They see the mind in all things."

I couldn't truly fathom what Louisa was saying. I found it unnerving to think that dreams and reality may not be so distinct.

"Any news from Juliet?" I asked.

"She's still in Vigo, researching a curious account of a monk who returned from Mexico in 1631. Apparently he possessed a tome or compendium of shamanic rites. The captain of the ship testified at an inquiry that the monk went mad on the return voyage and had to be locked away. His name was Ezio Tofana which is Italian. The tome was lost and the monk was confined to an asylum. He later escaped and was never found."

"Do you think that tome is what Madame LaFoy found?"

"Juliet thinks so but isn't sure," Louisa said. "Also, I asked Archy about the murder at Kilve. He said he was investigating but wouldn't say more and insisted I say nothing of it to anybody. I must go now, James, sleep well."

* * *

I awoke to Sophie shaking me vigorously.

"James, James, it's here," she whispered.

"Pardon, what, what is it?"

"It's here, the thing I felt in the forest. It's in the house."

"The grounds are well guarded. I'm sure nothing ..."

By the way Sophie squeezed my arm, I knew she was genuinely frightened. I also knew I shouldn't dismiss her premonitions as I might otherwise be inclined to do.

"Very well, light the lantern," I said.

I got out of bed, reached for my belt on the chair and drew my broadsword. Sophie handed me the lantern and I opened the door and stepped out into the hallway.

Fear knifed through my gut. I beheld a creature crouched before the door of Mr. Morgan's chamber. It had the shape of a man but was covered with a fine, gray fur with black spots. Its grotesquely large muscles rippled with feline power. It jerked its head toward me and hissed. I took a step back.

Large, round eyes reflected yellow in the lamplight. Its ears were pointed and a stub of a nose topped a protruding mouth snarling with small, sharp teeth and a pair of fangs like a viper. Elongated digits with curled claws made its hands seem like talons.

It turned its head away from me and exploded through the heavy oaken door.

It was going to kill Morgan, I thought. I willed my quivering legs forward and rushed into the room behind the monster. Morgan was upright in bed, terror-stricken. The violence of the door breaking free of its hinges had caused a wardrobe to fall on the creature. It hurled it off with a sweep of its arm and crouched to spring at Morgan. I yelled like a madman and charged, sword cocked to hew the beast.

It pivoted; its eyes catching mine. I felt like I'd been struck a blow. I staggered backward; my head burned and I collapsed.

Suddenly everything seemed so pointless. I realized at once what a pitiful, self-important creature I was, that we all were. Poor little Sophie stood over me, trying valiantly to lock minds with a being so horribly beyond her it was laughable. Why bother? Why strive against the futility of existence? The creature would destroy her mind and rend her body into pieces. Such an insignificant matter in a vast, indifferent creation. I supposed I could lift my sword again, make a feeble attempt to defend her. What would be the point? The result would be the same in the end - oblivion. There have been endless eons that preceded man's brief, absurd existence and there will be endless eons after he is gone. Why bother?

A loud crack jolted me and smoke billowed into the room.

Ears ringing and squinting through the smoke, I saw the monster stagger, its expression, if expression it could be called, was one of astonishment. Dark blood oozed from a hole in its massive chest. I got to my feet, sword still in hand and, overcome with a killing rage, I swung with all my strength. The creature's head came free from its body and it crumpled to the floor. I crumpled in turn.

* * *

The immediate aftermath was a blurry malaise. I was carried to a bed. I remember the negro princess, Hatchi, putting her hands on my head and chanting, then I dozed. It was dawn when I became fully awake, thrushes singing to the new day. I wondered what horrors this one had in store.

Kitten had fired the shot that defeated the creature. (My blow, I believe, was little more than an afterthought.) She had charged into the room with her carbine, Rackham behind her, and, for some reason, she had donned her hat.

Its band, Osceola claimed, protected her from the demon's mind magic.

Was it mind magic that made me falter, made me despair? Sophie, Louisa, Hatchi, they would all say yes, but I wasn't so sure. I had stood on the edge of the abyss and survived; the one I loved had survived. I should have been thankful, and I was, yet I was ashamed.

We ate breakfast at the kitchen table in brooding silence. Mr. Morgan was clearly shaken. I surmised he had suffered much the same as myself. A pistol had been on his nightstand but he had not reached for it when the monster burst into his room. He cleared his throat.

"I owe you my life, Captain LeRoque. If there is anything I can do for you, name it."

"You give me too much credit, I'm afraid," I said. "All I wish is that you succeed in your efforts to defeat Kratoka."

After eating we went to the bed chamber with several men and, for some time, just looked at the decapitated creature.

"There have been stories," Morgan said, "that Kratoka could perform a ritual that would transform a Leopard Man volunteer into a true monster. The Mayans believe in something similar, a kind of lycanthrope we would call a were-jaguar. I deemed it ridiculous until last night. You know, I left the roof hatch open. I wager that's how it got in."

I wondered what Sydow's former employer would think if he brought this abomination back to the British Museum. Then an idea occurred to me.

"I want its head," I said. "Could you put it in a box?"

"Certainly," Morgan said. "Do you want it as a trophy?"

"Good God, no. I have something else in mind."

* * *

Our things packed, we left the house to find our horses well brushed and looking better than when we got them. Kitten was already outside talking with Osceola. He slipped his knife and sheath off his belt and handed it to her. The knife was long, narrow and had a bone handle. The sheath was decorated with a leafy vine pattern.

"You are a warrior, Koahkotchee, you should have a warrior's blade," the young man said. "I will always remember you. Farewell."

Kitten seemed too struck to speak so she just kissed him on the cheek. Hatchi and Sophie embraced. I shook hands with Morgan and we were off. Mr. Hammer had two of his men escort us.

"That Indian boy really took a shine to you," I said to Kitten.

"He asked me to marry him, sir."

Despite my melancholy, I laughed.

"What did you tell him?"

"That I had a duty to the ship and to you."

"I appreciate that. I suspect we'll need you before we're done."

"Thank you, sir."

"No, Kitten, thank you."

* * *

Back in Kingston we returned the horses and parted ways with our escort. I hired a boat to take Sophie, Kitten and most of our gear to the *Bar Jack*. I asked a man where we might find the Shark's Tooth Inn. He pointed down the wharf and Rackham and I headed that way.

Mr. Morgan had given me the name of an agent whom, he said, had dealings with Jean Laffite from time to time. Apparently, the agent conducted much of his business at the inn. We found it near the merchant docks, an old structure out of place among the modern buildings. I gathered from the style that it was one of the original Spanish establishments. A jaw of a large shark hung over the door.

The inside was dark with wood paneling and ancient, well-used chairs and tables. The air was thick with the smell of tobacco and beer. The place was busy with people taking their noon meals. We walked by a table of men gambling at cards. One of the men, a bearded fellow, looked up at

Rackham with what seemed like recognition, if not surprise. I couldn't tell if Rackham noticed him or not.

I asked the barkeeper where I might find a Mr. Philip Nolte.

"Out on business, I think, should be back before long. Would you like a little lunch while you wait?"

"Yes, thank you," I said.

We found a small table and sat down.

"I think one of the men playing cards recognized you," I said.

"Yeah, I know him," Rackham said.

"A friend?"

"A crewmate."

"The *Vipere*?"

"Yes, he was wounded so we cut out his share and left him in Havana."

"Thoughtful."

"We took care of our own. That was the code."

I waited for Rackham to say more but she didn't, so I retrieved my pen and ink set and began writing a letter.

* * *

Letter dated 2 July, 1819:

To the honorable Duke of Manchester, Colonel William Montagu, Governor of Jamaica:

Your Grace,

Enclosed in the box is a foul thing. I do not send it as a jest but as incontrovertible evidence of something horrible in our midst.

I paid a call yesterday on Mr. Charles Morgan whom I believe you know. My purpose was in no way political. I was only seeking information about my friend, Dr. Paul Seymour, the lead natural philosopher on the ill-fated Squirrel expedition. However, last night, a loathsome, inhuman creature attempted to take Morgan's life. The effort was foiled only by the timely intervention of a member of my crew. As the beast was expiring from a gunshot wound, I hewed its head off with my broadsword. It is that head the box contains.

It is very likely that the creature was the contrivance of Kratoka, the rebel chieftain, one of his Leopard Men transformed by God only knows what power. I sincerely believe now that no cost should be spared to defeat Kratoka.

Mr. Morgan (who has no knowledge of my intention to send this letter and package) told me he has proposed making peace with the much more civilized and honorable Nashoba, chieftain of the eastern rebels, with a mind to combining efforts against Kratoka. From my limited perspective, I see this as a wise course.

I don't presume, however, to make any recommendation. I trust in your wisdom implicitly. I only wish to make you more fully aware of what Kratoka is and what he is capable of.

Your most humble and obedient servant,

Sir James Henry Ker LeRoque, Captain of the Bar Jack

* * *

Finishing the letter, I looked up to see Rackham eating while my soup and sausages had grown lukewarm.

"I need to use the head," Rackham said.

"By all means."

I dug into my meal and by the time I had finished my soup, Rackham had not returned. I looked around and saw the bearded man was no longer at the card table.

"Ah, hell," I muttered.

I went to the back hall, found the door to the ladies' facility and knocked.

"Ann. Ann! Are you there?"

There was no answer. I noticed the door to the back alley was ajar. I went through it and saw nothing. I went to the street and saw only a few people, none of them Rackham. I had a bad feeling, not so much about her running away. If she truly wanted to go, I wouldn't try to stop her. I hurried up the street, away from the wharf. Nearing the next alley, I heard a man's voice.

"Please, Ann, don't, you've got it wrong."

"You were the only one who knew who wasn't aboard the *Vipere*." The voice was Rackham's.

"It wasn't me, I'm telling you. Maybe it was Laffite."

"Laffite didn't know jack. Radan didn't trust him. You're a lying rat bastard and this is the end of the line."

I stepped into the alley to see Rackham holding the tip of her dirk to the bearded man's throat, a pistol cocked and ready in her other hand.

"Stop, Ann," I said. "Let the man go."

"Have to, LeRoque. The code is the code."

"You're not a pirate anymore. You said so yourself."

"Just one last duty to perform."

"You'll hang, Ann."

"I'm as good as dead anyway."

"No you're not. You have a fast ship and a good crew."

I could see the fury in her eyes, the blade drawing blood under the man's chin.

"You're a free woman, Ann. If you want to go, go. I won't stand in your way. But if you kill him, I'll have to turn you in."

She turned her head and glared at me. Would she kill me as well? I had to believe she wouldn't.

"Look, the *Bar Jack* is yours," I said. "When your business with me is finished, you can have her. You can buy her from me on installments, or captain her on commission, whatever arrangement you want. The ocean will be your lake to do as you please. Don't throw it away on a futile gesture, a point of honor now devoid of any relevance."

Rackham grimaced and withdrew the blade.

"You'd better go," I said to the bearded man. "And make yourself scarce for a time."

He nodded and hurried by me.

* * *

I was relieved to see the box under the table and the letter on top of it when we returned to the tavern. I had left them there in my haste to find Rackham. Mr. Nolte, the agent, had not returned.

We sat again to wait. I wrote two letters, one to my brother, the other to my friend, Darnsby, while Rackham borrowed a deck of cards and played solitaire. After sealing and addressing the letters, I asked the barkeeper again about Mr. Nolte.

"Business must be keepin' him away. Don't know when he'll be back. Maybe tonight. Tomorrow, for sure, I would think."

I turned to Rackham.

"Do you think it essential that we talk to the agent if we're going to visit Laffite?"

"Won't matter much," she said. "I say we get the hell out of here."

"Agreed," I said.

Chapter 11: Heavy Weather

2 July, 1819, Kingston, Jamaica

It felt good to be aboard the *Bar Jack*; it felt like home. Jamaica, however, did not. I ordered the crew to make ready to sail as soon as possible. I didn't want to spend another moment in this blasted place.

I found it curious that Captain Kearny and a few of his men were on board. I learned the *Bar Jack*, too, had received unwanted visitors during the night.

Sydow had agreed to another get-together with the *Enterprise* crew which, Sydow claimed, was conducted with moderation. Mrs. Kedward, who did not participate, kept watch when the others had turned in. She said a strange fog rolled in and, shortly thereafter, she heard whispers and paddling. She sounded the alarm and a groggy Sydow ordered battle stations. Polly, a keen-eyed girl, spotted what she thought were several canoes coming toward the ship. Sydow ordered the swivel gun crew and the musketeers to fire at the water in front of the canoes. That was sufficient to let the apparent attackers know they had lost the element of surprise and they turned about.

The gunfire had roused *Enterprise*'s crew and Kearny came over on a launch with several armed men. They stayed aboard the rest of the night but there were no further encroachments.

"Jamaica's turned into a damn, bloody hellhole," Kearny said.

"You'll hear no argument from me," I said. "That's why I want to set sail now."

"Where're you headed, if I may ask?"

“To pay a call on Jean Laffite. Charles Morgan thinks if anybody has information about the *Squirrel*, it would be him.”

“That may be but Laffite’s a wily bastard. I’d be careful,” Kearny said.

“Do you think our lives would be at risk?” I asked.

“Probably not. Laffite’s not known to be cold-blooded. He might take a shine to your ship, and your women will interest him. He’s trying to build a permanent settlement at Galveston, make it part of a new country that a bunch of filibusters want to carve out of Texas. A murderous reputation would hurt his plans. Mind you, I intend to nab the bastard and haul him to the gallows. He’s a lawless crook.”

“I’d appreciate it if you’d wait until I’ve had a chance to speak with him,” I said.

“Ha! You’d better move along then.”

As Kearny descended to the *Enterprise*’s launch, he looked up at me.

“You’re really going to head in toward Volcan Rojo?”

“It seems likely,” I said.

“Damned if I don’t want to do that myself. Good luck, captain.”

“Good hunting, captain.”

* * *

I told Rackham to take the *Bar Jack* straight out to sea to get out of range of any canoe sorties. The weather was fair with a light wind and we sailed close hauled on a southwesterly course. If the weather held, it would take us two days to reach the Straight of Yucatan. Rackham wanted to time it so we’d go through in daylight because that was where we’d be skimming the edge of El Radio.

The Admiralty had determined, somewhat arbitrarily, I assumed, that El Radio was a 300-mile radius extending from Merida, Mexico, which had existed near where Volcan Rojo had erupted. The city was presumed destroyed and all inhabitants killed. British naval and merchant vessels were forbidden to sail within the radius without the Admiralty's permission. I was the first one to receive permission since the *Squirrel* expedition, though I likely was the only one who had asked.

Working with Rackham we plotted a course that would take us north of the Cayman Islands toward Cape San Antonio, the western-most point of Cuba. We planned to pass within about ten miles of the cape as we entered the Gulf of Mexico. From there we would steer toward Galveston Island as straight as weather and currents allowed.

I took the middle watch, a mild breeze barely filling the sails. The sky was clear so I made star readings to check our position. Rackham relieved me at four to take the morning watch.

In my cabin I found Sophie still awake, sitting up in bed and looking out the stern windows.

"Can't sleep?" I asked.

She shook her head. I undressed and sat next to her. She rested her head on my shoulder.

"It was him," she said.

"Him, who?"

"The daemon that invaded my mind at Kilve Beach. He was there last night."

"You mean that monster was the daemon? Good riddance, I say."

"It's not like that," Sophie said. "He was a passenger, like Louisa is with me. He's not destroyed."

"Had he somehow followed us from England?"

"I don't think so. He seemed surprised that I was there."

"Did he attack you with mind magic like Hatchi said he attacked me?"

"No. He wanted me to join him."

"Join him? To what end?" I asked.

"Power."

For a time we just listened to the creaking of the ship. The idea of an other-worldly being tempting Sophie with an offer of power was more disturbing to me, somehow, than if it had outright attacked her.

"You call it a *him*," I said.

"He feels masculine to me."

"Mr. Morgan told me the Mayan Indians believe a powerful god of the underworld was released when Vulcan Rojo erupted, that a white witch released him. The god's name is Akabo, the darkness. Is that who this is?"

"I don't know," Sophie said. "When our minds met, I had a vision. I was back in Spain, my family's land and titles were returned, the monarchy was restored, and I held a high position at court. There were towering buildings of glass and ships that flew in the air. I was very old but my body was young. The vision was so vivid and, to make it real, I had only to allow the being to show me the way."

"You refused, I assume."

"Kitten shot the beast and the daemon was gone."

* * *

The weather being fair, we trained the next day – musketry, bayonet drills, fencing – and fired a few shots from the swivel gun. I was in an angry mood and the exercises abated it somewhat. As did the teasing the girls gave Kitten, calling her "squaw" and "Indian princess." She blushed and hurled insults back, but I could tell she enjoyed it. Rackham worked with her for a time, showing her how to handle the long-bladed knife Osceola had given her.

A strong south wind kicked up late in the afternoon. Rackham and I decided to shift course a little northward toward the Isle of Youth to take advantage of the wind. We made good speed through the night and into the following day. During the forenoon watch, Rackham summoned me to the deck. Her reason was obvious. A line of dark clouds filled the western horizon.

"A storm front," I said.

Rackham nodded.

"A little early in the season for a hurricane," I said. "Can we weather it?"

"Ain't a hurricane but it's a ship wrecker. We need to find shelter," she said.

"God damn it!"

It seemed the world was working against me.

"How about the lee side of the Isle of Youth?" I asked. "Could we find shelter there?"

"Too shallow, too many reefs, we'd be smashed to bits."

"Where do you suggest?"

"The Cuban coast, a place called the Bay of Pigs. I think we can make it but we need to turn now."

"Do it," I said.

Rackham ordered a northeast heading, the booms shifting as we crossed the wind. She helped the crew get the sails trimmed then ordered the outer jib flown.

"The wind's a bit stiff for that, isn't it?" I asked.

"We need all the speed we can get. We'll have to risk it."

That work done we went to my cabin to look at the chart.

"What about here, Cienfuegos Bay?" I asked. "There's a fort there, I believe."

"The French hold that fort now. I don't think we'd be welcome," Rackham said. "And it's too far."

"I see reefs marked between us and the Bay of Pigs."

"I know a channel we can get through."

"Does everything have to be such a near-run event?"

"That's life at sea, captain."

* * *

A long line of islands and reefs stretched eastward from the Isle of Youth. That's what lay between us and the Cuban coast.

"Kearny told me that coast is infested with pirates," Sydow said. He was manning the tiller, adding his strength to Maggie's in an increasingly rough sea.

"That may be but we have little choice," I said.

The storm loomed closer and as we approached the string of islands, the swell grew. I could see breakers up ahead. Rackham was at the bow using hand signals to make course corrections. I relayed them to Maggie and Sydow and kept an eye on the compass.

I was terrified but, at the same time, overcome with the splendor of it all: Lightning flashed to the west and thunder rumbled while the *Bar Jack*, under full sail in a heavy wind, glided along swells at astonishing speed. It seemed I could feel the masts straining; I hoped they would hold.

The breakers served as our guides and Rackham found her channel. Soon the reefs were behind us. The swell leveled some and the wind slackened but we still moved crisply. Rackham returned to the helm.

"The wind let up. A good sign, eh?" Sydow said.

"No, not a good sign," Rackham said. "It will be night soon and we won't make the bay before the storm hits."

She ordered the storm sails brought up and all hands on deck. On her signal the mains and jibs would come down and the short sails would go up. She waited, wanting to milk our speed until the last moment.

Sophie came on deck with the other women, out of place in her kitchen dress and apron.

"Sophie," I snapped. "Go to the cabin and stay there."

"It's all hands, captain. My place is with the crew. I want to help."

"Do you have the power to turn back the storm?"

"No."

"Then go to the cabin, now!"

Sophie complied and I immediately regretted my harsh words. I simply couldn't stand the thought of her getting swept overboard by a wave or blast of wind.

Night descended, the southerly wind slowly lost its force as I kept an eye on the chronometer, letting Rackham know the passing minutes.

Abruptly, the wind gave out and the sails went limp.

"Now!" Rackham shouted.

The crew rushed to pull down the sails. The *Bar Jack* lost momentum and, rather than riding the swell, was being buffeted by it. The helm became unresponsive and the ship lost steerageway. The mains came down briskly, but I watched the girls struggling with the main jib. Polly came running toward the aft deck, almost falling as a wave heaved the stern upward.

"The block is jammed, we can't get the jib down," she reported.

"Goddammit," Rackham hissed.

She and I went to the bow, the first patterings of rain moistening the deck.

"Looks like the block cracked and the cable's wedged between the spool and the housing," Rackham said.

"What do we do?" I asked.

"We have to unjam it or cut it down."

"I'll go," Kitten said.

"No," I said. "We should raise a ratline."

But she was already shimmying up the mast. I was going to order her down but Rackham clutched my arm.

"Let her go, it's our best chance."

The ship heaved with the swell while Kitten inchwormed upward. The block was attached about a third of the way from the top. Lightning flashed and to the west I saw the dark wall of rain and clouds enveloping the sea. The storm would be upon us in moments.

* * *

Without steerageway the *Bar Jack* couldn't hold course. Its heading drifted to starboard and it rocked awkwardly in the waves. Kitten hung on and continued her ascent. I could hardly stand to watch. She reached the block, worked it with one hand while clinging to the mast with her legs and other arm. She looked down and shook her head.

"Cut it down!" Rackham shouted.

Kitten drew her knife and sawed at the thick rope that held the block to the mast.

A blast of wind and rain swept the ship. The block gave way and dropped to the deck with a thud. The freed jib whipped violently in the wind while the crew labored to reel it in and raise the storm sails.

Kitten, somehow still clinging to the mast, shimmied her way down. Her straw hat had blown off her head and would have been lost if not for the chin cord. Lightning cracked, only yards from the ship.

"Hurry!" I shouted.

Lightning struck again, this time it hit the mast. Kitten dropped on top of me, bowling me flat on the deck. Blinded by the flash, the wind knocked out of me, I was stunned for a moment, gasping for breath. Kitten's body felt stiff and lifeless.

Recovering my senses, I saw Sydow lift Kitten off me. Mrs. Kedward was there, too.

"Are you all right, captain?" She asked.

"I'll be fine, what about Kitten?"

Mrs. Kedward shook her head. "Her heart stopped."

"Ah, nein, mein kleines krieger mädchen," Sydow sobbed.

"Take her to my cabin," I said. "Perhaps Sophie can do something."

Sydow hurried toward the stern, Mrs. Kedward supporting him across the rocking, slippery, wind-swept deck. I stumbled along behind. The storm sails were up and Rackham was at the helm with Maggie. The *Bar Jack* had steerageway again.

* * *

I reached the cabin to see Kitten on my bed and Sophie leaning over her. I was not prepared for the sight – Kitten's eyes were open and bulging and her tongue stuck out of her mouth. I turned away.

The storm raged outside and the ship pitched severely. Through the sound of the wind, I heard Sophie singing. I looked back to see she had her hands on Kitten's head. The singing turned to monotone, then it rose to a screech. Sophie staggered back and collapsed on the floor.

Kitten abruptly sat up and started gasping and coughing. Sydow patted her back. I picked up Sophie and set her on the bed. She mumbled unintelligibly and her eyes lolled in her head. Kitten's gasping eased.

"That was queer," she croaked.

Sydow laughed and hugged her. Sophie came out of her delirium, seemed awake for a moment, then fell unconscious.

* * *

I ordered Sydow and Mrs. Kedward to stay in the cabin while I went out onto the deck. I was met with a spray of water and nearly lost my footing. I climbed to the aft deck and took my place near Rackham and Maggie.

"How's the ship?" I shouted to Rackham.

"Hanging on," she said. "I hope we make the bay before the worst comes."

I didn't want to imagine what the worst would be. The *Bar Jack* crashed through crisscrossing waves that grew bigger by the moment. Rackham had ordered most of the crew below to take turns manning the pumps. Alice, Jenny and the sure-footed Clair stayed on deck to handle the rigging when the need arose. If the wind grew too intense, we'd have to bring down the storm sails, but then we'd lose steerageway and be at the mercy of the storm.

Rackham kept a northerly heading. I shouted compass readings to her and marked off the minutes. We sailed broad reach, nearly perpendicular to the main thrust of the wind., and the ship leaned heavily. We were sailing in darkness with little to guide us but the compass and Rackham's instincts.

The wind increased and the *Bar Jack* was dangerously close to foundering. Just when it seemed she would go over, Rackham turned to a course west by northwest. The ship straightened and the going became a little easier. Lightning flashed and I thought I saw land to starboard. If so it was worrisomely close.

The wind raged and I could see the rear sail ripping at its seams. If the sails gave way, we'd never make the bay. There was little to do but hope as the steep waves thrust the *Bar Jack*'s stern up and onto the peaks, then down into the troughs with a crash.

With curious suddenness the wind diminished, the swell leveled and the chop was manageable. Somehow Rackham had found the bay.

Chapter 12: Unsafe Haven

5 July, 1819, Bay of Pigs, Cuba

I slept longer than I had intended. With Sophie and Kitten occupying my bed, I had stretched out on one of the hammocks in the hold. The squawk of a tern woke me. I checked my pocket watch to see my nap had lasted three hours.

Several women were asleep in nearby hammocks. Groggy and stiff with bruises, I went to the head, then up on deck to see the squawking tern perched at the end of the bowsprit. We had anchored about a half mile from the western shore of the bay, obscured now by a thick fog. Rackham stood at the foremast looking up a ratline at Mrs. Kedward who was attaching a new block.

"How are we doing?" I asked Rackham.

"Not bad, a torn sail and a couple of leaks that need tending to."

"How about the mast? The lightning didn't hurt it?"

"There's a scorch mark but the Franklin rod saved it."

"I suppose we can spend the day getting tidied up, then set sail tomorrow," I said.

"We need to leave, as soon as there's any wind," Rackham said.

"The crew is exhausted."

"It isn't safe. We're vulnerable in the bay," she said.

"All right, we'll rouse the girls in an hour and hope we get some wind."

* * *

In my cabin Sydow snored in a chair, Sophie slept on the bed and Kitten paced the floor.

"You're supposed to be resting," I said. "You were struck by lightning for God's sake."

"I feel good, sir, really, and I can't sleep," Kitten said.

"Fine, go out and see what Master Rackham wants you to do."

"Yes, sir."

Sydow continued to snore but Sophie's eyes opened. I pulled up a chair beside her.

"How are you feeling?"

"Tired, drained," Sophie said, her voice nearly a whisper.

"Will you be all right?"

"I think so, I just need to rest."

"It appears you saved Kitten's life."

"I'm glad. I didn't know what I was doing; I just tried to enter her mind. It was like I was in a vast, dark chamber, only a tiny light at the far end, growing dimmer by the moment. I moved toward the light. It seemed like I was running but only slowly getting closer. Finally I arrived and the light was only a pinpoint. I reached for it and when I touched it, it exploded. I felt searing pain but don't remember anything else."

Sophie's experience was inscrutable to me; what a strange realm she could move in. I wondered what the philosophers would think – Descarte, Hume, Kant. They likely would have argued endlessly, Descarte claiming Sophie had snatched Kitten's soul back to her body, Hume countering that the claim would be sheer presumption, and Kant, I don't know what he would say. Was there a place in the mind where the phenomenal met the noumenal? Philosophy was never my strong suit. I leaned over and kissed Sophie's forehead.

* * *

When a trace of wind came and the fog began to lift, most of the women were on deck, scrubbing, tidying and making sure the *Bar Jack* was ready to sail. Sydow and Mrs. Kedward were below tending to a leak.

The shore came into view, a forbidding wall of mangroves. A good spot for crocodiles, I thought. Rackham appeared on deck. She had gone to her stateroom for a brief nap, but the wind, mild as it was, roused her.

"Time to go," I said.

"Yes, let's get the ..."

"Ship ahead!" Polly shouted. "Off the starboard bow."

Rackham and I reached for our spyglasses and extended them. The ship was a schooner, gaff rigged and smaller than the *Bar Jack*. She looked dingy with little paint left on her hull and her sails were weathered and frayed, yet she was armed. I could see two guns on her starboard side. She flew no flag. Several men scurried on her deck and I saw one looking at us through his spyglass. The ship was a half mile out and coming straight for us.

"Ah hell," Rackham muttered.

"Trouble?"

"Pirates, I'll lay to that. A bad slice of luck."

"Can we outrun her?" I asked.

"Ain't enough time. She'll be on us before we get any headway."

"She doesn't have many guns. Maybe we can take our lumps and hope for the best."

"Nah, they'll grapple us before we get clear."

Damn, I thought, this could be the end of the voyage. I supposed the sensible thing to do was to look after the lives of the women.

"Should we surrender?"

"This is a bad bunch," Rackham said. "They'll want the girls and the *Bar Jack*. I for one won't let them take me."

The women had stopped what they were doing and stared at the approaching vessel. A black flag went up. The women murmured and looked back at Rackham and me, anticipating orders.

That now familiar knot of fear returned to my gut. I imagined the horror the women would go through if they were captured. I might be spared, taken and ransomed, but then I would have to live with what had happened. Why couldn't I have left well enough alone and kept to my research at Cambridge?

I thought of the subject of my research, Scipio Africanus, the great hero of Rome who, with minimal forces, had wrested Spain from the Carthaginians during the Second Punic War, and later defeated Hannibal himself at the Battle of Zama. But I was no hero. Still, I wondered what Scipio would do right now. Ruses, misdirection, and surprise, combined with ferocious aggression – those were his tools. Could I make them mine?

"If we must fight, we'll fight," I said to Rackham.

"Aye, captain," she said grimly.

"All hands!" I shouted. "Down in the hold, now!"

Below deck I had no time for rousing speeches, nor did I have one to hand.

"I'll try to buy them off," I told the crew. "But if that doesn't work, we'll have to fight. Here's what I'm thinking ..."

* * *

While the women passed out weapons and got into position, I went to my cabin. Sophie was in a deep sleep. I had thought about asking if she could help with any sort of mind tricks but she was clearly in no shape to do so. I let her sleep and pulled out the strongbox from under the bed. On the way to the deck, I saw Rackham, Mrs. Kedward and Clair readying their weapons. Sydow was loading the blunderbuss. He slapped me on the shoulder.

"Today we fight together, eh, kaptian."

"Aye, and I may be the first casualty," I said. "Do your best for the women."

"Those pirates will know blood and death before I am done."

I stepped out of the door. The pirate ship was drawing close, men lined her deck – ragged, unkempt men. I set the box down a few paces away, then climbed to the aft deck and saw that Kitten had done her job. I knew she was now hiding in a coil of thick rope at the stern.

The crew of the pirate ship, no name was visible on her hull, lowered the sails, her momentum carrying her alongside the still anchored *Bar Jack*. I counted twenty men poised along the ship's gunwale, two groups of three manned the guns. A man with a bicorn hat I presumed was the captain. He had a cutlass in his belt and two pistols. Flanking him on one side was a sneering, lanky fellow with a long rifle and on the other a huge brute with a sandy beard.

Three men hurled grappling hooks onto our deck then pulled the ropes taut. The *Bar Jack* lurched as her mass stopped the other ship's momentum. I drew a deep breath.

The man in the bicorn hat shouted: "Do you surrender your ship?"

I shouted back: "I am compelled to tell you that we sail under the escort of the British frigate, *Pyramus*. We were separated in the storm but she should be along presently."

"Well, we better be along with our business quickly then," the captain said. "Do you surrender?"

He was English, his accent had a Cornish ring to it. His men were eager. I perceived greed and lust in their eyes.

"On the deck there," I said, gesturing with my arm, "is a chest with 500 pounds of coin and bullion. If you leave us unmolested, you may have it."

The amount, I knew, would be a fortune to them. Even so, I had little hope they would accept the offer.

"We'll have your money, and your women, and your ship," the pirate captain said. "Do you surrender? I won't ask again."

"No," I said. "Honor compels me to fight."

I drew my broadsword.

"I challenge you, captain, to settle this between ourselves in honorable combat."

The pirate laughed and his crew followed suit.

"You want I should shoot him, cap'n?" the lanky man asked.

"Nah, let me cut the pompous bugger in half," the bearded brute said, raising a broad-bladed scimitar.

"Aye, go ahead," the pirate captain said. "I want to see this."

The big man jumped onto the *Bar Jack* and headed toward me.

“The rest of you get the women and secure the ship,” the captain ordered. “I think we’ve got ourselves a pretty new home.

With a cheer the other men leaped on board, except the gun crews, the captain and the lanky man with the rifle.

* * *

Before I could assess the situation further, the bear of a man was upon me. A full head taller than myself and much broader, he swung his scimitar with maniacal fury. There was no technique, just a whirlwind of colossal strength and the sharp clash of metal on metal as I deflected the blows and hoped my blade would endure the onslaught. His attacks were easy to anticipate and I knew I could run him through, but only at the risk of being cut down by the momentum of his swings. I backpedaled and sidestepped, hoping for an opportunity to counterattack.

I heard a blast coming from the main deck, then a shot from behind me, then the bloody screams of women, then a cacophony of shooting, clanging and yelling. No time to hope or despair, I was locked in my own death struggle.

The blows kept coming. When would the man tire? I can’t claim it was stratagem, but something inside me said enough was enough; this fight had to end. I stepped into the man’s onslaught as his sword came down, lashing out with a backhanded cut that caught the man’s wrist. The scimitar dropped and struck my leg before clunking on the deck. We collided and I staggered back.

The giant man’s fury was replaced with horror as he looked at his now handless arm spurting blood. I advanced and drove my sword into his solar plexus at about the same time I heard the boom of the *Bar Jack*’s swivel gun.

I looked around. Kitten was behind me, crouched at the gunwale and reloading one of my dueling pistols.

The main deck was a smoke-obscured chaos of fighting – Sydow, Rackham, Clair, Jenny, Alice, Mrs Kedward swinging cutlasses and hotly engaged with the pirates. Any doubts I had regarding the women’s willingness and ability to fight were put to rest by the appalling ferocity of their assault. The pirates were retreating, one jumped into the water, others leaped back to their ship.

I went to the gunwale and saw the pirate captain was down as was the man with the rifle – Kitten's work, I presumed. Most of the men manning the guns were down also, the work of the swivel gun team and our musketeers who had come up the bow hatch when they had received the signal – Sydow firing the blunderbuss.

I saw a wounded pirate with a match crawling toward one of the cannons which was likely loaded with grapeshot. If he set it off, the blast would tear apart many of the women on the *Bar Jack*. I picked up one of the pistols Kitten had placed behind the gunwale before the battle. I aimed and pulled the trigger but the weapon fizzled and failed to discharge.

The pirate reached out with the match. Desperate I hopped onto the gunwale. With a yell I jumped toward the man and hewed him with my broadsword. I fell hard, my head slamming against the deck. I blacked out.

* * *

I came to, bleary-eyed and groggy, to see Alice kneeling over me.

"Are you all right, sir?"

"Yes, I believe so," I said, then saw my torn and bloody trouser leg.

"A pretty deep cut, sir. We should stitch that up," Alice said.

She helped me to my feet which were a little unsteady. Sydow approached holding my broadsword and wiping blood off the blade. He handed it to me.

"A sharp sword you have, kapitan."

"I've become a believer in Toledo steel," I said.

I surveyed the bloody scene of death around me; the smell of burnt powder lingered in the air. Six living pirates lay prostrate on the deck, their hands bound behind them.

"I see we carried the day," I said. "What's the butcher's bill?"

"One dead, Clair," Sydow said. "She took a bullet in the chest and a stab to her belly. Jenny has a bad slash on her hip. Mrs. Kedward is tending to it. Minor injuries, otherwise."

"I suppose we should be thankful. We were lucky."

"Not lucky, kapitan. They underestimated us and we attacked quick and lively like good Prussians."

Like Scipio Africanus, I thought, but I dreaded having to send the news to Clair's next of kin. My sense of triumph mingled with the question: Was this endeavor really worth it?

Rackham approached.

"We should get going," she said. "Another ship might be along that we can't handle."

"What about the cannons?" I asked. "Should we take them? They could be useful."

"No time. It would take most of the afternoon to rig a hoist and haul them over. We don't want to dilly with that. This is a bad place."

I looked at the water and saw many fins breaking the surface, sharks, dozens of them.

"All right, Ann," I said. "Push the guns overboard and confiscate the rest of their weapons. We can defang them at least. Take a party below and see what you can find, then let's be on our way."

* * *

I winced and took swigs of whiskey while Mrs. Kedward stitched the cut in my thigh. It was about three inches long and not overly deep. We were in a makeshift infirmary cordoned off in the hold of the *Bar Jack*. Jenny was lying on a cot. Her wound was worse.

"Such a shame about Clair," I said. "It breaks my heart. I wonder if the girls wouldn't prefer to just head home. It's so dangerous out here and the worst is likely yet to come."

“That’s not my sentiment,” Mrs. Kedward said. “Clair had a chance to do what few women could dream of doing. That’s true of us all. Death in the course of it is a part of life. We just proved we can hold our own against the weather and bad men. We’ve had our baptism of water and blood. We’re sailors now, through and through. Don’t deny us what we’ve now earned.”

Jenny clutched my arm.

“Brenda’s right,” she said. “This is our ship and you’re our captain. This *is* our home.”

* * *

I limped up to the deck, ignoring Mrs. Kedward’s admonishments to stay off my feet.

“The pirates had a prisoner bound up in the hold,” Rackham told me. “A black man, probably headed for the slaver’s block. What do you want to do with him? He’s in pretty rough shape.”

“Bring him over. We can’t leave him to the mercy of those fellows.”

The living pirates were still prostrate on the deck of their ship. Sydow and Maggie brought the black man over. He was tall, lean, naked and covered with bruises. He squinted and blinked in the brightness of the sun. Kitten trailed behind carrying a leather satchel with Indian-looking designs and a spear tipped with what appeared to be obsidian. They led him into the hold to have Mrs. Kedward look him over.

I wondered about Kitten, how she still seemed like a child. It was hard to align that with the fact she had shot four men dead, including the pirate captain. On Sydow’s signal, she had popped up and, wisely, shot first the lanky man with the rifle. The captain drew his pistol and returned fire but missed. Kitten killed him with one of my dueling pistols. With rifled barrels, they were accurate if well aimed.

“I found their logbook and a few charts,” Rackham said. “Looks like they’d been prowling the Mexican coast. Could be useful.”

“That’s good. Let’s cut the grappling lines and go.”

Rackham signaled Alice who shouted orders to weigh anchor and raise the sails. I drew my sword and did the honors of cutting us free of the pirate ship.

“Ann,” I said.

“Yeah.”

“Where are the sharks?”

She looked around. “They’re gone. That’s odd.”

The breeze filled the sails and the ship started moving. I watched the body of a pirate floating astern. The sharks should be feasting on it but there weren’t any. Then I saw a curious bulging ripple in the water moving toward the body. The water roiled and bubbled.

“What in the hell is that?” I asked Rackham.

“Don’t know. It’s big, whatever it is.”

A massive snake, or perhaps a tentacle, thicker than the heaviest cable, emerged from the water, coiled around the body and pulled it under.

I looked at Rackham. She shook her head. The wind freshened and the *Bar Jack* picked up speed. Thank bloody God, I thought.

Chapter 13: The Gulf

9 July, 1819, Gulf of Mexico

Although weary we had little time for rest after our departure from the Bay of Pigs. We had to navigate again the reefs extending from the Isle of Youth and through choppy waters and fickle winds. Then north through the Yucatan Channel where, despite our fatigue, we had to keep wary because we were skirting the edge of El Radio. Wary of what, I didn't know. We observed a thin band of gray haze on the western horizon, the ongoing spew of Volcan Rojo.

The passage went without incident, however. Favorable winds carried us into the Gulf of Mexico, then we made a northwesterly course toward Galveston. I ordered a return to normal shifts and I took the helm for my usual middle watch. The night was cloudless and the stars particularly vibrant. I thought about Sophie who was up and about these last two days, much to the relief of everyone. With both Sophie and Jenny laid up, the cooking chores had fallen to Polly and her friend, Esmerelda, otherwise known as Izzy. About all that could be said of their meals was that they were, for the most part, edible. Sophie's temperament was subdued and she was not talkative. I didn't press the matter.

Sydow climbed up the aft deck followed by the negro man the pirates had held prisoner. Perhaps an inch shorter than Sydow but of similar build, he moved slowly, still aching, I supposed, from whatever abuse the pirates had meted out. He looked better than when I had last seen him, however, and his eyes had gained a certain intensity. I felt a little anxious and was angered by the feeling because it stemmed solely from the fact the man was dark skinned.

"Mr. Cadmael would like to speak with you, kapitan," Sydow said.

"Of course," I said, reaching out my hand. "Mr. Cadmael, I'm sorry for not having had the chance to speak to you sooner."

"I am grateful that you freed me from the pirates," he said. "Thank you."

Cadmael's English was good with what seemed a Wessex accent but with a touch of Spanish inflection.

"I was curious, sir," he continued, "what you intend to do with me."

"Do with you? I hadn't thought of it quite like that. In fact I hadn't thought of it much at all. Now that I do, it does seem a problem. We're headed for a pirate stronghold. I think they dally with contraband slaves so I doubt you would want to disembark there."

"No, sir."

"After Galveston we're likely headed into El Radio along the Mexican coast."

"El Radio?"

"An imaginary circle around Volcan Rojo, a danger zone," I said.

"Being rescued by us may not have been so lucky for you," Sydow said.

Cadmael smiled, revealing a couple of missing teeth. The wind shifted and I noticed a flutter in the jib. I motioned for Izzy to deal with it. I looked at the compass and moved the tiller a bit to stay on course. Cadmael and Sydow watched Izzy and Polly trim the jib lines. The two were better sailors than they were cooks.

"Maybe I'm a lucky man," Cadmael said. "My home, I think, is in your El Radio."

"Is that so?" I asked. "Whereabouts?"

"A place the Spanish called Isla del Carmen."

"Hmm, I'll have to check my charts."

"Our island is at the entrance to Laguna de Terminos."

I remembered that name, a shallow bay near the shoulder of the Yucatan Peninsula.

"Well, then, Mr. Cadmael, you may indeed be in luck."

* * *

Sophie was still awake when I turned in. I put on my nightshirt and slipped into bed beside her.

"Have you communicated with Louisa?" I asked.

"Only to tell her we had to stop for a while."

"Why do you have to stop?"

She rolled over and rested her head on my chest.

"I'm afraid. I'm afraid he'll find me."

"The daemon thing?"

She nodded.

* * *

Letter dated 10 July, 1819:

Dear Mrs. Doris Hendry,

I regret having to say that your sister, Clair, is dead. She died 5 July, 1819, at a place called the Bay of Pigs, Cuba, of wounds suffered defending the Bar Jack from pirates. By all accounts she fought valiantly, taking down two marauders before succumbing. She was a respected member of the crew and I held her in the highest esteem. She had become a true sailor.

We committed her body to the deep waters of the Gulf of Mexico this morning. I presided over the ceremony and Mrs. Brenda Kedward read a few verses from her bible. It was a tearful event for all present. May Clair rest in peace.

Enclosed is a letter of credit that you may present to the firm of Baxter & Washburn in Bristol. An account will be set up that includes all wages due to Clair plus twenty-five pounds. You may draw on it at any time. I know this cannot replace your sister but I hope it represents some small compensation.

Please accept my sincerest sympathy,

Sir James Henry Ker LeRoque, Captain of the Bar Jack

* * *

Cadmael hunched over a chart in my cabin, pointing out to Rackham and myself the location of the island that was his home, Isla del Carmen.

"It is good for growing things and not touched by corruption," he said.

"'Corruption' is a word I keep hearing. What does it mean?" I asked.

"It's like a darkness that moves through the jungle and changes plants and animals. The jungle is very dangerous now, many strange creatures, some very deadly."

A cup slid along the edge of the table as the *Bar Jack* climbed a swell. I caught it before it fell off.

Cadmael went on to tell his story. He had been a cabin boy on an English merchant ship, a slave owned by its captain. The captain had promised Cadmael his freedom and even taught him to read and write, but when the captain's financial gambits failed, he sold Cadmael to a slave broker who in turn sold him to a Spanish plantation owner and he was compelled to work in the fields.

When Vulcan Rojo erupted, the plantation was not immediately affected but soon afterward people started going mad and senselessly attacking others like wild animals and eating their flesh. "Necrofagos," Cadmael called them, or ghouls. He said in time the ghouls would grow claws and fangs and hardly appear human, a notion at which I would have scoffed if not for recent experiences.

The Spanish fled and left most of the slaves behind. Cadmael and others went into the jungle and joined fragmentary groups of Indians. Every day was a fight for survival, Cadmael said. Eventually they made the shores of Laguna de Terminos and saw that the fort on Isla del Carmen was deserted. They fashioned rafts and took refuge there. Soon they were joined by others escaping the jungle, mostly Indians, but also a few sailors who escaped wrecked ships in dinghies and rafts.

"We call it 'Isla Lanza,'" Cadmael said, "Spear Island, after the spears we made to fight with during our time in the jungle."

"We brought a spear over from the pirate ship," I said. "Yours, I presume."

"Yes, but it is not much good for fighting. It's supposed to be enchanted and guide me to a new place to settle. Our numbers have grown and there are many children now. The island will not long support us all."

"The spear led you astray, it seems," I said.

"Maybe, but maybe not."

Cadmael explained he and a companion were in a canoe equipped with an outrigger, working their way along the coast, when the pirate ship overtook them. The pirates shot his companion, an Indian, and took Cadmael prisoner.

"I looked at the log," Rackham said. "They called the ship, the *Grouper*, and the captain's name was K. Jago. They were in El Radio because an American brig chased them there."

"The *Enterprise*, perhaps?" I said.

"Maybe, doesn't say," she said.

"I don't suppose, Mr. Cadmael, that you've ever seen a ship called the *Squirrel*, a sloop-of-war, three masts and 22 guns? It sailed into El Radio almost two years ago."

"No, sir. We see very few ships. If a ship like that had ever come close, I would know."

* * *

A fair breeze moved us along at a brisk clip in a steady sea. Rested now from our adventures with the storm and the pirates, I decided a little weapons drill would relieve the monotony. Whereas previous drills were carried out like a kind of game, there now was a pronounced seriousness to the activity, the women paying close attention to whatever Sydow, Rackham or I had to say.

Cadmael participated as well and demonstrated a peculiar sword-fighting style – a continuous flow of cuts combined with an open stance and fluid footwork. He punctuated his routine with occasional thrusts and upward cuts, rarely reaching out but keeping his elbows close to his body. It was a style quite different from the upright, extended techniques of saber fencing. Watching him I began to see the point was to beat away your opponent's attacks and step in close for the kill.

"Is that how the Mayan's fight?" I asked.

"No," he said. "A sailor taught us this. He is from the Philippine Islands and calls himself an escrimador."

"Impressive," I said.

"I had a blade called a machete that I liked better than this cutlass," Cadmael said. "Did you bring it over from the pirate ship? It had a carved handle with a cat's head."

"I don't know. We can go look in the weapons locker."

We found no such blade.

"Sorry, I suppose it went overboard with one of the pirates."

"Too bad, but thank you, captain."

* * *

"Wake up, James. We have land in sight," Sophie said.

I sat up, she handed me a cup of tea.

"Galveston?"

"That's what Ann says."

I sipped the tea, wishing we had some milk. I watched Sophie lay out a clean shirt and my shaving kit.

"Do you mean to marry me, Sophia," I asked.

After a pause, she asked in turn, "Is that what you want?"

"I'm asking what you want."

"I'm just a servant girl, and a Spaniard. You're a nobleman, a peer."

"What of it? I'm the second son in a minor family. Some might tsk tsk their disapproval but it would amount to little more than that. And you yourself have noble blood."

"It's what I dreamed of ever since I first saw you, even before, when Louisa would talk of you. But now, things are so confused, I don't know."

"I can't offer you immortal life or great power." I stood and put my hand on her cheek. "But I would like you to be my wife."

Sophie hugged me tight but said nothing.

* * *

I stood at the bow with Rackham, our spyglasses trained on the island that was Galveston. Seemingly just a long strip of beach with grass inland, it was difficult to discern from the Texas coast behind it. We sailed toward the channel on the eastern end that would take us around to the other side where the harbor was.

What kind of reception awaited us, I wondered. I found myself more excited than worried. Rackham was calm enough. Perhaps that's what fortified me. An old Spanish frigate came into view, painted red and bristling with an overabundance of guns. She was beached on the island side of the channel. They had turned her into a fort to guard the entrance.

"The Spanish used to call Galveston, Malhado, the Isle of Doom," Rackham said.

"Why is that?" I asked.

"Because of all the ships wrecked on her shore."

There being only the mildest of breezes, I saw little danger of being wrecked on this day unless the frigate's guns opened up on us. When we drew near, a man on the frigate waved flags, signaling us to heave-to.

"They're sending a pilot over," Rackham said.

"I suppose if we were to think better of things, now would be the time to turn around," I said.

Rackham gave me that annoying smirk that only came when I wanted her to ease my doubts.

"We've touched the spider's web already," she said. "If you catch my drift."

"I do."

"Orders, captain?"

"Find an anchorage. We'll wait for the pilot."

The pilot was a young Frenchman dressed in a striped shirt, brown trousers and a leather cap who spoke broken English and was glad when I spoke French to him. His accent was thick with the rough dialect of Southern France. He was tongue-tied in the presence of Rackham and our female crew. We weighed anchor and raised the sails. The pilot's attention wandered to watching the women do their work.

"Directions, s'il vous plait," I urged.

"Ah, oui, pardon, monsieur ..."

He guided us through the channel and past a narrower channel that separated Galveston from a smaller, marshy island. Rounding that, we came back down toward the north shore of Galveston.

"What is your business here?" the pilot asked. "Is this a prize? The *Terrier*, perhaps, caught another one?"

"We're not a prize crew," I said. "This is my ship. My business is with Jean Laffite. I wish to speak with him."

"The boss will like this ship, I think, no? And its lovely crew," the pilot said.

His words did not put me at ease. Sydow had asked if we should ready the "musketeers" below in case of trouble. I told him no, we would be at Laffite's mercy. He could apprehend us easily and any struggle would be pointless.

As it was we experienced no trouble upon arrival. We entered an excellent natural harbor and glided toward a quay. Beyond was a pretty town of new wooden buildings freshly painted in a hodgepodge of whites, blues and greens. The pilot told us to lower sail and he signaled a launch to come tow us dockside. The operation went smoothly and the place had all the appearance of a respectable little port, not a pirate's haven.

Except perhaps for the large, two-story house that loomed inland. It was painted red, had black shutters and a dark roof with generous eaves. On one side was built a tower that stretched up another story and, I presumed, commanded a good view of the entire vicinity. I remembered the name I'd heard – Maison Rouge.

* * *

Our pilot disembarked after telling us an agent would visit us soon to ascertain our business. As the women secured the rigging, men began to gather near the dock, some waving and smiling. "Hello ladies, welcome to Campeche," one man shouted. "We hope you can stay a while."

"A friendly place, it seems, eh, kapitan?" Sydow said.

"Hmm."

Rackham paid no attention to the onlookers but rather had her spyglass on a three-masted ship anchored in the middle of the harbor. I turned my spyglass on her and noted the name, *Frelon*.

"A corvette, French built, I gather," I said.

"Aye," Rackham said. "She's the sister ship of the *Vipere*. I wonder how Laffite got hold of her."

"I hope she doesn't stir up old longings," I said.

Rackham collapsed her spyglass. "Nope, just old memories."

Beyond the *Frelon* lay an Indiaman, a large merchant ship as big as a frigate. Workmen on her deck were raising a mast. She was British built, I knew, and I wondered how Laffite had obtained such a vessel. Indiamen were the pride of the East India Company and a lifeline of the Empire. Had we sunk so low we could let pirates take one?

The men on the quay dispersed, hurrying back to whatever they were doing before taking time to stare at the *Bar Jack* and her crew. Another man appeared, walking toward our dock in a purposeful manner. The agent the pilot spoke of, I thought. He wore a leather frock coat and a leather hat, much like Rackham's but pinned up on one side. On his belt dangled an old-fashioned hanger with a brass hilt. He stepped onto our dock, hands on hips and looked us over. He had a thin mustache and curls of brown hair that flowed from under his hat.

I was about to hail when Sophie hurried up from below to look at him, almost as if she were summoned. The man smiled, teeth white as snow. The hair rose on the back of my neck.

"Bonjour," he said. "It is true, this is the *Bar Jack*. I had heard of her not two days ago, a sleek schooner crewed by girls. I hardly believed it, but, ho, here she is docked at my port. Welcome. My name is Jean Laffite."

Chapter 14: Dinner With Pirates

15 July, 1819, Galveston Island

Maggie and Sydow lowered the gangplank and I stepped down to shake hands with Laffite. He was perhaps an inch or two shorter than myself.

"Captain James LeRoque at your service," I said.

He again showed those bewitching white teeth.

"Well met, monsieur. I'm impressed with the comeliness of your ship and crew. I would ask what brings you here but I'm pressed for time at the moment and would much rather talk when I am at leisure. Come to my house this evening." He motioned toward the red mansion. "And we'll dine together. Bring whomever you wish. In the meantime please avail yourself of our settlement. We should have whatever provisions or refreshments you need. Despite anything you may have heard, trust me, you, your crew and your ship are quite safe."

"Thank you. I accept your invitation."

"I very much look forward to it. Until then."

* * *

Soon a young man arrived and offered to show us where we might find provisions and necessities. Sydow and I went with him and he pointed out, among other establishments, a bathhouse to which we immediately headed and availed ourselves. I couldn't remember the last time I'd had a proper bath.

"I think the ladies will want a bath, too, eh, kapitan," Sydow said before he dunked his head into the steaming water.

I asked the proprietor if arrangements could be made for my crew to bathe. To this he readily agreed and said he would set aside the remainder of the afternoon as "ladies only." On the *Bar Jack*, the arrangement was greeted with enthusiasm. Naturally I worried about letting the women go ashore – this was a pirate haven after all – but Laffite had given his word and, as much as he made me uneasy, I doubted the men of the island would dare cross him. Furthermore, despite my protective instincts, I had come to accept the clear fact that the women could take care of themselves. I doled out wages and let them go ashore as they wished.

Rackham was as eager as any of them. She retrieved her duffle and headed for the gangplank.

"Ann."

"Yeah."

"We're invited to dine with Laffite. I thought you, Sydow, Sophie and I should go."

"Right, whatever you want."

"I don't know how formal an affair it will be but I also thought that, perhaps, you could wear the gown I bought you."

Had her eyes been daggers, I would have been pierced.

"Just a thought," I swallowed.

She went on her way. I went down to the hold and approached Cadmael who had strung his hammock in a curtained-off corner. He was reading *Frankenstein*, a book by an anonymous author I'd purchased in London.

"I've seen a number of black men moving freely in the town," I said. "I imagine it would be safe enough if you want to go ashore. We might be here a couple of days."

"Thank you, sir," he said. "Do you think I should disembark here?"

"No, certainly not, not unless you want to. I just thought you might like to set foot on land. I could give you some money."

"I prefer to stay down here for now."

"Understood. You might give one of the women your size. We can fetch you some fresh clothing."

"Thank you, captain."

* * *

I finished shaving and put on my best coat and top hat. The women below were laughing and carrying on. I believe Jenny was fixing Sophie's hair. I met Sydow on deck and he, like me, wore his sword. I could foresee no situation where they would be any use if Laffite had a mind to harm us – we were in his lair – but they were symbolically reassuring. We waited for our companions.

Finally Sophie emerged looking resplendent in her burgundy gown, hair pulled up to reveal her delicate neck. She was followed by Rackham who, astoundingly, wore the traveling gown along with a hint of makeup that hid her scar somewhat. The long dirk sheathed at her hip was incongruous yet, nevertheless, had a kind of appeal. I smiled and she may have even blushed.

"Who's this? A lovely woman I have not seen before," Sydow remarked. "Where is Ann, by the way?"

"Another word, Sydow, and I'll put my knife in your belly," Rackham grumbled.

Sophie took my arm and we stepped down to the dock. Sydow offered his arm to Ann but she ignored the gesture.

We strolled through the town, a pleasant evening, the sun lingering above the horizon. Folks eyed us as we passed; a few said, "howdy" or "bon soiree," none seemed unfriendly except perhaps a couple of women sitting on a porch outside what I presumed to be a brothel. A cobbled track led through a small glade of cedars, then to a bridge that spanned a moat surrounding Maison Rouge. Our boots clunked on the wooden planks.

"My Lord, what is that?" Sophie said, pointing to the water.

A huge reptile glided under the bridge.

"An alligator?" I inquired.

"Nein, a crocodile," Sydow said.

I imagined the beast could swallow a man whole. Why did Laffite indulge such a creature? Sophie held me close.

Sydow worked the brass knocker on a large oaken door and a well-dressed negro opened it. He motioned us into the foyer and I gave him my calling card. We proceeded into the drawing room where the butler announced: "Captain James LeRoque and his company have arrived."

Laffite and another man, who were smoking cigars, rose from their chairs.

"Welcome to my home," Laffite said.

* * *

The drawing room was large and eclectically furnished with different styles of chairs and divans. The walls were covered with a menagerie of paintings, mostly of the sea and ships, but one of Laffite himself. We shook hands and I introduced him to the members of my party.

"Enchante," he said to Sophie and kissed her hand.

"Miss Rackham," he continued. "I'm glad you are among the living, and what a rare treat to see you in a gown."

"Hello, Fita," Rackham said.

The pirate chieftain wore a long paisley jacket made of silk, double breasted with a sash instead of buttons.

"Allow me to introduce my friend and business associate, Mr. James Bowie."

Mr. Bowie was a stout young man with rugged features, broad side whiskers and a ruddy complexion. He wore a black frock coat, light brown trousers and weathered riding boots.

"Howdy, folks," he said. "Call me Jim if you don't mind."

"Earl," Laffite said to the negro man. "Fetch wine for our guests."

"Is that a broadsword?" Bowie asked, pointing at my hip.

"Yes, a family heirloom as a matter of fact," I said.

"My brother has a passion for blades. He'd love to get a look at that one."

I unfastened my sword belt and handed the rig to Bowie. He gripped the hilt and slowly withdrew the sword from its scabbard.

"Damn, that's a fine blade. Razor sharp, I reckon."

"Toledo steel," I said.
Bowie sheathed the weapon and handed it back.
"I like swords but they're damned cumbersome on the frontier. A lot of men prefer a tomahawk."
He pulled back his coat and withdrew a large knife with a wide blade at least a foot long. He handed it to me.
"This is my brother Rezin's latest design but he thinks it could be better. Not much to look at but it's stout and sharp."
The knife was hefty in the hand and resembled an oversized chef's knife. I passed it to Sydow.
"The goal," Bowie said, "is something that chops like an ax, shaves like a razor and parries like a sword. He wants to add a guard but he isn't satisfied with the blade's shape."
Sydow held it up to his eye and looked down the spine.
"What you want is a langmesser," he said.
"A what?"
"A langmesser. Add a guard like you say, drop the point and make it curve up slightly at the tip, then give it a false edge for good back-cuts."
"Huh, not a bad idea. I'll pass it along."
Earl returned with a tray of glasses and a bottle.
"Gentlemen," Laffite said. "Let's put our weapons away. You may hang them in the foyer. My wife will be down soon and they make her nervous."

* * *

No sooner had we seated ourselves with full glasses of wine than a man strode through the front door unannounced. He stamped his feet in the foyer and unbuckled his sword belt from which hung a cutlass and a pistol. He lingered a moment, apparently eyeing our weapons, then entered the parlor.
"Ho, I didn't know you had company, Fita," he said, voice growly and accent Italian. He was a lean man with long gray hair, clean shaven with a pock-marked face and hawk-like nose.

"Just arrived this very afternoon," Laffite said. "Noblemen, no less, a Scotsman and a Prussian, came in on that pretty schooner."

"I wondered what the hell that was. What's their business?"

"We haven't come to that yet, Vincent, but let me introduce you."

We stood and learned the man's name was Vincent Gambi, the captain of the corvette we saw in the harbor, the *Frelon*. He shook my hand with an iron grip. Looking at Rackham, a smile cracked his grumpy countenance.

"I'll be damned, Ann Rackham's back on the ocean."

"You might have some real competition now, Vincent," Laffite said.

Gambi poured himself a glass of wine and we seated ourselves again.

"Whose fancy broadsword is that?" Gambi asked. "Looks like blood on the tassel. It's seen action recently, I wager."

"That would be mine," I said. "And, yes, we had an encounter with a few pirates."

"Kapitan took the sword hand off a giant bastard and ran him through, cleaved another man's head open," Sydow interjected.

"Pirates, you say," Laffite said. "Whereabouts and when?"

"Bay of Pigs. Ten days ago," Rackham answered. "A motley crew on a shabby schooner waylaid us at anchor after a storm. Jago was the captain's name, I think."

"That had to be Kenan Jago," Gambi said. "A murdering shit he was, and none too bright."

"Your crew, Monsieur LeRoque, isn't it all ladies? How did you handle the pirates?" Laffite asked.

"We lured them into an ambush," I said and went on to tell the tale in full.

Laffite raised his glass: "Here's to the fighting ladies of the *Bar Jack* and to the vanquishing of pirates."

"Monsieur Laffite," I said. "Perhaps I've been misled but aren't you pirates yourselves?"

Laffite looked at me askance and I chided myself for speaking rashly, then he showed his teeth.

"I'm sorry that such is our reputation but, sir, we are not pirates, we are privateers. Everything we do is quite legal and authorized with letters of marque."

"Which country's letters of marque we apply can vary," Gambi said, snorting at his own joke.

"True," Laffite said. "And there are certain annoying officials who claim we break the law. Fortunately there exist magicians-for-hire the Americans call lawyers. With their sorcery they turn something that seems like a crime into something perfectly legal, assez merveilleux."

"Kind of like what we got cookin'," Bowie said. "Captain Gambi took a slaver as a prize ..."

"Quite legally," Laffite interrupted. "Under French law, slave ships are considered criminal and privateers bearing French letters of marque are free to capture them."

"The problem is what to do with the cargo," Bowie resumed. "Turns out the government will pay fifty dollars a head for contraband slaves. That's where I come in. I take them overland back to Louisiana and turn them over to the marshal. He has no use for slaves so he'll auction them off. But there ain't much demand for slaves on the frontier so I'll buy them back at $150 a head."

"Those numbers don't add up, Herr Bowie," Sydow said.

"Hadn't got to the good part yet. I'll then take the slaves across the river and sell them to planters in Mississippi for $1,500 a head, maybe more."

"All within the bounds of the law," Laffite said. "You see, Monsieur LeRoque, we are not criminals. We are simply businessmen."

I suppressed my rising disgust and nodded. "As you say, monsieur. In any case, your business affairs are not my concern. The point of my visit is to seek information regarding the H.M.S. *Squirrel* ..."

I was forestalled by the arrival of Madame Laffite.

* * *

A striking woman, tall with raven hair and white skin, she was introduced as Madame Madeline Regaud-Laffite. She wore a white, chiton-styled gown with a leaf pattern and a green sash cinched beneath her bosom. Around her neck was a string of pearls from which hung a small, gold pendant.

She was accompanied by a small man, somewhat rotund, bald with shaking jowls. He was introduced as Hector Guibourg and appeared more suited to the salons of Paris than a pirate's redoubt. He wore a foppish blue frock coat with a wide collar and flaring white cuffs. His breast prominently displayed a silver pendant – diamond shaped with the lower half elongated in which was set a small onyx stone. A sickle shape crossed the upper portion of the diamond. Odd, I thought, and noticed Madame Laffite's pendant was of similar design.

"Real nobility. My, why, we're very honored," she said with a tone suggesting she wasn't sure how to behave.

Monsieur Guibourg seemed drawn to Sophie and bowed as he kissed her hand. Madame Laffite took the arms of Sophie and Rackham.

"Come, it's so nice to have feminine company. Let me show you around the house while the men talk business," she said and led them up a broad staircase.

Rackham looked back at me with a pained expression. I shrugged and Sydow was unable to suppress a smirk.

* * *

Guibourg nestled himself into the plush chair Laffite had been sitting in and Laffite sat on the divan previously occupied by Sophie and Rackham.

"You were saying, Sir LeRoque, something about the *Squirrel*," Laffite said.

"Yes, that's why I'm here. I'm seeking information regarding its whereabouts. I'm led to believe that you know more about what's going on in El Radio than probably anyone."

I felt Guibourg's eyes upon me and the back of my neck tingled. Laffite glanced at him before answering.

"That may be true," Laffite said. "I do try to collect what news I can but I have heard nothing about what happened to the *Squirrel*, other than she sailed into El Radio after calling at Veracruz. I had heard she was going to attempt to approach Volcan Rojo itself and had carried many scientific instruments on board."

"A fool's errand, if you ask me," Gambi said.

"Why?" I asked. "The *Squirrel* was a sloop of war with a crack crew. Do you believe in sea monsters that could threaten her? Or French frigates protecting Bonaparte's big secret?"

"Bah to both. Volcan Rojo is still erupting. Get close and you're dealing with smoke, ash, roiling waters, maelstroms and rocky reefs that weren't there before. No ship would be safe."

"Vincent is correct," Laffite said. "Her fate may never be known but that she was lost is no surprise."

"What specifically was the *Squirrel* after?" Guibourg asked.

I felt an urge to tell all I knew of Paul's discoveries but a wary instinct interceded.

"I actually know little and what I do know I'm not at liberty to say."

"Come now, sir," Laffite said. "You are here for information. Like for like as they say."

"The *Squirrel*'s natural historian, Dr. Paul Seymour, was a good friend and a brilliant chemist. He thought, as many do, that there was a connection between the eruption and the strange events that followed. He wanted samples of the volcano's effluvia to study and test his ideas. I am no chemist and understand none of the details. My only intent is to try to find him, or at least learn for certain that he perished. I consider it my duty as a friend."

Guibourg gave me a pursed, squinty grin. "We all should have such friends."

"I'm sorry we cannot be of more help," Laffite said. "Where do you plan to go from here?"

I sensed an uneasy bond between Laffite and Guibourg. I couldn't guess what a man like Guibourg was doing here or what influence he might have over Laffite.

"We sail for Veracruz, I suppose," I said.

"You don't want to be going to Veracruz," Gambi said. "A French fleet has blockaded the harbor. You'd be turned away or interred, like as not."

"The Spanish Republic and France want to seize Veracruz as a steppingstone to Mexico City," Laffite said. "But the Royalists have a talented young general, Antonio Santa Anna, who turned back a landing attempt. He won't hold for long, however, if Bonaparte gets serious."

"I appreciate the warning," I said. "It is frustrating news."

The ladies returned and Madame Laffite announced supper was ready.

* * *

While not elaborate, the meal – steaks with a peppercorn sauce, potatoes and steamed peas and carrots – was flavorful and satisfying. Claret was served in generous portions and our glasses were never left empty. The dining room was rather spare, there being no art on the walls save a painting of the Taj Mahal.

"I couldn't help notice an Indiaman in your harbor," I said to Laffite who sat at the head of the table and I next to him. "A prize of yours?"

"We cannot claim credit for that one, I'm afraid," he said. "The French navy took her while the war was still on and handed it over to the Spanish Republic. Not long ago a group of royalists commandeered her in Buenos Aires and sailed her to Veracruz. Santa Anna, knowing it would be taken by the French if she stayed, sent her here to sell to me. I gladly paid and he needed the money."

"What will you do with her?"

"Arm her. It will be the first frigate privateer and Vincent will be her captain. What shall we call her, Vincent?"

Gambi looked up while chewing a bite of meat. He swallowed and took a drink of wine.

"*La Tigre*," he said.

The thought of these pirates loose on the ocean with a modern frigate was appalling, yet part of me couldn't help but admire them. Mayhem was their element and the world was full of it.

"Miss Rackham," Laffite said, raising his voice so he could be heard across the table. "Soon, the *Frelon* will need a new sailing master. What do you say? You could become rich and you wouldn't have the world on your tail like old Radan."

"I already have a job as sailing master," Rackham replied.

"Captain, then," Laffite said. "Imagine it, a corvette of your own and a fine one at that. You'd be queen of the sea. I can't imagine you'll just go dig up Radan's treasure and retire."

Rackham squinted. Laffite laughed. His last words stung me. Much of the *Vipere*'s plunder had not been recovered. Did Rackham know where it was?

"I've got a job to do, Fita," she said. "After that, who knows?"

"Your loyalty recommends you," Laffite said more somberly. "There will be a place for you here if you want it."

* * *

Sydow and Mr. Bowie sat across from each other and I listened to some of their conversation. Bowie talked of Texas and of buying large tracts of land to parcel out to settlers.

"A cavalry man, you say. Do you know how to raise horses?" Bowie asked.

"That was my family's business," Sydow said. "Our barony was known for its horses and I was all but born on one."

"Then think of it, man," Bowie said. "You could have your own barony in Texas, as big as you please – lush, rolling grasslands that never end, just begging to be settled. A good horse breeder would make a fortune."

"Wouldn't there be Indians to contend with?" I interrupted.

"There's danger, no doubt," Bowie said. "But that's what makes it exciting, eh? A company of good men and a veteran cavalry officer to lead them – I think the Indians could be brought to heel."

Bowie's enthusiasm was having an effect on Sydow; even I felt its infection. This was the spirit of the New World, I thought. The possibilities seemed endless and the land inexhaustible.

* * *

The conversation moved on to Bowie's adventures on the frontier, then Sydow talked of his experiences fighting the French army, then, as we moved back to the parlor for brandy and tobacco, Laffite and Gambi talked of their efforts helping Andrew Jackson prevail at the Battle of New Orleans. I think they wanted to provoke me, given that Britain lost the battle, but I never favored that pointless war, so I didn't take the bait.

"Where will you go from here, captain?" Laffite asked.

"You say Veracruz is denied us," I replied. "So my thought is we'll steer wide of the port and venture into El Radio along the coast, though I will need to confer with Miss Rackham on the specifics."

"I would be wary. That coast is wild now. You're likely to see things that are quite frightening. Do you plan to venture far into El Radio?"

"As far as we need to. As for frightening sights, we've seen a few already."

Laffite smiled: "Well, sir, if you must go, perhaps we should ask Hector to give you a reading. What do you say, Hector?"

"Why certainly, Jean, if Sir LeRoque so wishes," Guibourg said.

"Hector is very gifted," Laffite said. "He has steered us clear of much trouble and led us to some valuable opportunities. Perhaps he can help you find what you're seeking."

"Are you a soothsayer?" I asked Guibourg.

"I have studied the occult all my life," he said. "In recent years my efforts have borne fruit. I would not use the word, 'soothsayer,' rather I am a seer of tangible possibility that we cannot divine with our normal intelligence."

My first thought was that Guibourg was a charlatan who had charmed his way into the graces of Laffite and his wife. But I thought of Louisa and her tarot cards and her remarkable visions. I sat next to Sophie on a divan and she squeezed my hand. A warning, I assumed, but it let me know that Guibourg likely had real ability. Could I turn down the chance he might learn something useful about the *Squirrel* expedition?

"All right, Monsieur Guibourg. I'm game if you are."

* * *

"There are many forms of divination," Guibourg lectured as we moved back into the dining room. "Cartomancy, or tarot cards, of course; acultomancy, the dropping of needles on flour and reading the patterns; botanomancy, the burning of herbs and reading the smoke; and many others, but I prefer carromancy, the dripping of wax into cold liquid and reading the shapes. They have a dynamism to them yet move slowly enough to ponder their significance."

We sat at the table again, I across from Guibourg and Sophie beside me. Earl, the butler, brought in a copper bowl half filled with water. Guibourg lit a candle and set it next to the bowl. He poured a fresh glass of wine and set it before me.

"Earl, put out the lights, if you please," Guibourg ordered.

The room darkened; only the candle provided light. Mr. Bowie made a joke and Gambi and Sydow guffawed. Guibourg ordered silence.

"Do as he says," Laffite said softly.

The room quiet, Guibourg closed his eyes, spread his hands expansively and began to hum, a near monotone that only gradually rose in pitch, then lowered. He opened his eyes and looked at me.

"Take a drink of the wine, Sir LeRoque, and pour the remainder into the bowl."

Guibourg had set the stage like a good performer. It felt like a parlor game, the kind Louisa liked to play in our youth. Sophie gripped my hand tightly. I took a drink and slowly poured the rest into the bowl.

"Now lift the candle and let three drops fall into the liquid."

I grasped the brass holder and tilted the candle over the bowl. Plop, plop, plop, the drops formed dendritic patterns that spun and circled each other. Guibourg placed his hands on the bowl, gazed into it and resumed his humming. The wax patterns swirled apart and reformed in a continuous motion not unlike the furling and unfurling of Dr. Seymour's projected smoke images.

"Now that's queer," Bowie muttered.

"Hush," Laffite hissed.

Guibourg's gazing and humming continued for some time. The candle flickered. Suddenly the wax sank and a depression formed in the liquid. Guibourg groaned, Madame Laffite screeched, Sophie gasped. The depression rebounded like a released spring, spewing liquid into Guibourg's face. He stood abruptly, eyes wide, pink water trickling down his head.

"Medusa!" he screamed.

Then he fell to the floor.

* * *

"Get the damned lanterns going, Earl," Gambi commanded.

Madame Laffite was leaning over Guibourg, patting his face, but he was out cold, though still breathing. Laffite remained seated and bore a pained expression.

"This is getting out of hand, Fita," Gambi said.

"I know," Laffite said wearily.

"You're playing with fire, monsieur," I told him.

"So are you, LeRoque, so are you."

* * *

Sydow and Bowie lifted Guibourg and carried him up to his bed followed by Sophie and an anxious Madame Laffite.

"I don't think he liked what he saw," Rackham said to me.

"No, I don't think that he did."

Gambi left to fetch the town's surgeon. Rackham and I went to the foyer and strapped on our weapon belts.

"You know, you do look out of place in that gown," I said.
"Really? I was just starting to get used to it."
I laughed.
Laffite approached and appeared to have regained his spirits.
"Please let me accompany you back to your ship," he said. "I'd like a word with you, LeRoque."
The rest of my party returned from upstairs. Sydow and Bowie bade each other goodbye and Bowie let Sydow know how he could be contacted.
"Think about it. Texas is ripe for the picking."
"I certainly will, Herr Bowie."
Laffite strapped on his hanger and we left Maison Rouge.

* * *

A full moon was rising, glowing large on the horizon. Laffite and I walked a ways in front of the others.
"One of my ships," he said, "after being chased into El Radio by an American brig ..."
"The *Enterprise*?" I interrupted.
"The very same. You know of her?"
"We anchored alongside her at Kingston. I became acquainted with Captain Kearny."
"That bastard gives me no end of trouble."
"He says he's going to see you hang."
"He may at that, but with the *Frelon* and *La Tigre* at my disposal, he's going to need a bigger ship. I have him outgunned."
"I suppose you do. You were saying?"
"Yes, my ship took refuge in a small harbor a couple hundred miles along the coast from Veracruz. They found a crude fort and some Mexican soldiers occupying it. They heard tell of two Englishmen who had come ashore in a battered dinghy."
"Were they from the *Squirrel*?" I asked.
"Possibly. I don't know. The region is known as Tabasco and it's gone wild. The governor, however, is holding out in the town of Villa Hermosa, about 30 miles inland from the

harbor. Angel del Toro they call him, an unpleasant man, I'm led to believe. He has the Englishmen, that is if they still live."

"This is news, our first substantial lead," I said. "Can you show me on a chart where the harbor is?"

"Certainly."

I grew excited but was left wondering why Laffite hadn't told me earlier. I'm sure he had his motives, but no matter.

"I have a question, monsieur," I said. "Do you know anything about where Ann came from?"

"What I know of her past I couldn't speak of it."

"The code?"

"Yes, the code. But I will tell you I know nothing of where she came from before Captain Radan took her on. I've even made inquiries. Hector has wild ideas but he doesn't know. Does it matter to you, LeRoque?"

"No, it would change nothing. I'm simply curious."

We reached the quay and could see torches and lanterns lit dockside of the *Bar Jack*, an impromptu gathering of men on the island and my crew. For my part, it was no surprise. I hadn't forbidden it. Laffite seemed amused.

"Many of my men have grown rather rich and are looking to settle down, either here or stake a claim in Texas. Good, strong women would be very welcome."

"I imagine so," I said. "I need to see my errand through. After that the women can go where they wish."

"If it weren't for Rackham," Laffite said, "I'd have little hope any of you would return, but with her as sailing master, I'd say your chances are decent."

The din of the party quieted when we approached, the men clearly not expecting Laffite to arrive himself. He motioned his men to be at ease. We waited for Sophie, Rackham and Sydow to catch up, then waded through the crowd and went aboard. I saw Kitten sitting on the gunwale of the aft deck, the carbine on her lap.

Chapter 15: El Radio

16 July, 1819, Galveston Island

After breakfast Rackham, Mrs. Kedward and Sydow went to arrange the purchase of victuals to supplement our supply. Rackham had seen a battered dinghy for sale the day before and wanted to buy it as a spare. I thought it was a good idea.

The sky was clear and a stiff breeze blew in from the west, a good sailing day, and I was eager to be on our way. After handing a bundle of letters to one of Laffite's agents, I took a walk along the shore and saw a group of Indians crabbing in the shallows. I paused to watch them and think.

"Is Hector Guibourg a charlatan, or does he have real ability like you?" I had asked Sophie the night before.

"Both," she said. "Laffite has the ability, too, and his wife, though I guess they are only beginning to get to know it. Monsieur Guibourg has had much practice. His divination was a performance; he wanted to impress us, scare us, too, I think."

"I think he scared himself," I said.

"He saw something he didn't expect, something horrible."

"Did you see it?"

"No, I was shielding myself as best I could."

"Do you think it was Akabo, or the daemon thing, or whatever it is?

"No, it felt different."

"Medusa ... what could it mean?"

Sophie shook her head.

The Indians started looking askance at me so I walked on, turning inland across grassy terrain honeycombed with game trails. I made a circuit of the town and returned from the opposite end. I came to an open market with various wares laid out under a broad canopy. I stopped to browse and saw a table with an array of knives and swords.

"Would you happen to have a blade known as a machete?" I asked the vendor, an old man with a toothless grin.

"No, sir," he said. "I do have a fascine knife, French made. Should serve for clearing brush."

"Hmm, that might do. What's this?" I asked looking at a thick, curved scabbard with an odd wooden handle protruding from its mouth.

"Ah, that, a curious thing, don't know what it's called."

The man unsheathed it revealing a fat-bellied blade about 15 inches long with a pronounced forward curve. I then knew what it was, a kukri knife from Nepal. Darnsby had brought one back from a tour in India, though his was smaller. I suspected this was plunder from the captured Indiaman. I handled the weapon a bit and found it blade-heavy but very sharp. Darnsby had told me Gorkha warriors used kukris for all sorts of things including fighting. It had a distinctive notch at the ricasso, the purpose of which no one seemed to know.

"How much?"

"It's a nice piece, brass hardware, copper inlay, rosewood handle," the man said. "I can let you have it for ten dollars. Very rare, from India, you know."

"Nepal, actually. Here's two silver schillings. They ought to more than cover the price."

"Yes, sir, I believe they would."

* * *

Returning to the pier, I saw the women loading stores onto the *Bar Jack*. I also saw Laffite standing next to Sydow near several powder kegs, crates and a small cannon on a wheeled carriage.

"Bonjour, monsieur," I said. "What is all this?"

"A field gun," Laffite said. "I'd like you to do me a favor and deliver this to Angel del Toro. Tell him it is a gift from me in the hopes we might begin a trading partnership. I suspect it will help smooth your dealings with him should the Englishmen still live."

"A good gun, kapitan," Sydow said. "Even a few canister rounds, which are very deadly."

I wasn't keen on trafficking arms or getting involved with the wars between Spain and her rebellious colonies. If we were boarded by the French or Spanish, the gun would look suspicious. I also suspected Laffite had other motives. Nevertheless, I was in no position to deny his request.

"Very well," I said. "It may indeed help. Thank you. By the way, how is Monsieur Guibourg?"

"He is on his feet but remembers nothing about last night, or so he says. Bon voyage, LeRoque."

"Farewell, Laffite. It has been an interesting meeting."

He flashed his white teeth and walked away.

* * *

I found Cadmael in the hold helping to stow the newly acquired victuals. He wore a fresh pair of trousers and a white shirt.

"Mr. Cadmael, a word in my cabin if you don't mind."

"Certainly."

Once there I invited him to sit.

"We're departing this afternoon and heading straight into El Radio. I intend to take you home."

"Thank you, sir. If there's some way I can pay you ..."

"You owe me nothing," I said. "I would, however, like to hire you. We plan on making landfall before we reach Isla Lanza. We'll probably need to travel inland about thirty miles. It's wild country, I'm told. I'd like you to be our guide. What do you say? I can pay a fair wage for the service."

"I will do it happily but I probably won't know the area."

"But you know the jungle and the dangers therein."

"Yes."

"Excellent. That's what we need. By the way, I looked for a machete but couldn't find one. I did find this, however."

I handed Cadmael the kukri and he withdrew it from its sheath.

"This is beautiful but strange," he said.

"From Central Asia, used by a warrior people known as Gorkhas. They gave our army serious trouble not long ago."

Cadmael smiled. "I think this might do, captain."

"I'm glad. For the moment we have a cannon to load on board, if you wouldn't mind helping."

"Of course, and thank you."

* * *

We tacked against a gusty south wind in a choppy sea. I wanted to get beyond the main shipping lanes as quickly as possible in order to avoid any dangerous encounters. Rackham kept the crew on its toes sailing as close hauled as she dared.

The wind died down at dusk and Rackham spotted a ship off our starboard bow sailing a course perpendicular to our own.

"She's turning toward us, captain," she said.

"I see that. A brig."

We both had our spyglasses trained on the vessel.

"Can we evade her?" I asked.

"Maybe. She's got the wind of us and she's handled well."

To my relief I saw the stars and stripes of the United States flag.

"American, unless it's a ruse," I said.

"Nah, it's the *Enterprise.* I thought she might be."

When the *Enterprise* neared, we exchanged signals and hove-to.

* * *

When Captain Kearny came aboard, I invited him to dinner but he declined. He did accept an offer of coffee, freshly obtained at Galveston. We sat in my cabin with Rackham and Sydow catching up on events since Jamaica, a chart of the Gulf spread on the table.

"So you had your audience with Laffite," Kearny said. "I'll be damned."

"He was actually rather polite," I said.

"He's still a scoundrel."

"I don't doubt it. He is frightening in a way, though I never felt any threat from him."

"I bet he's working an angle," Kearny said and took a sip from his cup. "Damn, that's good coffee. Hard to come by these days."

"Laffite seems to have the best of everything," I said.

"What all does he have back there?"

"Am I to be you informant?"

"If you had to make promises, I won't press the matter."

"I'm under no obligation," I said. "Laffite probably expects me to talk about him."

I told Kearny about the harbor and its ships including the *Frelon* and the Indiaman being converted to a frigate. Rackham gave him more detail and estimated the ship would be ready to sail in two or three months.

"Blast, we'll need a fleet to flush him out. But Washington is playing coy. Laffite has friends in Congress."

"He dabbles in the occult. A Parisian soothsayer stays at his house," I said. "The way things are that may be more worrisome than his warships."

"I have trouble giving credence to that stuff."

"I wouldn't take it lightly."

I told Kearny of the two Englishmen Laffite said were at Villa Hermosa and showed him on the chart our plan to sail to a nearby harbor and trek inland.

"Seems risky but at least you have something to go on," Kearny said. "Tell you what, I'll provide escort to the edge of El Radio. That should keep any Spanish or French warships from being tempted to board you."

"Very much obliged, captain."

* * *

The warm south wind picked up again in the morning and we continued tacking, though not so close hauled in order to remain near the *Enterprise.* The American ship was expertly handled but her square rigging made her sluggish before the wind compared to the *Bar Jack*. Three days passed without incident.

On the fourth, however, Polly spotted sails off our port bow. I was roused and went to the deck without shaving.

"A French corvette," Rackham said. "At the head of a fleet, I reckon."

My spyglass revealed the sleek lines and low profile of the three-masted ship. More sails emerged on the horizon behind her. I saw Captain Kearny on the *Enterprise* looking in the same direction. Not wanting to sail into the midst of the fleet, I ordered a course west by southwest so we would pass well in front of it and told Rackham to signal our course change. The *Enterprise* signaled first, suggesting the same course. I admit I felt satisfaction that Rackham did not object to my order and that it agreed with Captain Kearny's signal. I went back to my cabin, shaved and ate breakfast with Sydow.

We returned to the deck with lit pipes only to stare agape at the extent of the French fleet that had appeared – four ships-of-the-line, three frigates and two corvettes escorting four large merchant ships. The towering masts full of wind were quite a sight. We likely would pass about a half mile in front of the nearest ship.

"Should we be worried, kapitan?"

"I'm guessing they have bigger fish to fry," I said. "Ann, what's their heading?"

"Southwest on a slow tack. Sailing for Veracruz, no doubt."

"Bonaparte is getting serious, I think," Sydow said.

"Very," I said, wondering what would happen if Mexico fell to Napoleon.

After crossing in front of the fleet, we returned to our southerly tack. The French ignored us and I was happy to be ignored.

* * *

On the morning of 23 July, we crossed into El Radio. We sailed through a squall, then the sun came out and the wind became westerly. The *Enterprise* signaled Godspeed and turned away to a course north by northeast. We kept our southerly heading.

Rackham announced that a frayed halyard of the aft rigging needed to be replaced along with a block. The work took most of the afternoon. I ordered an extra watch but we spotted nothing that day.

I took my usual middle watch at the helm. We shortened sail and the *Bar Jack* kept her line coursing close reach to a perpendicular wind. Low clouds hid the stars. I put a match to my pipe, shrouding it with my hand. With the *Enterprise* gone, I felt vulnerable and the inky gloom of the night amplified the feeling. I could see the hands on deck were scared. Izzy reported she saw something to port but I could make nothing out with my spyglass. I thought about having the swivel gun crew ready the weapon and stand watch. Instead, my mind drifted with the sound of the sea, the sway of the ship and the feel of the tiller. Rackham relieved me early as usual and I retired to my cabin to find Sophie sleeping.

I was about to put out the lantern when she started grunting and thrashing about. "No! No! Get out of my mind! Go!" she shouted. Abruptly she sat upright, eyes open, flushed and breathing heavily. She looked more angry than frightened. There was a knock on the door.

"Is all well in there?" Sydow asked.

"Yes, Leo, just a nightmare," Sophie said.

"We're all right," I followed.

"Good night, then," Sydow said.

I turned to Sophie. "It wasn't a nightmare, was it?"

"I don't think I want to talk about it."

"The daemon?"

She shook her head but said nothing. She turned away and put her head back on the pillow. The ship rocked and jerked as it struck a wave at an awkward angle. I put out the lantern and tried to get some sleep.

"It was Louisa," Sophie said.

"Louisa? What do you mean?"

"She wanted to communicate, live through me like she had done before. I told her not now, not here. It was too dangerous."

"But something else happened."

"She ..."

Sophie was lying on her side. I stroked the curve of her hip.

"She tried to force herself on me, dominate my mind. We struggled. I shut her out."

I had no words. I was pained that the two people I loved most were at odds and in a way I couldn't imagine. Had Louisa really assailed Sophie's mind?

"She's lonely," Sophie said.

"I don't think people are made for the intimacy you and Louisa have shared," I said, having little else to say.

"I think Juliet stopped communicating, too."

"What happened?"

"I don't know."

* * *

After two more days sailing, we spotted land at first light of the third, a shore of forbidding jungle. Rackham timed the landfall impeccably but we had to cruise the coast about two miles before we spotted the entrance to the harbor, a wide channel but I could see no signs of the fort beyond.

Rackham ordered sails shortened and signaled a course change to Maggie who had the tiller. A southwesterly breeze blew and the *Bar Jack* angled slowly toward the channel. As we approached Rackham ordered soundings to get our depth. We struck the center of the channel and the depth read seven fathoms.

The bay opened and the breeze freshened. Standing at the bow with Rackham and Sydow, I could see a beach and, on a rise just beyond it, stood the fort. The gate was down and no flag flew.

"It's deserted," Sydow said, looking through my spyglass.

"That's disappointing," I said.

I'd hoped to meet a garrison, learn if the Englishmen still lived, and negotiate passage inland. It appeared we'd have to make the trek alone. I ordered the shore party to get ready and Rackham to take us in as close as she dared.

The shore party consisted of Sydow, Cadmael, Mrs. Kedward, Kitten, Sophie and myself. I loathed depriving the ship of her carpenter but Mrs. Kedward was adamant, hoping one of the Englishmen was her husband. I hated including Sophie, or Kitten for that matter, but I couldn't deny the possibility their skills would be needed. Cadmael recommended traveling as light as possible but, at the same time, taking as much water as we could carry. Stream and river water should be avoided if possible, he said.

We stood on the deck ready to descend into the dinghy and saying our farewells. I was armed with my long hunting rifle and broadsword; Sydow with his saber, pistol and the blunderbuss; Cadmael with a musket and his kukri; Mrs. Kedward a musket, pistol and cutlass; and Sophie with naught but a small knife.

Kitten was a sight in her trousers, blouse, straw hat with Osceola's headband, the long Seminole knife at her hip, the carbine rifle slung on her shoulder and my dueling pistols on a bandolier. Our thought was three quick, accurate shots from her could make all the difference if it came to a scrape, though I very much hoped it wouldn't.

* * *

With eight of us and our gear in the dinghy – Jenny and Izzy worked the oars – I was glad the water was calm. I scanned the fort ahead. Clearly a battle of some kind had taken place. The jungle beyond looked unwelcoming.

"Mein Gott!" Sydow exclaimed, pointing to an outcropping of rock jutting into the bay.

What I had thought was a boulder perched on the end of the outcropping was not a boulder. Looking now I saw the neck of a creature craning toward the sky. The boulder was actually a massive turtle. I put my glass on it. A thick, leathery neck extended from a shell about five or six feet in diameter. Webbed feet with long claws dangled from its side. The turtle's head had a predatory beak.

"A snapping turtle but so huge," Sydow said.

I looked at Cadmael. He shrugged. "Not a worry if you keep your distance."

"Well, I don't intend to bother it," Mrs. Kedward said.

Kitten had her carbine trained on the beast. Sydow gripped her shoulder.

"I think you would only make it angry," he said. He then got out his notebook and made a sketch.

The beach, thankfully, was free of monsters and we disembarked without issue. We shouldered our rucksacks and trudged across the white sand toward the fort. My rucksack was quite heavy. I had hoped we might procure a donkey or mule but that wasn't to be. Kitten was the only one who didn't carry a rucksack. Aside from her weapons and ammunition, she only carried a waterskin and a small pouch. Sydow wanted to keep her burden light so if trouble came she could act quickly. I agreed.

The fort was crude, a palisade of thick timbers built on an earthen berm. What had been the gate was knocked over. Sydow was taking a close look at the surrounding ground.

"Marauders?" I said.

"No sign of cannon fire. The gate was pushed over, I'd say."

"By what?"

We cautiously entered, firearms ready. To our right toward the shore, was the toppled remains of a guard tower. There were bits of timber scattered all around and, in the center of the fort, the crumbled remnants of a building. A shed behind it appeared intact. Weeds grew amid the rubble. Whatever happened had happened at least a few weeks prior.

Mrs. Kedward knelt and picked up a plate-like object.

"What in Heaven's name is this?" she asked.

The plate was triangular, had a dark, coppery color and was larger than my hand. Though hard it was not metal and had what seemed like bits of dried flesh on one edge. I waved Cadmael over.

"What do you make of this?"

“What I was afraid of,” he said. “It’s a scale from a snake we call titanaconda.”

“Titanaconda?”

“Yes, captain, like an anaconda only much larger.”

Sydow examined the scale.

“An anaconda is like an African python,” he said. “They grow 20 feet or longer. But this, I don’t know, big enough to destroy a fort. I have seen several muskets and spent balls. They tried to shoot it.”

I found it disheartening that, armed as we were, there were creatures around that we could not stand against.

“They could have used that field gun,” I said. “We were too late.”

“Ja.”

“Mr. Cadmael, did the snake come from the jungle?”

“They say the titanaconda keeps to the shore and the big rivers. I doubt it came from the jungle.”

I looked out over the light blue waters of the bay to the *Bar Jack* lying at anchor. Was the great snake prowling out there?

The shed contained a few muskets, a keg of powder, food stores, a couple of barrels of water and two kegs of wine. I said we should leave the provisions be. They might come in handy later on.

We found large mounds of scat, presumably from the snake. It must have stayed a while to digest its meal. Sydow held up a portion of a skull, clearly from a man who had been devoured.

Chapter 16: Tabasco Road

26 July, 1819, Tabasco Region, Mexico

"Here we are," I said. "I don't think it's possible to overstate the danger. I feel I have to go on, so I will. None of you need come with me. I don't know what our chances are. Not good, I suppose."

"For Christ's sake, captain, nobody's backing out now," Mrs. Kedward said.

Thus chastened I nodded and returned to the beach where Jenny and Izzy waited by the dinghy. I looked toward the outcropping and saw the turtle was gone.

"It slipped into the water a little bit ago," Izzy said.

"We're proceeding inland," I said. "Tell Master Rackham the fort was destroyed by a massive snake. It could threaten the ship. With luck we'll see you in five days. Farewell."

"Be careful, captain," Jenny said.

"I intend to be."

The two women pushed the dinghy into the water. Jenny rowed while Izzy scanned the water with her musket to hand.

* * *

I met the others at the trailhead. Cadmael was stooping, picking long, narrow leaves from small plants growing at the edge of the trees. He gave us each a handful.

"What's this?" I asked.

"It will help keep the bugs away," Cadmael said. "It's called yerbaniz. Rub it on your face and neck and hands. The less you get bit the better."

We followed his example. The leaves smelled like tarragon. We each gathered a couple more handfuls for later use.

"We should get going," Mrs. Kedward said.

Cadmael led the way into a forest of tall, dark palms. The track was wide, rutted and, at one time, must have been frequently used. The going was level for perhaps a mile, then we began to climb up a ridge where the palms gave way to cedars.

We were all sweating and respiring heavily when we reached the crest. The weight I carried had seemed manageable at first but now seemed twice as heavy. We rested briefly then started our descent on a series of switchbacks. Parts of the road had crumbled and we had to watch our steps else tumble into the ravine below.

Up a rise and down another set of switchbacks, the road leveled and skirted a marsh to our left edged by thick willows entangled with parasitical vines. A splash in the water caused us to train our weapons in that direction but we saw nothing.

The road traversed an area of rolling ridges and humps and we came to a deep gully with a fast-flowing stream. Fortunately there was a crude but sturdy bridge. We rested on it, eating a lunch of bread and cheese. Soon the flies became so thick that, tired as we were, we had to move on.

Beyond the bridge the ground leveled and we entered a forest of huge mahoganies. It was dark and cool and the flies weren't so ferocious. We spread out as we plodded along, Cadmael and Mrs. Kedward at the front, Kitten and Sydow bringing up the rear.

"I communicated with Louisa last night," Sophie said, walking beside me.

"Oh."

"She apologized. She was ashamed of what she'd done."

"That's good. I hope you two are back on friendly terms."

"I think so."

"Anything else? Any news? Any word from Juliet?"

"When she told Louisa she had to stop communicating, she was in Milan staying with friends. She learned there is probably more than one copy of that book Giselle LaFoy found in Spain."

"The one that priest wrote back in the 16th century?"

"Yes, I think so."
"What happens if Juliet finds a copy, I wonder."
Sophie shrugged. "We learn more."
If the book really was a key to some kind of power, what would the temptations be? I kept the thought to myself.
"Did Louisa say anything about the incident at Kilve Beach?"
"Your brother is keeping mum on the subject but Louisa believes it's caused a stir in the government."
A group of monkeys shrieked and passed overhead in the canopy, leaping from limb to limb.
"If you really wanted to take over someone's mind, could you do it?" I asked.
"I don't know. Not now. Maybe in time."
"But that sort of thing is possible."
"I think so."

* * *

Our pace slowed entering an area of many orchids on the ground mingling with the buttress roots of the trees. We beheld an array of reds, purples and yellows. Some flowers were solid in color, others striped or spotted. My nose was bombarded with odors rank to sweet, musty vanilla to minty fresh. We halted when Sydow knelt to observe closely a particularly splendid example.
"It would fetch a fortune in London," he said.
"The Mayans would say this place is touched by Ixchel, the moon goddess," Cadmael said.
"I suppose we should leave it be," I said.
Cadmael, acting like he caught scent of something, left the road and went into the trees. Sophie followed.
"Wait, where are you going?"
Irritated and uneasy, I followed with my rifle ready and thumb on the hammer. About 50 paces in I saw Cadmael and Sophie standing at the edge of a clearing. The air was heavy with a smell akin to bergamot.
"Ho there," I said. "Things are dangerous enough, we don't need side adventures ..."

Then I saw what they saw – a large ground plant a couple of yards away. The more I looked, the more I was left in wonder. Two great oblong leaves, lying flat and hinged together, projected long, needle-like spines, giving the impression of open jaws. The leaves were dark green and spines white. Hundreds of short, tubular growths, reddish-purple in color, rose from the area where the leaves hinged.

Soon the others appeared and were similarly dumbfounded.

"A giant Venus flytrap," Sydow said. "It could swallow a horse."

"It does not take life," Cadmael said. "It gives it. They call it mandíbulas curativas. This is the first time I've seen one. They say it can restore health to those on the brink of death, but they must be pure of heart."

Sophie seemed especially entranced. She stepped forward and reached out to touch one of the spines. Cadmael pulled her back.

"It is bad luck to disturb it unless the need is great."

"I concur," I said, though I was unconvinced by Cadmael's story. The thing was clearly predatory. "We should get back to the road."

* * *

Before long we were in the midst of a rain squall. We slogged our way up a slope where mahoganies gave way to cedars. Fortunately the rain didn't last long.

When the slope leveled off, we found ourselves on a plateau and an expanse of savanna stretched before us. The sun dried our clothes and our firearms which we re-primed to make sure they would discharge if needed. The road was damp and mud clung to our boots. Cadmael put up his hand and we stopped.

"Aves del terror," he said, pointing to the ground.

We gathered close and looked at a huge track in the mud, like a bird's but two feet long. More of them stretched ahead.

"Terror bird," Sophie said, translating.

“Unglaublich,” Sydow muttered, taking out his measuring string.

“These tracks are fresh,” I said. “What on earth is it?”

“A giant bird,” Cadmael said. “This one is maybe eight feet tall.”

“Are they dangerous?”

“Very. They’re hunters.”

“Can they fly?”

“No, but they run very fast.”

Sydow measured the track and the length between strides, then made a quick sketch. We walked on, keeping wary. Kitten could hardly see over the grass. After a few hundred yards, we saw where the terror bird had turned off the road to our right but we could see nothing in that direction. I checked my pocket compass; the road was running southeast.

“We need to camp soon,” I said. “This is wearisome travel. I don’t know how much longer I can go on.”

“I was hoping to find a village, or the remains of one,” Cadmael said. “I don’t think we want to camp in the open if we can help it.”

We kept going and after a mile or so, we came to an area of once cultivated fields, maize and barley now mixing with native grasses. We ascended a low hill and at the top, looked down on a small valley with a stream meandering through it. We saw the burnt-out remains of a large house, a barn and a few outbuildings. Several antelope grazed in their midst. The road skirted the ruined settlement and snaked its way toward a gap in tree-covered ridges.

“Camp here?” I asked, almost pleading.

“Yes, camp here.”

* * *

We cleared an area in the rubble of the large house, built a campfire and ate a passable meal of roasted sausages, bread and a few greens Cadmael had picked along the stream. When night fell, despite the warm, humid air, the fire was a welcome comfort. The sky was clear and we hoped for a rainless night.

I lit my pipe for a smoke before I turned in, Sophie beside me, softly singing a Spanish ballad. Sydow had propped himself up against the remains of a wall making notes in his field book. Kitten reclined on his lap and occasionally poked the book with her finger. Sydow finally slapped her hand.

"Hör auf," he snapped.

Cadmael was already asleep. Mrs. Kedward was making a braid with a ball of twine she had packed. To what end I wasn't sure, probably something to keep her hands busy. I only half finished my pipe. Soon I was asleep.

* * *

Sophie woke me with a kiss.

"Your watch, captain."

I grunted, blinked and pushed myself up, every muscle stiff, and she handed me the pocket watch. She reclined where I had been lying and was soon snoring softly. She had kept the fire blazing and I paced circles around it to get my blood circulating.

I walked around the perimeter of the ruins. A partial moon was up but I could see nothing but the rustling of grass in the breeze. The trees on the ridges beyond were a dark, forbidding mass. Returning to the fire, I sat down to smoke. I'd hoped we'd make Villa Hermosa during the coming day. I'd figured we'd traveled fifteen miles at least but Cadmael said it was closer to ten, if that far. He was likely correct and we'd have to spend another night in the wilderness.

It was quiet and I gazed at the stars. I admit I drifted into a torpor but came out of it when I heard what sounded like singing, distant and faint, but it was gone when my senses fully returned. I attributed it to an illusion of a type that occurs between sleep and wakefulness. Then I heard it again, coming from the ridges, high pitched, melodious like a bird call but slower, not a bird but not human either. Another voice sounded in answer, and another, a flowing melody, sometimes harmonious, sometimes discordant. I could make out little clicks and thuds, too, like drumming. The rhythm was there but I couldn't catch the time of it. What a strange world we had entered.

Cadmael had the last shift and it was almost time so I thought I'd wake him but his eyes were already open.

"You hear it?"

"Yes," he said and sat up.

"What is it?"

"It's the song of the Alux, the little people."

"Do you mean little men and women?"

"No, not men and women. Creatures, deep jungle dwellers. The Mayans say they have magic powers."

"Are they dangerous?"

"Very, so I am told, but they do not attack, usually, unless provoked."

"What do they look like?"

"I don't know. Few have seen them and stories vary. They say they walk upright like people and use tools. Some say they have feathers; others say they just wear them."

"Do they know we're here?"

"They can't have missed the fire."

We listened to the singing a while longer. I thought about waking the others, the sound was so intriguing, but it faded into silence.

* * *

I slept until the sun was well up, later than I'd wanted. Sydow stood on a crumbled portion of wall holding my long rifle.

"What's going on? Where's Cadmael?" I asked.

"He thought he saw someone skulking in the grass."

I hoisted myself onto the wall and saw Cadmael walking back toward camp.

"Someone was there but slipped away," he said.

"What does it mean?" I asked.

Cadmael shrugged. "Who knows?"

We roused the women and ate the last of the sausages. The farmstead had a well and Cadmael pronounced it good so we refilled our skins and pressed on.

* * *

I walked with Cadmael at the front this time, Sophie and Mrs. Kedward were in the middle and Kitten and Sydow brought up the rear. The road wound through the ridges and descended from the plateau into deep jungle dominated by huge mahoganies. The caw of birds or cackle of monkeys erupted from time to time.

"The plateau is good land," Cadmael said. "It would be a good place to settle."

"Perhaps," I said. "It seems dangerous."

"Everywhere is dangerous."

Our progress was interrupted by the appearance of a snake, a six-foot brute with black and brown trapezoidal patterns on its back. It was sunning itself on the road where a rare ray of light found its way through the canopy. Cadmael stopped abruptly and pushed me back. The snake reared and hissed, mouth open, showing long fangs dripping with venom.

"A fer de lance," Cadmael whispered.

He shouted at it, "shoo, shoo," but the viper didn't give up the road. I waved Kitten up. She took aim with the carbine and fired, hitting the snake square in the head. The blast set dozens of birds to flight and caused monkeys to scream and scramble away through the canopy. The snake writhed a moment then stilled.

Sydow measured the fer de lance and made a few notes in his book. Cadmael chopped the head off with his kukri and slung the body over his shoulder.

"We should eat it," he said. "Doesn't taste too bad."

* * *

The jungle seemed to grow darker and deeper but the road remained clear and the ground level. We took a break around noon and Cadmael gutted the snake. Later we found a large paw print and Cadmael pronounced it the spoor of a jaguar. Yet another dangerous creature, I thought. Sydow measured the track and made a note.

The road became narrower and the ground more rugged. We occasionally had to duck under a low hanging vine. The air was still and thick with humidity. At a bend, where the road circumvented a large boulder, Cadmael halted the party. He was sniffing the air and I could smell it, too, a sickly odor of rot and sulfur.

"Another orchid patch?" I whispered.

Cadmael shook his head. "Shh." He looked worried. He moved at a tiptoe around the bend. I motioned the others to wait and followed.

On the other side of the boulder, we saw a black pool of muck and beside it, growing up in the middle of the road, was the strangest tree I'd ever seen. It had a broad trunk of gray, leathery bark and from it sprung five branches that arced upward and over, each ending with a long, black tusk. The tree had no leaves.

A bubble rose in the pool releasing a puff of yellowish gas.

"Bad luck," Cadmael whispered. "We're too close."

He took my arm and began to back away slowly. Suddenly a root or tentacle sprang up and wrapped itself around Cadmael's leg, yanking him down and dragging him toward the tree. He cried out and tried to clutch the ground.

I drew my sword and and hewed at the root. The branches of the tree aligned toward us, thrusting out with their tusks. My third stroke severed the root and the remaining length sprang back toward the tree. I pulled Cadmael up but another root caught my leg and yanked me off my feet. I vainly tried to jab it as it dragged me. The black tusks thrust out as if eager for me to get into their range. Soon I would be skewered.

With one stroke Cadmael severed the root with his kukri and we scrambled away. The others had come around and leveled their weapons at the tree.

"No, no! Run! Run now!" Cadmael yelled.

* * *

I trembled so much I had to kneel, those jabbing tusks fresh in my memory. We had run about a hundred yards from the boulder.

"What in God's name was that?" Mrs. Kedward asked.

"A'rbol espada," Cadmael said. "A sword tree. They always appear by the black bogs and grow very quickly. A trail that was clear the last time you walked it may have a sword tree next time. They have killed many people."

Sydow picked up the end of one of the roots that must have come off my leg while I was running.

"Be careful, Leo," I said.

"It's not really a tree," he said. "A fungus, perhaps."

Sydow sliced the tip off with a pocket knife and put it in one of the snuff tins he kept for samples. He turned to me and handed back my rifle. The remains of the fer de lance had dropped from Cadmael's shoulders during the struggle. We wouldn't be eating viper fillets that evening.

"The road is blocked," I said. "We'll have to find a way around."

Cadmael was already searching, presumably for a trail that someone else had blazed. My trembling abated. I stood and Sophie put her arm around my waist. Cadmael found vines that had been cut, probably within a fortnight, he said.

The meager trail seemed our best option and we left the road, walking single file with Cadmael leading. He kept his kukri out and trimmed away intruding brush. I took compass readings to keep our direction and Sydow made slash marks on the trees with his saber to mark our way.

I began to worry because, assuming the road kept its southerly course, we were continuing to veer away from it. Mrs. Kedward screamed when a large spider dropped on her shoulder. Kitten brushed it off with her hand and crushed it with the butt of her carbine.

"Bloody spiders, I can't stand them," Mrs. Kedward said. "I hope we don't have to camp in this thick stuff."

We came to a clearing dominated by a huge mora tree with a trunk as wide as a small house. Liana vines twisted their way up and into its broad expanse of leaves. We stopped and rested for a time.

Cadmael spotted two trails exiting the clearing, one eastward and the other westward. We took the eastward one and it wasn't long before we were back on the road.

"I don't suppose we'll make Villa Hermosa by nightfall?" I said.

"No, we may have to camp on the road," Cadmael said.

"We should push on a bit further."

We continued, my feet and back aching. After about another quarter mile, we approached a fork in the road. There was no sign to let us know the correct way, though the left path had seen more use.

"Left looks like the best bet," Mrs. Kedward said.

"Agreed," I said.

"Wait," Sophie said. "Look at this."

She was examining a tree trunk near the left fork and on it was carved a symbol - an oblong diamond shape with a crescent bisecting the top portion. The lines were filled with a kind of black pitch. The curves of it and strange asymmetry gave it a sinister feeling.

"Like a bull's head, kind of," Mrs. Kedward said. "Maybe it stands for Angel del Toro."

"Maybe," Sophie said. "But when we dined with Monsieur Laffite that night, his wife wore a pendant that looked like this. So did Monsieur Guibourg."

"Whatever it pertains to," I said, "perhaps Angel del Toro is part of it. I don't much care. I just want to find the Englishmen or learn who they were if dead. The sooner we do, the sooner we can get out of this blasted place."

We walked on, though Sophie only reluctantly. I had to take her hand which, after a short distance, began to tremble.

"What's wrong? Do you sense something?" I asked.

"I'm afraid. I wasn't, even after all we've seen, but I am now."

"We have to go on."

"I know."

We rounded a bend and I, too, felt a chill, whether due to Sophie's fear or the dark ambiance of the jungle, I didn't know. Then someone shouted from behind us, the voice familiar.

"Stop! Stop! You don't want to go that way!"

I turned and saw two men running toward us. One was clearly an Indian; the other was Dr. Paul Seymour.

Chapter 17: Castaways

27 July, 1819, Tabasco Region, Mexico

We stared at each other. Seymour at least as amazed as I was. His beard was long and he was as thin as ever but otherwise appeared fit. His lip quivered.

"You're right, Paul," I said. "I don't want to go that way, not now. Now I want to take you home."

"James, my good friend ..."

We shook hands.

"You of all people," he said. "But, really, hum, I should have known you'd be the one to come. How did you find me?"

"A tip from a pirate. It's a long story. I imagine yours is even longer."

"Dr. Seymour," Mrs. Kedward said. "Is my husband with you? Do you know? Is he still alive?"

"Your husband, ma'am?"

"This is Mrs. Brenda Kedward," I said. "She is the wife of Mr. Thomas Kedward, the *Squirrel*'s carpenter."

"Ah, oh, hum, no, I am sorry, very sorry, he perished. I ... didn't know him well but I can say he helped save my life."

"Señor, debemos irnos," the Indian man said in an urgent tone.

He was small and wiry and wore only a breechclout and a belt with a knife and a pouch. He carried a small spear.

"Abund is right, we must go," Seymour said. "This is a dangerous place. We can speak later."

We hurried back the way we came. Soon we were at the clearing with the mora tree and Abund and Seymour seemed less anxious. We slowed our pace and took the westward trail we had declined to take earlier.

"A stroke of luck you found us, it seems," I said to Seymour.

"Not entirely. Abund was out foraging and spotted your camp at the old Paraiso Ranch. He returned quickly and said he saw two white men, a black man, and three white women. The news was, hum, hard to believe but Abund is an expert scout. We set out immediately to intercept you."

After about a mile, the trail twisted its way over a rugged ridge then came to a deep gully spanned by a fallen tree. A rope had been strung across as a handhold. Not far beyond we had to make a steep climb over another ridge. The trail at that point would have been very difficult to follow unless one already knew it.

We then descended into a grassy meadow, bright and beautiful after the gloom of the deep jungle. A mule grazed and paid us little attention. The other side of the meadow was bordered by a sheer cliff and at its base was the entrance to a cave or grotto. The entrance had a facade built from large, finely hewn blocks with symbols chiseled into them. Above the opening was carved a face of a monstrous god very similar to the stone block possessed by Charles Morgan in Jamaica.

"This is our home at the moment," Seymour said. "It's safe for now."

A small black man came out of the cave entrance and Seymour introduced him as Pablo. We made introductions all around and proceeded into the cave. Daylight coming in through the entrance revealed a high, arching cavern room with eldritch pictographs painted in neat rows along the walls. At the back was a small tunnel.

"Did the Indians make all this?" I asked.

"Their ancestors, long ago, or so they say," Seymour said. "We were lucky Abund knew about it."

"Where does the tunnel lead?"

"To an underground pool that's spring fed. It's clean water."

"This is a fine place to hole up but I thought you'd be in Villa Hermosa. Two Englishmen were said to be there."

"What you heard was correct but, hum, Villa Hermosa was overrun. We escaped here, barely."

There was so much to discuss it was hard to know where to begin. We settled in to stay the night and Pablo cooked a savory bean stew over a small fire in the cave. It was spicy and made my nose run. Sophie stayed close to Mrs. Kedward to console her grief but she never lost her composure. We boiled coffee and Seymour began his tale.

* * *

The *Squirrel*, after a stop at Veracruz, entered El Radio and cruised the eastern shore of the Yucatan. Landing parties found strange creatures but no significant quantity of anitite. The captain, anxious to complete the mission, decided to head straight for Volcan Rojo.

Near the volcano they discovered a maze of shoals, reefs and small, rocky islands that weren't on the charts. Seymour and a geologist named Bernard Bloom scanned the islands for signs of anitite and eventually found a good candidate. A shore party found chunks of meteoric rock and Seymour's tests confirmed they were indeed anitite. They loaded two large crates and returned to the *Squirrel*.

With little wind, the ship was slow extracting itself from the maze. Seymour worked with Bloom in a small laboratory below deck.

"It was foolish," Seymour said. "We should have waited until we returned to England but we were both so eager."

The *Squirrel* became becalmed and the crew was lowering a launch in order to tow the ship through a channel between reefs. Seymour was on deck stretching his legs along with the captain who chatted with Mr. Kedward about minor repairs.

Something struck the boat and the jolt nearly knocked Seymour off his feet. Whether it was a rock or a creature, he didn't know. An explosion below deck sent plumes of smoke rising from the hatches.

"I'm sure it was Bloom," Seymour said. "He was brilliant but, hum, always in too much of a rush. I should not have left him alone in the laboratory."

Men ran up on deck. The captain struggled to marshal them into some kind of order. More men came up, faces red with fury and attacked the others, clawing and pummeling and biting like rabid animals. Soon the sane men were fighting for their lives. A group formed around the captain and Mr. Kedward. They fought valiantly but were overwhelmed.

"Get to the launch, get the doctor out of here!" was the captain's last order.

"A sailor all but hurled me over the side," Seymour said. "He jumped in, cut us loose and rowed. 'Aren't there others? Shouldn't we wait?' I asked. The sailor shook his head and kept rowing as fast as he could. A few of the insane men leapt into the water but, hum, didn't catch us."

* * *

"Do you know what caused the men to go mad?" I asked.

"I suspect when the ship was bumped, some purified sodium came into contact with water. The gas from the explosion had high concentrations of anitite. Small quantities in the bloodstream do no apparent harm and may even be helpful, but, at a certain point, it causes insanity and the effect is immediate. I, hum, have since learned the victims in time grow claws and fangs and their skin turns gray. The locals call them ghouls."

"Excuse me, doctor," Mrs. Kedward said. "Are you sure my husband died? Is there no chance he survived?"

"No, ma'am, I saw him go down, saw him get ... no ma'am, he could not have survived."

Mrs. Kedward took the news without tears. Sophie clutched her hand. Seymour continued his narrative.

* * *

Seymour and the sailor, whose name was Sydney Johnston, rowed well away from the shoals and reefs before Johnston set up the launch's small sail. They were then at the mercy of wind and current. The launch had no food but did have a keg of water.

"We were carried out to sea but didn't expect to see other vessels so deep in El Radio. Johnston was a competent sailor but, hum, had little notion of navigation. I assumed we were doomed."

Adrift for three days, badly sunburnt and out of drinking water, they were swept up in a storm and had to use what energy they had left to keep from being swamped. But the storm blew them toward land and they were able to row to a beach on the edge of the jungle.

They tried to press inland and found fruit to eat but the jungle was too thick and insect bites sapped what strength they had. So they returned to the boat and rowed along the shore hoping to find a settlement or at least fresh water. As it happened they were not far from the bay where Angel del Toro's men were building the fort. They were picked up and, after a few days rest, taken to Villa Hermosa.

"We met the governor briefly but he had little interest in helping us get home, nor means to do so."

Johnston caught a fever and died. Seymour escaped the fevers and, after regaining his strength, decided to try to make himself useful. He figured out the town was short of gunpowder. When Seymour told an officer he could make gunpowder, Angel del Toro became interested. Seymour was moved from a dirt-floor hovel to a pleasant house with a cook and Pablo, who knew English, became his personal servant.

"The governor gave me every comfort, hum, sometimes more than I wanted. He promised if a ship came to the harbor, he would ask to have me taken as a passenger. I don't think he kept his word."

The world around Villa Hermosa was dangerous. There were ghouls, which had thinned out since the eruption but were still a threat, and ulaks.

“Ulaks are like ape-men. They are, hum, not very bright, but they wield clubs and throw stones. They rove in small bands and like to raid crops or groups of unwary people. They usually run if confronted by armed men. I’m not sure where they come from, or whether they are a separate species or corrupted human beings.”

Villa Hermosa seemed safe enough with its walls and surrounding farmland, but it wasn’t.

A huge swarm of ghouls emerged from the eastern jungle, crossing the fields to attack the town. People panicked but Angel del Toro mustered his troops and beat back successive waves. The corpses of the ghouls piled on top of each other, allowing others to ascend the wall. When the fighting was at its peak and it appeared the ghouls would be repulsed, an army of ulaks attacked from the south. They were equipped with crude ladders and soon overwhelmed the thin line of defenders on that side.

“I knew little of what was going on at the time. Abund and two soldiers appeared at my door and said they had orders to take me to the fort on the coast. Angel del Toro would try to join us later.”

The small party escaped through a secret tunnel dug under the north wall.

“We haven’t seen anybody from the town since.”

* * *

“The attack was planned,” Sydow said.

“By whom?” I asked.

“Abund says it is a demon they call Akabo,” Seymour said.

“I’ve heard the name,” I said. “From Charles Morgan whom you’ve met. But it is myth.”

“Undoubtedly just a name from legend but, hum, it fits whatever is out there, something with intelligence and an agenda.”

* * *

Abund led the small party, including a heavily laden mule, along back trails. When they picked up the road again, they were many miles from Villa Hermosa. One soldier was bitten by a snake and died, the other was taken by the sword tree which Abund didn't know at the time was there.

The party did make it to the fort on the bay only to find the garrison gone and the gate toppled. Abund approached cautiously and saw the titanaconda coiled within.

"I didn't get a look at it but Abund thought its girth to be around five feet. I suspect it was, hum, eighty feet long, perhaps more."

Abund knew of the hidden meadow so they retreated back into the jungle.

"This place is sometimes occupied by the Alux," Seymour said. "But, hum, fortunately they were not here when we came."

"What would they have done had they returned?" I asked.

"They did return. We, hum, did not see them but their songs were angry. Abund suggested an offering so on a fallen tree we set out a few knives, a hatchet and a saw. The next morning the items were gone and the Alux have left us alone."

Chapter 18: The Painted Bird

28 July, 1819, Tabasco Region, Mexico

I had nearly done what I set out to do. Now it was a matter of getting home safely. We decided to wait a day at the meadow. It would take two days to get to the bay and by that time Rackham should have returned with the *Bar Jack*.

My party rested while Seymour, Pablo and Abund made their preparations. The weather was very warm and the humidity clung like a film but the cave was a cool and welcome respite. Cadmael and Abund talked frequently in the Indian language.

Seymour and I talked of the things we'd learned. He knew the story of the white witch and was intrigued by the idea that it was Giselle LaFoy, Napoleon's mistress. I filled him in about what I knew of Friar Cossio and his book.

"Such a book could be useful," Seymour said. "I hope young Juliet finds a copy."

I took a stroll around the meadow while Seymour finished packing his things. I found Mrs. Kedward petting the mule's flank while it grazed.

"I don't mean to disturb you," I said. "But I haven't had a chance to convey my condolences regarding your husband. It is clear he was a brave and honorable man. I'm very sorry."

"Thank you," she said.

She fell silent and I took that to mean she wanted to be left alone. I started to walk on.

"It's a relief in a way," she said.

I stopped. "At least you now know."

"More than that, and I maybe feel a little ashamed. Working on the *Bar Jack* and going through all that we have, I'm seeing things differently. What would happen if we did find Thomas? Could I go back to our cottage in Portishead and be content there? There's so much more I can do. I wanted desperately for him to be alive but I dreaded being his housewife again. Now that I know he's gone, I feel free, and guilty about feeling that way."

I wasn't sure what to say.

"I don't think Thomas would have understood but I think you do, captain."

"Perhaps, an inkling," I said. "I've certainly learned there is little, if anything, men can do that women cannot."

"A couple of girls want to go back to Galveston, take up with a rich buccaneer, maybe settle in Texas. Most like being sailors and want to keep doing it. I know now why Thomas loved the sea and took such pride in his work. Is there a chance we can remain sailors when our job with you is done?"

"We have a ways to go yet," I said. "But I should think so. I promised the *Bar Jack* to Ann. I'm not sure what the arrangement will be but I imagine she'd be happy to keep the crew intact. That would be up to her, however. In any case, the way things are, captains may be more willing to take on women. I'll do what I can to help."

She took my arm and we returned to the cave together.

* * *

Rested and with a mule to help, we set a brisk pace the next morning. I was glad we had so far avoided any sickness short of mild bowel trouble. Cadmael often urged us to rub ourselves with the leaves of insect-repelling plants. He seemed to think there was a connection between tropical diseases and insect bites. Seymour thought the idea might have merit.

"Too bad we can't get another look at that sword tree," Sydow said.

"It's positioned so if you can see it, it can grab you," I said.

"Ja, ja, but it is fascinating."

"I don't care to ever see it again."

“Herr doctor, I think it may be a kind of fungus. What do you think?”

“Well, hum, no. I would say it is a primitive kind of animal, like a sea anemone or starfish.”

“I have a sample cut from one of its roots,” Sydow said. “Putting it under a microscope might tell us more.”

“I should be, hum, very careful with that sample.”

“Sealed up tight in a tin.”

“Excellent.”

* * *

Well into the afternoon, we emerged from the pass between ridges out onto the grassy plateau, the westerly breeze refreshing after the closeness of the jungle. We headed for the ruins of the Paraiso ranch where we planned to camp.

Sophie walked a few paces ahead of me. She had spoken little for most of the day, keeping her eyes on the ground, the jungle seeming to have a brooding effect on her. I watched her look over to her right, scanning the grass as if something was there. I saw nothing at first, then a dog appeared on the slope of a nearby hillock.

“Oh, look,” Sophie said and walked through the grass toward the animal.

“I don’t think you should approach it,” I said.

“It’s friendly,” she said. “It won’t hurt me.”

The dog waited for her and wagged its tail. It was a peculiar dog with brown fur so fine it appeared hairless. It wasn’t large, perhaps 30 pounds. Sophie knelt in front of it. It licked her hands and she petted it.

From over the hillock, like out of a nightmare, a huge creature raced toward Sophie and the dog. It was a terror bird, feathers brown with streaks of red and yellow, its crest blue and red. The dog bolted. Sophie ran but the monster snatched her up in its massive beak. Its vestigial wings flared and it shook her violently.

Kitten fired her carbine, striking the beast in the flank. The terror bird let go of Sophie and swung its head around. Cadmael and Kedward fired their muskets. Snapping out of my stunned state, I raised my rifle and fired. The shot was high but struck its thick neck. The terror bird turned and ran. Kitten got two more shots off with the dueling pistols before the creature disappeared over the hillock. Gunsmoke hung in the air.

I dropped the rifle and ran to Sophie. She was unconscious, her limbs akimbo, a horrendous, bloody gash in her chest. I sank to my knees. My vision blurred.

* * *

I recovered my senses enough to see Seymour and Kedward hunched over Sophie trying to staunch the bleeding. Sophie's face was deathly pale.

"Will she ..." I couldn't finish the question.

"The damage is too great. I'm sorry," Seymour said.

"Damn it, no ... Sweet Sophie, what have I done?"

Kedward put her hand on my shoulder.

"It might not be too late," Cadmael said. "We may be able to do something. The mandíbulas curativas, it's not too far."

The big ground plant, Cadmael had said it could heal the stricken. My mind grasped at the hope.

"Yes, yes, we should at least try," I said. "I'll carry her myself."

I stooped to pick up Sophie but Sydow pulled me back.

"You're in no shape to take her, kapitan. I'll do it on the mule. It will be faster."

Sydow barked an order, a full-throated Prussian officer's order, and the rest of the party hurriedly unpacked the mule. Sydow hopped on deftly and grabbed the rope that served as a rein. Seymour and I lifted Sophie to him and he held her upright on his lap, her head leaning on his shoulder.

"Can you find it?" Kedward asked.

"It's near the orchid patch. I can find it," Sydow said. "Cadmael, what do I do when I get there?"

"Lay her where the big leaves meet then step away quickly. They will fold over her."

Sydow nodded.

"Make haste, man," I said.
"Javol."
He kicked the mule and galloped away.

* * *

I stared after Sydow, blunderbuss slung on his back, saber flapping at his side, arm around Sophie. I unslung my rucksack, retrieved my waterskin and slung it over my shoulders.
"I have to follow him," I muttered.
"I'll go with you, captain," Cadmael said.
I nodded.
"I want to go," Kitten said.
"No," I snapped. I squeezed her shoulders and bent down close to whisper. "You need to stay and protect the others, especially Dr. Seymour. We need to keep him alive. If anything happens to me, the most important thing is to get him on the *Bar Jack*."
"Yes, sir."
I told the others to camp at the ranch and we'd bring the mule back in the morning. With that Cadmael and I began our run. I started with a near sprint but he urged me back into a jog.
"Steady pace, captain. That's the fastest way."
Reaching the edge of the plateau and descending into the jungle, I tripped and fell. Cadmael helped me up. I panted with my hands on my knees.
"We should walk now, then run again when the ground is level. We want to get there before dark," Cadmael said.
I realized my only weapon was my broadsword and Cadmael only had his kukri.
"I don't suppose these will do much good if a terror bird attacks," I said.
"Terror birds like land where the trees meet the grass. You don't see them in the deep jungle very often. Snakes are our main worry, and jaguars, maybe, but they mostly hunt at night, and ghouls sometimes can surprise you ..."
"Yes, I take your point."

* * *

My world became a blurry tunnel of trees and vines. My lungs burned. The sunlight faded and we had to slow our pace to a brisk walk. By the time I caught my breath, the jungle was nearly pitch dark.

"We're close but I don't know how much further we should go without light," Cadmael said. "We may want to stop and make a fire."

"Let's go as far as we can, snakes be damned."

Not much further on, however, we perceived a dim flickering ahead. We rounded a bend and saw a fire in the road illuminating a beautiful array of orchids. Sydow sat against a tree, head bowed and blunderbuss on his lap. The mule was tethered to a tree limb, head bent as if dozing. Cadmael and I stepped behind a tree.

"Leo," I hissed.

Sydow grunted and raised the blunderbuss.

"Don't shoot. It's us."

"Ah, oh, ja, ahum, sorry, I must have nodded off."

"Sophie? What about Sophie?"

Sydow shrugged and inclined his head toward the trees.

"Did the plant take her?" Cadmael asked.

"The leaves folded over her, like you said. I'm not sure if she's being healed or digested ... Ah, entschuldigung, kapitan, I should not have said that."

"No need to apologize, Leo. And thank you, whatever happens."

I took a burning ember from the fire and headed into the trees. Cadmael followed. The odor of bergamot hung heavy in the air. The dim light offered little detail and Cadmael cautioned me not to get too close. The enveloping leaves had formed into a kind of cocoon which appeared filled with fluid. It rippled from time to time.

"A good sign, captain. It has taken her."

"Will she live?"

"I don't know. All I know are the stories."

"How long before it opens?"

"They say it can be hours or days."

* * *

Exhausted, the three of us slept near the road without taking watch. Undoubtedly foolish but the bergamot odor had a soothing effect and the place felt safe.

Morning brought no change in the cocoon which continued to ripple periodically. I was famished but we'd brought no food. Cadmael dug a few edible roots and we ate them without relish. Sydow headed back to the ranch, leaving the blunderbuss with me. The mule moved stiffly and Sydow led it instead of riding.

The hours passed with no change in the cocoon. Near nightfall the others arrived.

"Sorry we're late, kapitan. The mule needed to water and graze."

Sydow carried a large, heavy sack that held a strangely shaped object. Seeing huge feathers sticking up from the mule's baggage, my intelligence wasn't taxed to figure out what was in the bag.

"You didn't."

"Ja, kapitan. We found it dead about a hundred yards beyond the rise. It's for science."

"I see," I said, wondering what sum the British Museum would pay for the specimen.

We camped again on the road and for supper ate meat from the monstrous bird. Other than two snakes we shooed away, we were not molested. I sent the rest of the party on to the bay so they could signal Rackham. Cadmael stayed with me to keep vigil on the cocoon.

"If you had your choice, Cadmael, would you and your people choose to stay in El Radio?"

We sat against trees in the little glade that contained the mandíbulas curativas.

"Yes, I think so. Here we are free."

* * *

Late in the afternoon, Abund arrived and handed me a note from Sydow. I read it aloud: "Made camp at fort. No sign of snake. No sign of *Bar Jack*."

What had delayed Rackham? I couldn't imagine her abandoning us deliberately. I worried more she'd run into trouble.

"It's only been a day," I said. "We can't expect these things to work out perfectly. I'm sure Ann will ..."

I was interrupted by a whooshing sound and turned to see fluid draining from the plant, the bergamot odor nearly overwhelming. I heard coughing coming from the cocoon and rushed toward it, my instinct urged me to pry it open. Cadmael held me back.

"Patience, captain."

I stood in frenzied anticipation, Cadmael and Abund beside me. Sophie's coughing abated.

"We have to get her out of there!"

"Please, captain, let the plant do its work."

Several interminable minutes passed before the enveloping leaves unfolded and there she was, lying naked between them. Her clothes must have dissolved away. She sat up, blinking, then she stood.

There was no sign of any wound but her skin, instead of a pale olive, had turned a lustrous brown. I had adored the beauty of her skin but now, if possible, it was even more beautiful. Sophie looked herself over and seemed bewildered by the change. Abund knelt and bowed and muttered words in his own language.

"Ixchel," Cadmael whispered.

Sophie sighed.

"Do you have any clothes I can wear?" She asked.

* * *

Kedward had indeed thought to leave a blouse, a pair of sailor's trousers and a pair of sandals. I quickly retrieved them from my pack.

"Get back to the road," I ordered Cadmael and Abund. "Go now, please."

“Of course,” Cadmael said. Abund was so awe-struck, Cadmael had to pull him along.

I gave Sophie the clothes and she dressed hurriedly.

“I’m very glad you’re alive,” I said. “I can hardly believe it but I’m very glad.”

She embraced me and I held her for a long while.

Too late to reach the bay before dark, we built a fire on the road and ate our supper, more meat from the terror bird.

“They say no one comes out of the mandíbulas curativas unchanged,” Cadmael said. “Sometimes the change is big, sometimes it is small, but life is life.”

Sophie tried to smile. “I have skin like yours now, Cadmael.”

“No, not so dark,” he said.

“Do you know what happened to that dog?” Sophie asked.

“I believe it approached the others back at the ranch but Kitten sent a bullet over its head and ran it off,” I said.

“She should have killed it,” Sophie said.

“Why?”

“She just should have.”

* * *

We made the bay before noon the next day. The party had managed to prop up the fallen gate, leaving a small gap a person could slip through. It was buttressed with beams and stones scavenged from the rubble inside the fort.

“Do you think it will hold back the titanaconda if it comes?” I asked.

“Hum, probably not,” Seymour said.

“It should buy us time,” Sydow said, “so we can escape over the wall. We made a ladder.”

Everyone was pleased Sophie survived but her change in appearance was a source of awkwardness. She put on a brave face and did her best to make light of it.

“My punishment for being a fool,” she said.

The *Bar Jack* had not returned.

“We saw a ship in the bay this morning,” Kedward said. “A schooner flying a French flag. It didn’t stay long.”

"We kept hidden, kapitan, but if the *Bar Jack* is lost, perhaps we should have hailed it."

"I'm glad you stayed out of sight," I said. "Ann will come. We just have to be patient."

I spoke the words with more conviction than I felt and wondered why a French schooner was prowling the coast. Perhaps its presence was why Rackham had not returned.

* * *

There wasn't much to do but sit tight behind the walls. One of us always kept watch over the bay and we had a flag ready to use as a signal.

That night I took the last watch along the wall and Sophie rose to join me. The sky was clear and stars twinkled beautifully above the humid tropical air. The mild surf whispered on the beach.

"I dread the thought something has happened to the *Bar Jack*," I said.

"They're alive," Sophie said.

"How do you know?"

"Jenny has the ability. I haven't told her. It seemed she had enough to worry about. But just now I caught a glimpse of her perception. The *Bar Jack* is under sail. Where she is, or what direction she's going, I don't know."

I held Sophie close.

"That is good news."

We kissed.

"Just in case you have any doubt," I said. "I still want to marry you."

"Don't be foolish, James, it can't happen now. People could get used to you marrying a Spanish servant girl, but you can't marry a negress. People just wouldn't have it."

"I don't care. To hell with them. We can live elsewhere. I don't know, perhaps take up with Nashoba in Jamaica or go to Angola in Florida. There are people who would accept us."

Sophie didn't reply and we just held each other.

"That dog," I said. "Something happened with it."

"I didn't realize what was happening until it was too late. Its mind is possessed by a daemon. It was subtle, a projection of friendliness. I was caught off guard. When I was petting the dog, I thought why am I doing this. I don't even like dogs. Then I sensed the daemon and knew, but the monster was upon me."

"The daemon of Kilve Beach? Akabo?"

"A different one. It felt feminine."

"What a damned bloody place this is."

* * *

Weary of standing we decided to sit for a bit, backs against the wall. We dozed off.

I was roused by the first glimmer of the morning sun. I stretched my legs and looked out over the bay. There lay the *Bar Jack*, beautiful on the blue water in the golden light of dawn. She must have slipped in during the night and anchored. I was struck by the thought that she was the finest ship in the world and that I would know no greater honor than having had the chance to be her captain.

I could see Maggie and Jenny rowing toward the beach. I nudged Sophie.

"Wake up, darling. We're getting out of here."

Chapter 19: A Ship of Fools

2 August, 1819, Tabasco Region, Mexico

Rackham didn't want to tarry and I agreed. Speaking through Cadmael, Abund said he wanted to stay. The land was his home and he would take care of the mule.

"He'll be all alone," I said.

"I'll return with some of my people," Cadmael said. "We'll start settling here, and at the ranch."

"Wouldn't you face the same threat as Villa Hermosa?"

"They didn't know the ways of the jungle like we do. We can fare better, I think."

I didn't argue. It was hardly my place in any case.

* * *

Rackham eased us out of the bay and only when we were well out to sea did she pause to chat. She explained they had encountered a French schooner with eight guns. It signaled for the *Bar Jack* to heave-to but Rackham ignored the order and fled.

"It was quite a chase. The schooner's topsail rigged and fast downwind. I put some distance between us by nightfall but she spotted us again in the morning. Late in the day we lost her in a squall and by morning she was nowhere to be seen. I figured she might prowl the shore to see if we'd holed up somewhere so I stayed out to sea a couple more days. Sorry I was late, captain."

"Your instincts, as usual, were correct," I said. "We saw the schooner yesterday."

"The crew's dog tired."

"We should be able to rest at Isla Lanza, assuming all's well there."

* * *

Kedward, Kitten, Cadmael, Sydow and I took over the handling of the ship in order to give the rest of the crew a respite. Seymour and Pablo helped as best they could and Sophie got to work in the kitchen. Some of the crew seemed genuinely spooked by her change of appearance. The more superstitious women had long concluded she was a witch but maintained she was "our witch." Her now brown skin was more difficult medicine to swallow. Sophie was determined to shrug it off and resume her duties.

The crew's respite didn't last long. A storm approached and soon it was all hands. The women handled the ship efficiently and Rackham guided it with her usual aplomb.

The worst of the weather behind us, I took a break in my cabin and talked with Seymour over coffee.

"This is a fine ship you have, James," he said. "I'm very impressed, and Miss Rackham seems, hum, frightfully competent."

"Indeed," I said.

"I had my doubts, you know. She is a pirate. I don't think I would have trusted her with the ship."

"Ann, I've come to learn, is very loyal by nature, if not to me, then to her word. Also she has much to gain by this mission, which, I hope, is nearly over. I promised Cadmael I'd take him home. With luck we'll be there tomorrow, then we're homeward bound."

"Ah, hum, yes, regarding that. It occurs to me that this ship, with its fine crew, is the ideal vessel to navigate the shoals and reefs near Volcan Rojo. I'd like to fetch some anitite to take home."

"You're not serious, Paul."

"I am. We need anitite to study. We need, hum, to understand what's happening. Things are going to get worse."

"Yes, I know, but ..."

"England is in trouble. Our survival may be at stake. France, I believe, is far ahead of us. This may be our best chance."

"My crew, I've asked so much of them already."

"I think the danger is, hum, manageable. The *Squirrel* wasn't lost because of a sea monster, it was lost because of carelessness, my own included. You've got an iron lock box, true?"

"Yes."

"We put the anitite in it with material that will deaden its effects and leave it there until we get back to England and can handle it in a specially prepared laboratory."

"Let me think about it," I said.

"You'll be compensated, I can assure you."

"That's really the least of my concerns, Paul."

* * *

I poured another cup of coffee, went out on deck and joined Sydow at the helm. The wind remained blustery and a misty drizzle made everything damp.

"The storm blew us off course but Ann thinks we'll make Laguna de Terminos tomorrow afternoon," Sydow said.

I nodded, watching Rackham and Sophie who stood at the bow talking. Sophie had a pea coat on over her kitchen dress. Rackham leaned toward her ear and said something. Sophie's head turned abruptly, as if surprised, then she grinned, said something, and rubbed Rackham's back.

"Well, Leo," I said. "I thought we were nearly on the home stretch."

"Ja, what now, kapitan?"

"Paul wants to go in close to Volcan Rojo, find some anitite. He thinks it essential if we're going to counter Napoleon."

Sydow guffawed. "He's more of a fool than you are."

"He fits right in."

"We're a ship of fools, kapitan. What's one more foolish errand? I say what the hell."

"I fear our luck may run out."

"Our luck may run out anyway."
"True, but we'd be tempting fate, really tempting it."
"Ah, kapitan, but there's poetry to it – the *Bar Jack* accomplishes what the Royal Navy could not."
"By God, Leo, you're a bloody romantic."
"Ja, would I be here if I wasn't?"

* * *

Lying on my cabin bed felt wonderful after the nights on hard ground and having Sophie beside me was a pleasure beyond what any man deserves. I told her what Seymour wanted to do.
"I think he's right," she said.
"You're not afraid?"
"I'm terrified."

* * *

I called a morning meeting in my cabin. Snugged into the space were Rackham, Sydow, Kedward, Alice and Maggie. I thought about including Seymour to let him make his case, but I decided the discussion should be between only the leaders of *Bar Jack*. I plainly spelled out the proposed errand.
"We've accomplished what we set out to do so I don't see how I can honorably require you to do more," I said.
No one responded immediately. I tried to read the others' faces but could not. Sydow was about to speak but I motioned him not to. I didn't want to convince them with rhetoric and part of me wanted them to demur. Rackham stared at the chart spread on the table but said nothing. Kedward was looking at Alice and Maggie.
Finally, Maggie shrugged. "Sure, captain, I'll go."
"Why not?" Alice said. "We've weathered storms, beat back pirates, eluded a French warship and snatched Dr. Seymour from the jungle. I think we can manage to pick up a few rocks on the way home."
"I see it as our duty," Kedward said.

I looked to Rackham, without whom the venture would be idiocy, but she kept looking at the chart as if calculating a course.

"Ann?"

She looked up. All eyes were upon her.

"Yeah, I'm game."

Chapter 20: The Music of Isla Lanza

3 August, 1819, Isla Lanza

The old Spanish fort was smaller than I anticipated yet still a formidable structure built of stone. Four large guns protruded from its battlements and an embroidered flag of many colors flew above it, the pattern a kind of sunburst. The island itself appeared to be mostly grassy hillocks with occasional clumps of palm trees. Huts lined the broad beaches.

We glided in, flying the Union Jack. Cadmael was at the bow holding high the spear with the obsidian head that we'd salvaged from the pirate ship. Sophie stood beside him wearing a simple green gown; her hair was undone and flowed like a mane.

People soon appeared on the battlements, along the crumbled pier and along the beach. About a hundred yards out we struck the sails and lowered anchor. It dragged the sandy bottom and we eased to a stop. We lowered the dinghy and Jenny and Izzy rowed Sophie, Cadmael and myself to the pier. Cadmael climbed out first and helped us up to the promontory. A dozen or so ragtag soldiers marched toward us, two armed with muskets and the others spears. The leader appeared of Asian descent. I was unarmed. Cadmael carried his kukri and held the obsidian spear. I wanted to give the impression that he was in no way a hostage or prisoner.

The leader stopped and looked us over. He wore a short sword in a wooden scabbard and a pistol on his belt. Cadmael spoke words in Spanish. The leader smiled and clasped Cadmael's arm. They chatted briefly then Cadmael introduced us and I learned the leader's name was Ruy

Saylas, the Filipino sailor Cadmael had said taught him to fight with a machete.

"Ruy says you have a beautiful ship," Cadmael said.

"Gracias," I said and bowed.

"Come, we'll take you to Manuel, our headman. The chief of the Maya is not here but his wife sits in his place."

We walked toward the fort, the crowd making way, all eyes upon us. I was nervous; all the people were blacks or Indians.

* * *

We passed through the fort's courtyard, climbed a broad staircase and entered a large room that must have been the Spanish commander's office. Except for Saylas, the soldiers stayed outside. Paintings that must have once lined the walls were gone but a large mahogany desk remained and a long table surrounded by several chairs. A black man and an Indian woman rose to greet us.

They spoke Spanish with Cadmael. I wished I knew the language better. The Indian woman had long raven hair and a weathered face that was nevertheless appealing. She wore a long tunic with thousands of beads woven into colorful geometric patterns. The man was tall, had very dark skin and gray hair. He wore a frock coat over a white blouse.

"Parlez-vous Français?" The man asked me.

"Oui, monsieur," I replied.

"Excellent, pleased to meet you, Captain LeRoque. I'm very grateful you have returned Cadmael to us. I am Manuel and this is Sacnicte, wife of Balam, together they lead the Mayan people of this region."

"I'm honored," I said and bowed.

"I would reward you but we do not have much to give other than our hospitality," Manuel said.

"I told Cadmael he owed me nothing. Nevertheless he saved my life, and Sophia's, and was instrumental in keeping us alive during our trek through the jungle. If anything, I am in his debt."

"Cadmael is, no doubt, a good man to have to hand," Manuel said. "You are welcome to stay as long as you like. We can offer food at least and comfortable places to rest for your crew."

"Thank you. We may stay a day or two but we have a long journey ahead and the hurricane season approaches."

We exchanged further pleasantries and settled into conversation. Sacnicte was very interested in Sophie and the two, along with Cadmael, talked amongst themselves. I found myself liking Manuel and we talked at length. Saylas listened politely but I don't think he understood French well. Manuel was intrigued when I told him Villa Hermosa had been overrun and Angel del Toro was likely dead.

"It grieves me the town succumbed to Akabo but I cannot feel sorry for Angel del Toro. He was a brutal man and he treated slaves and Indians poorly. My former master was often appalled by his actions."

"What do you know of Akabo?" I asked.

"Only what Balam, Sacnicte and Yaxkin have told me."

"Yaxkin?"

"He is a very old Mayan priest who lives among us. His health is bad and likely he'll die soon. He'll be greatly missed. He has, how shall I say, powers that are helpful."

"I know something of those powers. Tell me about Akabo."

"They say he is an ancient spirit who came to this world a very long time ago, before the coming of men but was trapped in the depths of the earth. Many other spirits, called the old ones by the Maya, were with him. When Volcan Rojo erupted, he was released along with his kin."

"He is the leader of these spirits?"

"Yaxkin says Akabo is among the most powerful and commands many other spirits, but not all. Some are malicious, but not all. Some are as powerful as Akabo, or more so, but he is the most intelligent, the most able to influence events."

"Is he mankind's enemy?"

"Yaxkin says he is indifferent, like one might be indifferent to animals – employ them if they are useful, ignore them if they are not, slaughter them if they get in the way."

"What does Akabo want?"

"His ends are inscrutable, Yaxkin says, as are the minds of all the old ones."

I sighed. Despite all I'd seen, this kind of talk seemed outlandish.

"Do you believe all this?" I asked. "Perhaps there are other explanations."

"Perhaps, but what other story do we have? In my experience white people want explanations laid out in sequences of cause and effect. But what has happened may be beyond explanation. The Mayan stories may have to suffice."

* * *

I returned to the *Bar Jack* while Sacnicte took Sophie to visit the old shaman, Yaxkin. I was uneasy about it but didn't object. Cadmael went to his home where his wife waited. I found Rackham, Sydow and Seymour smoking and drinking coffee on deck.

"We were beginning to worry, kapitan."

"All is well," I said. "The leader here, Manuel, is an interesting man. We are welcome to stay. They're planning a celebration tomorrow evening."

"Can we trust them?" Rackham asked.

"More than we could trust Laffite, I'd say."

"To Laffite the *Bar Jack* is just a pretty trinket; to these people it's much more valuable."

"You have a suspicious mind, Ann," I said.

"Aye, that I do."

"Cadmael is my friend, our friend. We saved his life and he saved ours," I said. "If it turns out to be a ruse so his people can commandeer our ship, so be it."

* * *

I hung my coat, removed my collar and unbuttoned my blouse. Sophie sat on the bed, staring into nothingness, a common behavior since she emerged from the mandíbulas curativas.

"Are you going to sleep in your gown?" I asked.

"I think my place is here," she said softly.

"Pardon?"

"I mean my place is with these people."

I struggled to comprehend.

"James, look at me. I can't go back to England or Scotland."

"Of course you can."

"There could be no life that I'd want there. Yes, I could be your servant and we could remain secret lovers but it couldn't last. I want more than that. One of the girls called me a tuft-hunter and she was right."

Flummoxed, I sat on the bed beside her, shaking my head.

"I was just a steppingstone," I said.

"No, you were the prize. More than that, you're a man I can't help but love, much more than a girl's dream."

"You can still have me. We don't need to live in England, like I said."

"It wouldn't be right. You belong with your people. Maybe you don't see it but I do. Your family needs you. Your country needs you."

"I'm just a scholar and not a particularly brilliant one at that. I think my family can do without me and so can Cambridge."

I spoke the words feeling like the world was slipping away and my luck had finally run out.

"Don't be so dense, James," Sophie said.

"Now you sound like Louisa."

"You'll soon be taking this ship to the gates of Hell and you have a crew that will happily follow you. They do it because they want to. They have confidence in themselves and you gave it to them. That's power, real power."

"You're flattering me."

"Yet it's true."

She slid her fingers through mine and we kissed.

"It's more than just the change of your skin's color," I said. "Something else happened."

"The jungle claimed me, James. I don't know how else to put it. I can't leave. I just can't."

* * *

Seymour, Sydow and I toured the island with Manuel, walking through fields of maize, barley, beans and peanuts, and orchards of lemons, limes and other fruit. We reached the south shore and, standing on a rise, we overlooked the beach where there was a large yacht undergoing repairs and an array of canoes, some quite large and all equipped with outriggers.

"Mayan canoes don't have outriggers," Manuel said. "Another thing Señor Saylas taught us."

"Cadmael says he was shipwrecked and came ashore on a raft," Sydow said. Sydow's French was good but his accent peculiar.

"That is true," Manuel said. "We were fortunate he did."

"I see a few others who appear to be of Oriental descent. More castaways?"

"Yes."

"But I see no whites," Sydow went on. "Were there no white castaways?"

"Leo ..." I grew alarmed; the question was impertinent.

"There were," Manuel said. "Come, let me show you something."

We walked inland a ways then east along a trail that passed through a small village. From there we went up a slope to a grassy area where we found a large mound. The mound was littered with bouquets of flowers and on top stood a large wooden cross with a carved Jesus figure nailed to it. It had a wound on its side and painted blood dripping from it. The carving was primitive but the effect was poignant. Manuel spoke:

"Not long after we arrived on the island, a launch from a wrecked Spanish warship came ashore. The people were in bad shape, yet they still expected us to serve them despite the fact their ship had carried them away and abandoned us to the terrors of the jungle. Regardless, I was inclined to help them. They would come around to their predicament soon enough.

"But that was a dark time; anger seethed in our people. One of our men, in a rage, killed one of the white men with a spear. Soon others followed. There was no holding them back. We slaughtered them all, even the women who were with them."

I struggled to think of something to say.

"So now you know our great sin," Manuel continued. "I make no excuse, but it was a dark time."

"You buried them here," I said.

"Yes, Yaxkin was very angry. He said we must atone or the helpful spirits would abandon us. So we carried the dead to the highest point on the island and created this mound. We consider it a sacred place."

* * *

We took a trail north then veered around toward the fort. We neared a low, rocky escarpment, a portion of which was an old quarry. Two men with pick hammers were scrounging the rocks.

"We find crystals here and sometimes other semi-precious stones," Manuel said.

Seymour broke off from the group and went to the quarry. We stopped to watch him. He returned with a small bit of rock.

"Quartz," he said. "It, hum, could be useful."

"Take what you want, doctor," Manuel said.

* * *

I stood on the battlement with Manuel overlooking the island. People below prepared for the feast. Sydow and Seymour had fetched a bag and pick hammers from the *Bar Jack* and returned to the quarry to hunt for crystals. A few of the women from the crew walked the beach. Rackham, so far as I knew, remained on board.

"Will you send your people to settle the place we came from as Cadmael suggested?" I asked.

"Once the yacht is seaworthy," Manuel said.

"You know a titanaconda broke down the gate and killed the men at Angel del Toro's fort."

"We will have to deal with it as best we can."

"I think I can help. A pirate named Jean Laffite gave me a field gun that I, in turn, was to give to Angel del Toro as a diplomatic gift. Now I may as well give it to you."

"I gladly accept but we haven't much powder. The big guns you see here, we could only fire them once or twice."

"We have several powder kegs that came with the gun as well as ball, grapeshot and canister rounds. When we rescued Cadmael from the pirates, we took in a store of arms. You can have anything we don't need. Also, Seymour's servant, Pablo, now knows how to make gunpowder. I think he would be happier staying with you than returning with us to Britain."

"Such generosity, captain ..."

"It isn't much in the grand scheme and I really have no use for the field gun. It's actually a liability."

"If my people should survive and prosper, we'll long remember the coming of the *Bar Jack* and Captain LeRoque."

"I'm honored, but our coming is likely a prelude to others. I'm reasonably sure Laffite's ships will come calling soon. I suspect he wants a base within El Radio. He isn't brutal but he's manipulative and may resort to force to get what he wants."

"A fair warning, captain. That will be a challenge to face when the time comes."

"Another warning and I don't know what it means if it means anything at all. In the jungle on the road to Villa Hermosa we found a strange symbol carved into a tree – a narrow diamond shape crossed by a sickle."

"We have seen it, too. We believe it is the mark of Akabo or one of his minions."

"Laffite's wife and his occultist friend, Hector Guibourg, wear pendants of similar design. Laffite himself didn't wear one and seemed wary of Guibourg. Yet Laffite is beholden to him in some fashion."

Manuel smiled. "Laffite wants to use Guibourg, but who is the cat and who is the mouse?"

"Indeed."

* * *

The feast was set in an open area near the fort surrounded by palm trees. We ate clams, crab legs, lobster tails, fish of all sorts, fruits, and barley meal concoctions. There were no tables so we sat on the grass in groups around open fires, Sydow, Seymour and I with Manuel, Cadmael, Saylas and other men. Sophie, Rackham and Kedward sat with Sacnicte and other island women. Most of the women of the crew sat apart, still uneasy, I assumed, about mingling with their dark-skinned hosts. We drank a punch of fermented fruit. I didn't find it immediately pleasing but it went down well enough after a while.

"One thing I would ask you, Manuel," I said. "Does the word, 'Medusa,' mean anything to you?"

"The monster of Greek legend?"

"Yes, Guibourg was trying to tell our fortune when he screamed the word and passed out. We could get nothing else out of him."

"I'm sorry, captain, the word has no special meaning here."

"I think it may have been an act so I'm not overly concerned. Another question, and please tell me if I'm being too forward: You are an educated man. I wonder how you come by it."

"My father was the butler of a plantation owner and I was raised to replace him. I learned to read and write so I could keep accounts. The owner's son, Alfonzo, and I were friends. He liked to read and he would share books with me. We spent much time discussing the things we read and that continued when he became the master and I the butler."

"Alfonzo abandoned you in the end, I gather."

"He didn't have the opportunity. His wife went insane and killed him while he slept. Alfonzo's brother led us to the port of Campeche but the town was burning. There were two warships taking on survivors but only whites. The other slaves and I were left behind."

"Abominable behavior," I said. "I'm sorry."

"Don't be. That is when I became a free man, though it was galling at first having led a life of gilded servitude."

* * *

The meal over, Sydow, Cadmael and Saylas were up and showing off their respective weapons: Sydow's saber, Cadmael's kukri and Saylas' peculiar kris sword with wavy edges. The women of the *Bar Jack* began to mingle, though few spoke any Spanish.

Two men began playing guitars, the song a Spanish ballad that Sophie liked to hum. Three men with drums seated themselves nearby. Sacnicte stood and another woman handed her a short wooden tube and a narrow solid stick. When the ballad ended, she started tapping out a rhythm: tock_tock ... tock_a_tock_a_tock ... tock_tock ... tock_a_tock_a_tock ...

"The clave, a sacred rhythm from Africa," Manuel whispered to me.

People started to clap, a half time to Sacnicte's beat. It created a strange tension that tugged one's body to move. Then the drummers played, pounding out layered rhythms with their hands. I had read accounts of African drumming but had never heard it. The effect was beguiling. People danced in place to the hypnotic sound, then the guitars entered again, Spanish chords and melodies winding their way through the rhythms.

A man stepped into the center of the circle wearing a feathered mask and carrying the obsidian spear. He danced a high-stepping dance, sinewy limbs radiating power and suppleness. He ended the performance by planting the spear into the ground.

Sophie then stepped out and performed a folk dance, waving her green skirt, showing her legs and doing jig-like steps with her feet. Shouts from the crowd encouraged her and some of the women sang eerie, high-pitched trills. The pace of the clapping and drumming quickened and the guitarists plucked rapid arpeggios. Sophie moved from a jig to a kind of waltz, rounding the circle while she spun, her arms going up and down and her hair twirling. She seemed lost in a trance of motion.

A wind picked up and grew stronger as the music intensified. Then a fierce gust blew through, bending the palm trees and blowing sparks from the fires. The music stopped and people braced themselves against the torrent. Sophie sank to her knees, hands in the air, the wind streaming her hair back like a wild brush stroke. The look on her face was maniacal.

The wind gave out abruptly and Sophie collapsed, gasping. I ran to her and picked her up. She clung tightly and buried her face in my chest. It was then that I saw Yaxkin, the priest, hunched, beardless, impossibly old, leaning on a staff, wearing a colorful poncho cloak and looking at us.

I knew in my bones at that moment the woman I held in my arms had become something beyond me.

Chapter 21: Volcan Rojo

8 August, 1819, Gulf of Mexico

Gloom followed me, us, from our anchorage at Isla Lanza. Low clouds and drizzle blew in on an easterly wind. We sailed close reach on a due north course, seeking the relative safety of open ocean and planning our approach to Volcan Rojo.

Rackham, Sydow and Seymour sat hunched over the chart in my cabin. Seymour was talking. He had studied the *Squirrel*'s charts and was mining his prodigious memory for details. I wasn't paying close attention, distracted by my own thoughts.

We had probably lingered too long at Isla Lanza – Rackham and Kedward helped with the repairs of the yacht, others took to playing a stick ball game with some of the islanders, Kitten and Sydow hunted for exotic birds and ranged the south shore for glimpses of the strange creatures said to haunt Laguna de Terminos – but I was loathe to leave Sophie. She spent her days with the priest, learning God knows what, and her nights with me. We talked little but tried to squeeze a lifetime of love into two evenings. I was a fortunate man but didn't feel fortunate, knowing it would end soon.

It ended when we embraced on the pier and I boarded the *Bar Jack*. Cadmael, Manuel and Yacnicte were there, too, and I went through the motions of courtesy. The crowd of islanders waved when the wind caught the sails and the *Bar Jack* began to move. I went to my cabin and stayed there until we were well away.

"Captain," Rackham said.

"Pardon?"

"Seymour thinks the *Squirrel* approached from the west starting about here," she said, pointing to the chart, "and set course east by southeast toward the volcano."

"Yes, hum, if so we should come upon three pillars of rock about ten miles out," Seymour said. "From there I think I can find the island that had the anitite."

"There's nothing on the chart," I said. "I assume the rocks and islands sprang up during the eruption."

"Yes, most likely," Seymour said. "The *Squirrel* charted them but, sadly, that work is lost. The captain complained of unpredictable currents and eddies."

"I think we can handle it, captain, if it ain't too weathery," Rackham said. "The worst thing would be a storm. Even a mild one would put us in trouble."

"Set your course accordingly and we'll keep our eye on the barometer," I said.

"Aye, captain."

* * *

The weather turned fair and the wind southwesterly. The *Bar Jack* continued its northerly course. Kedward and a few of the women took to painting the second-hand dinghy purchased at Galveston and making it look smart.

Seymour commandeered my strongbox so I had to put the money and bullion in a drawer. He filled the box with a base layer of a concoction he'd produced on Isla Lanza composed of chunks of quartz, sand and copper shavings. It was similar to what he'd given me before he embarked on the *Squirrel.* He recommended each of us sprinkle some in our hatbands.

"The concentration of anitite in the air is high near the volcano and can play tricks on the mind," Seymour said. "I believe this will help."

No one gainsaid him when he distributed the mixture. Only Rackham seemed dismissive.

In two days we reached our waypoint and made our turn eastward. Late that night two tiny red streaks of light appeared on the horizon and by morning it was clear they were lava streams flowing down the dark mass of the volcano. There were no clouds as such, just the miasma of Volcan Rojo's ongoing spew. Looks of confidence turned to apprehension.

Seymour peered through Rackham's spyglass, the German optics.

"There, I see them, to the left, hum, ten o'clock."

He handed the telescope to Rackham.

"I only see two pillars. You said three."

"Perhaps one is hidden, hum, by the angle."

Rackham gave instructions to Alice who barked orders and the *Bar Jack* swung seventy degrees to port. About fifteen minutes later another column of rock appeared, a little larger but positioned back from the other two.

"That's it, that's them," Seymour said. "Take us in on the left side."

Rackham gave the order and the *Bar Jack* turned again. We passed the nearest rock at about two hundred yards. It was a ragged obelisk, set there as if by an angry god. We entered a region of dark water; a shifting black substance lingered beneath the waves and, increasingly, gray rocks protruded above them.

Rackham stood at the bow and gave a hand signal that let the helmswoman, Maggie, know to turn the ship two degrees to port. The deck crew adjusted the trim of the sails without needing orders. Rackham had her hat off, letting her hair flutter in the mild breeze, as if doing so helped her read the intentions of the wind. Her eyes were on the water ahead, watching for odd ripples or out-of-place swells that would suggest rocks near the surface.

Sydow, Seymour and I made readings and gauged distances to the rocks and the reefs we could identify, doing so in the hopes of creating a useful chart. Rackham, usually studious with her chartwork and notations, had given herself over to her more trustworthy faculty – her instinct for the sea. It seemed she was in a competition, the opening round in a struggle with an unseen opponent.

* * *

"There, hum, yes, I think that's it." Seymour pointed to a low, barren island of gray rock.

Volcan Rojo loomed much closer now, towering a mile above the sea. A colossal pillar of black smoke mushroomed into the sky; red rivers flowed down its sides. Steam rose from its base where the lava met the water. A rumble rippled through the air like the sound of thunder. Rackham looked at me and I looked at the barometer.

"Still reads high."

If the barometer began to drop, we would leave, anitite or no anitite.

"We heard that sound on the *Squirrel*," Seymour said. "Probably electrical discharges from the plume."

"Take us in, Master Rackham," I said. "Let's get this over with."

* * *

The *Bar Jack* hove-to about a hundred yards from the island; Rackham did not want to get any closer, nor did she want to anchor. We lowered a dinghy into the water. Seymour and I got on board with Sydow and Maggie who took the oars.

The sheer, jagged shore of rock did not look promising. Seymour steered us a little starboard then pointed to a small cove where the rock met the water at a shallow angle. We coasted into the cove and eased to a stop at the water's edge. Sydow threw a grappling line and, on the second attempt, got the hook to hold fast. He stepped onto the island and I handed him the strongbox and two pick hammers. Maggie stayed near the boat to make sure the hook didn't work its way free. The rest of us ventured inland.

The island was a treacherous surface of fissures and bits of volcanic glass. We moved slowly, Seymour scanning ahead, Sydow and I keeping our eyes on the ground at our feet. Seymour stopped at a jut of rock, looked it over, shook his head and moved on. He stopped again at another rock that looked like a huge, chiseled egg jammed into the granite. This one had a metallic sheen to it. Seymour took out a small vial and poured a few drops of liquid onto the rock's surface. The liquid sizzled briefly then turned purple.

"This is it, anitite," he said.

At Seymour's instruction we tied kerchiefs over our faces. "You don't want to, hum, breath any of the particles."

Sydow and I proceeded to chip off pieces of the rock. They did not come easily. Irrationally, I worried about the noise we were making, but who was around to hear us? The place was utterly lifeless, unless the volcano itself could take umbrage.

Seymour tested the pieces as they came off and set them in the strongbox. He was wearing my dress gloves. Sydow and I were sweating profusely when he announced he had all that could fit safely into the box. From a bag he poured more of his mineral concoction over the chunks so they were completely buried, then he closed the lid and secured the padlock with a key.

"Do you have a spare?" He asked me.

I did and handed it to him. He threw the keys as far as he could.

"So there will be no temptation."

I surmised he would be the only one tempted to open the box before we reached England. Sydow and I hefted our cargo and we returned to the boat and an anxious Maggie.

A bright flash dazed us. Instinctively we looked around for the source. Looking back at Volcan Rojo, we saw two balls of fire arcing through the sky trailing flame and smoke.

"Get down," Seymour ordered.

Several seconds later a crushing boom assailed our ears and an invisible force nearly toppled us. I looked out over the water and saw a rippling line that made the *Bar Jack* shudder when it passed.

"The shock wave, from the explosion," Seymour said.

We watched the fireballs descend to the sea, too far off to see the impact, but we could see plumes of steam and, several seconds later, heard thunderclap booms. After the last echo died away, it was Maggie who broke the silence.

“This place is like a festering wound on the face of the earth itself. It shouldn’t be here.”

“I think you speak for us all,” I said.

“Hum, indeed.”

“Javol.”

Maggie and Sydow rowed with alacrity. Maggie was a strong woman when I met her but she was stronger now, stronger than me, stronger than I thought a woman could be, yet still not quite Sydow’s steely strength. They both dipped their oars deeply and pulled with smooth, powerful strokes. The dinghy skimmed the water briskly on the return to the *Bar Jack.*

* * *

A low mist settled over the water; puffs of fog accumulated with a diminishing wind that now blew from the north, directly against our route back through the rocks and shoals. We had to tack frequently to keep our course. The rocks were obscured by the fog, the water hidden under the mist. Rackham, now at the helm, guided us by instinct and memory alone. I tried to gauge our position on our crude chart but the compass was behaving erratically. The barometer dropped a bit.

The unseen opponent I imagined earlier flourished again in my mind. We were so damned close to the safety of open water, yet our progress was achingly slow.

“We may be getting close to a rock on our port side,” I said.

“Shh,” Rackham responded, then made a turn to starboard.

A puff of fog passed and the suspected rock was indeed only yards from us. Minutes later we tacked to port, passing close to another rock. Rackham handed the tiller to Maggie.

“Steady as she goes.”

Rackham checked the chronometer, leaned against the gunwale and took a drink of water.

“We’re through the worst,” she said. “I’ll lay to that. On this heading we should see the pillars within the hour.”

“Thank God you’re a bloody genius, Ann,” I said.

"We ain't home yet."

* * *

The fog to the northwest cleared some and, on the horizon, I could just make out the three rocks. Soon we'd be in open water. How Rackham did it, I had no idea.

"Ship!" Polly yelled. "Ship! Ship to starboard, three o'clock."

Rackham and I peered through our spyglasses. The fog was thicker to the east.

"I don't see anything," I hollered back. "Are you sure it was a ship? These rocks have strange shapes."

"It was a ship, I'm sure of it," Polly said. "Three masts but no sails."

Sydow was at the helm. Seymour came up beside us. Rackham wiped dew from her lens and looked again.

"I see it now, bearing one-ten," she said.

Soon I had it in view, a low, black silhouette, small in the distance, with three masts.

"Odd," I said. "She has no yardarms. She must be a derelict. Could it be the *Squirrel*?"

"Nah, it's a frigate, French by the lines of her," Rackham said.

"What's it doing in this damnation?"

"Looks dead in the water to me."

"Let me look," Seymour said.

I handed him my spyglass.

"A French frigate, you say; we should, hum, investigate."

"What we need to do is leave this place, Herr Doctor," Sydow said.

"Could there be survivors?" I asked.

"I doubt it," Rackham said.

"Even so, hum, it could have charts, log books, information that could be very useful."

"What do you think, Ann?"

"She may be grounded but I could get us close safely enough for a better read. It's your call, captain."

I sighed.

"Nothing is easy, is it? I suppose we should at least check it out. That would be maritime custom. If it looks even modestly dangerous to approach, we'll head out to sea."

* * *

The *Bar Jack* made its turn and we sailed broad reach toward the black silhouette. Something was nagging me, some points of memory that should connect but weren't. I thought of our time at Galveston and Guibourg's performance but nothing gelled. I thought of the things Louisa had told me – Giselle LaFoy sailing for the jungles of Mexico, sailing on a French warship. Then it occurred to me – a frigate, she sailed on a frigate called the *Méduse.*

"Ann, I think it's the *Méduse*," I said. "The Admiralty considers her lost from the French order of battle. She carried an expedition to the Yucatan five years ago and never returned."

"Could be. Makes sense, I guess."

"I'm getting a bad feeling. Remember what Guibourg screamed?"

Rackham looked through her spyglass.

"Yeah, me too, captain. There's something wrong with her – too bulky, her masts are too thick."

Jenny came running up on deck still wearing her cooking apron. She looked terrified, which was disconcerting because she was among the pluckiest people on board. She leaned over the gunwale and looked out at the ship.

"Captain!" She shouted. "We have to go! Turn us around!"

She ran up onto the aft deck.

"Please, please. Something horrible is out there."

"What is it?" I asked.

"I don't know. I just feel it. It's terrible. Please, captain. We need to get away."

"Okay, calm down," I said. "Ann, that settles it. Take us about. Let's get the hell out of here."

"Helm," Rackham said. "Make course north by northwest, heading three-three-zero."

"Aye, ma'am, gladly, ma'am," Sydow responded.

The *Bar Jack* turned and we headed for open ocean. Rackham kept her spyglass fixed on the frigate, now behind us. Maggie was trying to settle Jenny.

"You're turning away because of a frightened woman?" Seymour asked.

"I have reason to trust her instincts," I said.

"She isn't wearing her hat and this area plays tricks on the mind, hum, like I said."

"I'm sorry, Paul, we're just going to have to pass on this one."

"She's moving, captain. She's turning," Rackham said.

"Pardon?"

Chapter 22: The Dance Charybdis

11 August, 1819, Gulf of Mexico

It simply could not be. With little wind and no sails, the *Méduse* moved, turned toward us and gained speed.

"Raise the jibs!" Rackham shouted. "I want full sail now!"

The crew scurried. Rackham and I looked on at the frigate. My mind struggled to comprehend how she could move at all. A freak current perhaps?

"She's not moving very fast at least," I said.

"Fast enough. We need to catch a decent wind."

As if her words were a magic spell, telltale ripples on the water in the distance behind us signaled a change. A brisk easterly was blowing in. The wind parted the mist obscuring the *Méduse* and seemed to radiate out from there.

"That wind ain't natural," Rackham said.

"It's just what we need, isn't it?"

Before Rackham could answer, the *Méduse* unfurled her sails, not white sheets raised on lines of rigging, but great, leathery, trapezoidal segments stretching out like the wings of an inconceivable bat. They unfolded in sequence – spreading out from the mizzenmast, then the mainmast, then the foremast – as if the stage effect of some macabre opera.

I lowered my spyglass, wanting to confirm what I saw with my naked eyes. The spyglass slipped from my hand, clanked on the deck and rolled to Sydow's feet. He picked it up, turned to hand it to me and saw the thing that was behind us.

"Heileger fick."

* * *

Our northerly breeze died completely and the *Bar Jack* was becalmed. The *Méduse*'s speed increased and she loomed ever nearer, ever larger. The new east wind was stronger than I'd judged and when it hit, it buffeted the *Bar Jack*. With a crack the main jib block broke free.

"Goddammit all to Hell!" Rackham yelled.

The crew scrambled to reel in the free flying jib sails. I took the helm and Sydow went down to lend his strength to the effort. Rackham hurried from point to point, adjusting the mainsails to the new wind. They, at least, had held and the *Bar Jack* gained speed. The *Méduse*, however, continued to close the distance.

Izzy and Polly raised a ratline on the foremast. Kedward strapped on her tool belt and hooked a spare block to it. She was getting ready to ascend and fix the damage once the jibs were under control. Rackham returned to the aft deck.

"Brenda is really going up there?" I asked.

"We have to get the jibs up," Rackham said.

She took the helm and adjusted our course some to milk as much speed as we could from the mainsails.

The *Méduse* still gained. Through my spyglass, I could see her hull was covered with dark, metallic scales. Instead of a bowsprit, it had a massive horn shaped like that of a rhinoceros. What seemed like fleshy nubs bulged from the gunports. The bow was most uncanny, covered with knobby growths that gave the impression of a face of some preternatural carnivore. She opened her eyes.

* * *

Terror gripped me. I turned and hunched over, hands on my knees. Rackham let go of the tiller, crouched on the deck and put her hands to her face. Activity on deck stopped as the others did much the same. Seymour, standing at the aft gunwale, stared out at the monster and laughed as if he had just grasped God's divine joke.

I knew what was happening. I'd felt it before in Jamaica, the sudden despair, but this was more powerful. Yet, perhaps because of previous experience combined with the buffering effect of Seymour's mixture in my hatband, I was able to function. I grabbed the tiller and made sure we stayed on course.

"Ann, get up," I said. "It's an attack. The thing is sowing despair in our minds."

She didn't wear her hat so I imagined the effect on her was worse. Nevertheless she stood up. She bared her teeth, something between a smile and a snarl.

"Despair and me are old friends, captain."

She drew her dirk, went over to Maggie who was huddled against the gunwale and kicked her in the hip.

"Get up, you fat whore. We got work to do."

The sight of the snarling Rackham pointing the long dagger jolted Maggie out of her torpor and she got to her feet. Rackham ordered her to add line to the boom stays, then went to the next inert sailor.

Rackham had the right idea, shock them into action. I reached out and yanked Seymour toward me.

"Snap out of it, doctor, and take the tiller," I commanded. "Just hold it steady until relieved. Can you do that?"

He blinked rapidly. "Yes, I, hum, can do that, captain, yes sir."

I hurried down to the main deck and found Sydow sitting against the foremast, the jib halyard limp in his hand, staring at nothing. I slapped him hard.

"Get up you miserable Prussian dog!"

He stood abruptly, fury on his face, and drew his fist back.

"Mr. von Sydow," I said. "Would you please beat to quarters if it isn't too much bother?"

I could see the light of his right mind returning to his eyes. He drew a deep breath: "Battle stations! All hands to battle stations!"

His booming voice had the desired effect. The crew began to stir. Rackham had Alice up who was blowing her whistle and yelling orders. Kedward got up and climbed the ratline.

Kitten and a couple of others emerged from below carrying their weapons. I told them to help with the rigging. The swivel gun team emerged and I directed them to mount it at the stern. A futile gesture, I was sure, but we couldn't leave anything untried.

I relieved Seymour at the helm and soon Rackham joined me. We judged the *Méduse* to be about 700 yards behind us.

"You're cooking up something," I said.

"It might buy us some time," Rackham said.

Alice signaled Rackham that all was ready.

"Okay, turn us due west, captain, heading two-seven-zero."

"That will put the wind directly behind us and spill our sails."

"Just do it."

I made the turn as directed and Rackham signaled Alice who relayed further orders. The mainsail booms swung outwards, the rear boom to starboard, the fore boom to port, until they were perpendicular to the ship's beam. The triangular sails, now spread out, caught the full force of the strong tailwind.

The *Bar Jack* gained speed. We were maintaining our distance from the frigate, perhaps outpacing it slightly. Moving directly downwind, the *Méduse*'s rear wing prevented the other two from catching the wind. Rackham had spilled her sails.

The *Méduse* opened her jaws and roared.

* * *

The sound was like a distorted eagle's screech combined with a low booming tone and a peculiar buzz. The crack of her jaws opened just below the horn, revealing yellow, shark-like teeth. Some of the women held their ears; some seemed paralyzed with fear.

"You are the crew of the *Bar Jack*. Do your jobs!" I yelled.

The screeching abated but the rumbling and buzzing remained.

"Three pillars ahead! One o'clock!" Polly shouted from her post at the bow.

From the aft deck we couldn't see forward because our sails, spread like wings, blocked our view.

"On this course we'll pass south of the rocks," I said. "We haven't traversed that water. There could be reefs."

"We'll have to risk it," Rackham said. She was looking up at Kedward who was trying to fasten a new block to the foremast. Kitten shimmied up to help her.

"Once we get by the pillars, we'll make our break north," Rackham continued. "If we time it right, the thing might get hung up on the rocks."

The supply of tricks in Rackham's bag seemed endless. The buzzing and rumbling continued. I could feel the *Bar Jack* vibrating.

"Whirlpool! Whirlpool!" Polly shouted, frantic this time. "Dead ahead!"

"What now?" Rackham growled.

I waved Maggie over to take her place at the helm while Rackham and I hurried to the bow to see this fresh horror.

A maelstrom formed before our eyes, water rotating around a depression that grew deeper by the moment. It was just south of the pillars and we were headed right for it.

Rackham ordered the mainsails brought into normal positions then signaled Maggie to turn hard to starboard. The *Bar Jack* leaned over, now sailing broad reach on a northerly course. The *Méduse* closed rapidly.

"How's it going up there?" Rackham shouted at Kedward.

"A couple minutes if you can hold the goddamned ship steady."

Soon the *Bar Jack* stopped making progress against the current flowing toward the maelstrom. The water passed at speed but we were going nowhere. With the *Méduse* 500 yards away, we were quite literally trapped between Scylla and Charybdis.

Four hundred yards now. I ordered the swivel gun crew to open fire, though likely it would be little better than throwing pebbles. The shot splashed short but the *Méduse* did close her eyes.

Rackham ordered the steerage hands to stand ready at the sails. She was going to make another turn. I followed her back to the aft deck. Three hundred yards, another shot from the swivel gun bounced off the frigate's bow. Rackham took the tiller from Maggie and looked up at Kedward and Kitten.

Two hundred yards.

"Whatever you're going to do, you really ought to do it soon," I said.

"I'm going to drown the bitch."

What we saw next crushed the remnants of any normal sense of reality I'd had. The fleshy nubs that had been the *Méduse*'s gunports, 40 of them, sprouted tentacles – long, thick, snaky appendages, each ending with three toothy fingers like a flexing tricorn mouth.

I was beyond horror. A line from Job came to mind: "Behold the hope of him is in vain; shall not one be cast down even at the sight of him." Except this leviathan was a she and she was closing for the kill.

One of the girls of the swivel gun crew, Wanda, I think, screamed and fled below decks. The other two cowered behind the gunwale.

"Here we go, captain," Rackham said, and turned the *Bar Jack* hard to port, straight for the maelstrom.

* * *

The turn gave us a little distance but the *Méduse* didn't slacken her pursuit. Rackham nudged the *Bar Jack* to starboard, then later made a harder turn. I surmised she was maneuvering for the best angle. I wasn't sure what she hoped to accomplish. Even she had never done this before. From time to time, Rackham glanced up at Kedward and Kitten.

"We need the jibs or I don't think this will work," she said.

It was clear to me that once the ship went round the maelstrom, the two women on the mast would be flung out to sea.

Kedward waved her hand. The block was repaired.

"Get down from there now!" I shouted.

Kitten slid part way then leaped, landing in Sydow's arms, and they both rolled on the deck. The *Bar Jack* was at the edge of the great eddy. Kedward grabbed the jib line with both hands and jumped, pulling the jib sails up with her fall. She landed with a grunt but on her feet. She and Alice quickly secured the line.

"All hands to port side and hang on!" Rackham shouted.

The *Bar Jack* sailed straight for the three pillars. I didn't know how far back the *Méduse* was, I didn't look, but I could feel she was close.

The *Bar Jack* entered the swirl at a tangent, on the edge of the bowl but not down into it. She canted to port and I wondered why Rackham had ordered the crew to that side. Rackham turned the ship hard to starboard. The circling current caught the *Bar Jack*'s flank and she rotated around the abyssal eye of the maelstrom like a pointer on a compass traversing the directions – north, northwest, west, southwest, south, southeast ...

Rackham heaved on the tiller. The east wind caught the sails from the port side and the *Bar Jack* lurched to starboard. The centrifugal force of her rotation plus the sudden thrust from her sails hurled her away from the whirlpool like a stone from a sling. Running four points to the wind, the *Bar Jack* leaned heavily, the starboard gunwale skimming the water.

The crew, clinging to the port side gunwale, cheered as the *Bar Jack* drew away from the maelstrom and the *Méduse*, tentacles flailing, spun in her own trap.

Rackham held the course only a few minutes before turning northeast. The *Bar Jack* crossed the wind beautifully without losing momentum and we sailed close hauled toward open ocean.

But the *Méduse* did not go under. The maelstrom stopped spinning and a huge bulge of water heaved up from below it. The *Méduse* rode the crest of the wave, maneuvering away from the rocks. It was then I saw she had a tail protruding from her stern like that of a behemoth shark. She turned toward us and continued her pursuit.

I then heard the ripping of cloth, looked up and saw the aft mainsail tearing away. My hope went with it.

* * *

"Bad slice of luck," Rackham said.

We had to change course to level the ship so the crew could take down the remnants of the aft mainsail and put up the shorter, but sturdier, storm sail. We lost speed and the *Méduse* had the wind advantage again.

Wanda came up from below deck, red-eyed and somber, and took her place at the swivel gun. The *Méduse* was a ways out still, too far to shoot. Beyond the pillars now, the inky substance below the waves was gone. The afternoon sun appeared, burning away the lingering fog. The sea was once again blue and beautiful.

"I think I'm out of tricks," Rackham said. "We can zig and zag but we're hobbled. The bitch is faster than us, and can turn better, and she's got the weather gauge."

"Keep going; it's all we can do," I said. "Perhaps she'll tire out."

Rackham laughed.

We needed help but we were alone on a part of the sea where no one ventured. I watched Jenny pull on a halyard. The storm sail went up. That would give us some speed but not enough. I went down to the main deck and took Jenny aside.

"I want you to try to contact Sophie," I said.

"What, captain?"

"With your mind, try to communicate with Sophie. You have the ability like she does. She told me and I suspect you already know."

"I don't know how."

"Neither do I but you need to try. Like as not we won't escape this monster. Perhaps Sophie or the old priest can do something, distract it perhaps. I don't know."

Jenny pursed her lips in confusion.

"Go to my cabin and try it there where it's quiet," I said. "Sophie left some clothing. Perhaps something familiar to her and you both will help. I admit I grasp at straws but you must try."

Jenny nodded and left the deck for my cabin. I issued an order to ready both dinghies. Once overtaken we could attempt to abandon ship and hope the *Méduse* would be satisfied with the destruction of the *Bar Jack* and not pursue the boats. I had little confidence in the plan.

I returned to my place on the aft deck and found Seymour staring out at the creature. Its tentacles were withdrawn except for a few feet of the ends that stuck out from the nubs like flagella on an anemone.

"I'm sorry, James," Seymour said. "I was a fool to ask we undertake this errand."

"We all knew it would be dangerous, Paul. We're all fools. I think my main regret is that there will be no one to recount the bravery and skill shown by the crew today. They have been simply marvelous, and Master Rackham has shown she has no peer."

"Yes, hum, I quite agree."

* * *

The *Méduse* was twice as long as the *Bar Jack*, twice as wide and displaced a thousand tons. Soon she would be upon us. At 400 yards I ordered the swivel gun crew to commence firing.

There was a shift in the wind, easterly to north easterly. Rackham had the helm and adjusted course a few degrees to port, hoping to milk just a little more speed. Maggie had summoned her musketeers to the aft deck. Kitten was there with her carbine and Sydow with my long rifle. We all knew it was for naught but the *Bar Jack* would go down fighting.

"Sails ahoy! Sails ahoy!" Polly shouted. "Two ships, to port, ten o'clock!"

I rushed to the bow for a better look. The ships were closer than I anticipated. Polly must have been distracted from her lookout duty. They were sailing a southeasterly course, one in front of the other, on a different wind, a northwesterly. A gun flash from the trailing ship let me know it was in pursuit of the other. The leading vessel was a smallish, gaff-rigged schooner, the other a two-masted war brig.

On their current course, they would pass in front of us. My first instinct was to turn to intercept them, seek safety in numbers, but could I in good conscience deliberately bring the abomination upon them?

Through my spyglass I saw frantic activity on the leading ship's deck, then it turned hard away. They must have seen the *Méduse* and thought it better to face the guns of their pursuer.

The trailing ship, however, did not turn to continue its chase; it turned the other way, toward us. The turn brought its bow square against a wave and water splashed high into the air. At that moment I made out its flag, stars and stripes rippling in the wind, and I knew. She was the *Enterprise.*

* * *

The swivel gun boomed again. Izzy and Alice drew up seawater in a bucket and poured it on the barrel. The water sizzled and steamed while the gun's crew reloaded. The last shot must have stung. Within a hundred yards now, the *Méduse* opened her mouth and let forth a deafening screech. Maggie and her musketeers let go a volley, some balls pelting the monster's pointed tongue. The tentacles sprouted forth again in all their fantastic menace and the *Méduse* surged forward.

The *Enterprise* passed our port side at close range on an opposite course. The *Bar Jack*'s women screamed their war cries and the *Enterprise*'s men answered with theirs. A leading tentacle swept our aft deck, causing the women to duck or stagger back. Another tentacle clutched the swivel gun and ripped it from its mount along with a chunk of the stern.

Still at the bow, I saw Captain Kearny with his saber raised in the air. The *Enterprise* was now parallel with the *Méduse.* Kearny lowered his sword, his gunnery officer yelled, "Fire!" Seven big guns barked out a booming, staccato barrage of flame, smoke and speeding hot iron.

It was hard to see what damage, if any, the salvo had done but it got the *Méduse*'s attention. She roared and veered away toward her new adversary. I cheered with joy along with the rest of the crew.

Captain Kearny displayed his own sailing skills. The *Enterprise* turned crisply 180 degrees and unleashed another salvo from its starboard guns. Undeterred the *Méduse* kept coming. The monster frigate and the much smaller brig conducted a kind of slow waltz, circling and turning. All the while the *Bar Jack* sped away, each minute carrying us closer to a chance of returning home.

The *Enterprise* fired a third broadside, and a fourth.

"Die, you loathsome bitch, die," I hissed.

The fifth broadside, the last, sheared a tentacle away and the bat wings on the foremast fell limp. But the *Méduse* had caught her prey, ramming the *Enterprise* and rending it with her tentacles.

* * *

"I'm sorry, Ann, I don't think I can just stand here and watch them die while we sail away."

"I hear ya, captain."

"Take us about."

"Aye, captain."

* * *

The ship of fools had its encore to perform. The crew went at it with grim determination. The plan was to sail within fifty yards, lower the dinghies and fetch as many men as we could before making a break for the sea. Men screamed, muskets flashed and the *Enterprise* was disintegrating, but the *Méduse* was thoroughly entangled. That was our hope.

In a pretty swing, the *Bar Jack* hove-to broadside the mayhem. The wind was calm, the natural northwesterly beating back the *Méduse*'s conjured easterly. The dinghies splashed into the water. I went into one with Maggie; Sydow and Alice climbed into the other. Ropes were tied to the sterns so they could be pulled back in need. We rowed with utmost dispatch.

Many men were already in the water, swimming frantically toward the *Bar Jack*. We told the stronger ones to keep going and hauled in the weaker ones. I saw Captain Kearny, still on the *Enterprise*, dueling a tentacle with his saber.

"Kearny! Get out of there!" I shouted.

With a titanic roar, the *Méduse* heaved herself onto the *Enterprise*. Kearny slid into the water. I told Maggie to row hard. She was joined now by a man we'd hauled from the sea. I threw Kearny a line. He grabbed it and I pulled.

Just as he reached the dinghy, a tentacle grabbed him. I drew my broadsword and slashed with all I had. Sparks flew as the blade struck the steely scales and the tentacle dropped Kearny. My blade was notched.

I hauled him in, then unhooked the rope from the stern, attached it to the bow and shouted for the crew on the *Bar Jack* to pull us in. We hauled in more men as we went and others hung on to the sides.

I looked to the other dinghy. A tentacle descended on Sydow but a well-aimed shot sheared one of its digits and it withdrew. I didn't need to look back to know who'd made that shot.

Soon we were scrambling on board. I ordered Rackham to set sail immediately and we cut the dinghies loose once all the men were up.

* * *

Under the weight of the *Méduse*, the *Enterprise* broke in two with a cacophonous racket of splintering wood, each half sliding under the water. The toothy digits of the tentacles cut away entangling lines and the *Méduse* lurched forward. The *Bar Jack* could only creep along. With so little wind now, she could barely make steerageway.

"You were a damned fool to come back for us, Captain LeRoque," Kearny said.

We stood on the aft deck, leaning against the gunwale, exhausted, drenched and bloodstained. Rackham remained at the helm.

"You were a bloody fool to come to our aid, Captain Kearny," I said.

The *Méduse* moved toward us, propelled, I assumed, by its great fin. I could feel the wind freshening but there was no hope of picking up speed in time. I drew my sword and saw on its tip a clinging, inky fluid.

"It bleeds red, anyway," I said.

"Aye, captain, it does," Kearny said.

The *Méduse* was wounded – a broken wing, at least two tentacles missing and several punctures in its sides seeping fluid. It seemed to wheeze through its open mouth and bloodied tongue.

"I bet she won't soon forget the *Enterprise* and the *Bar Jack*," Kearny said.

"No, I doubt she will."

Yet she was still alive, still huge and still coming, a relentless malice. Volcan Rojo towered on the horizon behind her, spewing smoke and fire. The *Méduse*, once again, opened her eyes – orange orbs streaked with red, and black, depthless pupils.

I felt the terror and the despair but was unmoved. Captain Kearny went to his knees. The men of his crew went down, too, but most of the *Bar Jack*'s crew continued their work. I waited with my sword in hand, knowing there was no hope. I wondered what hope there was for any of us. Was mankind's time on earth coming to an end?

A strange quietude prevailed. It occurred to me that for every hero whose tale could be told, there were a dozen whose tales were untold. Were their deeds less noble for being lost to silence?

I heard a door open and close, then saw Jenny walking on the deck, stepping around the huddled, terrified men. She wore one of Sophie's kitchen dresses which was too small. She moved with a graceful sway to the port side gunwale and looked out to the northwest. Her hair was undone and the breeze fluttered her skirt.

Jenny's eyes seemed to track something in the water but I could see nothing. She turned her head slowly toward the stern. I looked again and saw a bulge of water, like a rogue wave, moving toward the *Méduse*.

The whale broke the surface at speed and rammed the frigate's side near the bow. The *Méduse* screamed, a colossal, anguished bellowing. Water exploded near the frigate's stern and another whale careened into the air, snatching two tentacles in its long, toothy jaw. It landed with all its bulk on the *Méduse* then slipped back into the water, yanking the tentacles out from their roots.

The *Méduse* turned away, back toward the volcano. The massive sperm whales rammed her again and a third time. She thrashed with her tail, raised her two good wings and withdrew her remaining tentacles as she sped toward the three pillars in the shadow of Volcan Rojo.

No cheers, the crew of the *Bar Jack* could only look on in awed silence. Kearny and his men rose, shaking off their despair.

The whales pursued the *Méduse* for a time then veered off. I wondered if perhaps they were repulsed by the inky waters near the volcano. They lingered near the surface, frequently blowing tall spouts as if catching their breath. Eventually the *Méduse* disappeared into the haze surrounding Volcan Rojo. The whales headed west and slipped under the waves.

Jenny was still standing at the gunwale. I skipped down the steps to the main deck and went to her. I put my hand on her shoulder.

"Sophie?"

She shook her head as if coming out of a trance.

"Excuse me, captain."

"Sorry, Jenny, I just thought ..."

"What the hell am I doing in this dress?"

I laughed.

"Saving our lives, Jenny. Saving our lives."

Epilogue

29 August, 1819, Bridgetown, Barbados

We made landfall in the late afternoon, the setting sun shining a golden light on the palm trees, beaches and tall ships of Bridgetown's harbor. The crew gave a weary cheer, along with our guests, the thirty-seven men we'd saved from the clutches of the *Méduse*. Thirty-one of the *Enterprise*'s crew had perished.

The voyage to Barbados had been taxing and started out in uneasy fashion. The pirate ship the *Enterprise* had been chasing lingered and kept a parallel course to our own. At that point in time, we would have been an easy prize.

"I'm pretty sure it's one of Laffite's boats," Captain Kearny had said.

"She is," Rackham said. "I saw her in the harbor at Galveston."

Eventually, however, the ship turned away, sailing northwest while we kept a northeasterly course. I suspect its captain recognized the *Bar Jack* and knew we had left Galveston on good terms with Laffite.

"I thought you weren't allowed to pursue ships into El Radio," I said to Kearny.

"I just couldn't bring myself to let the bugger go."

Kearny advised us to sail straight for New Orleans but I wasn't going anywhere that wasn't in the direction of home. Barbados was much further away, however, and we had thirty-seven extra mouths to feed. Fresh water was our primary concern and we started rationing immediately. Fortunately a couple of rain squalls along the way helped supplement our supply.

* * *

We didn't bother with the crowded harbor and steered instead for our previous anchorage near the beach. The frigate, *Pyramus*, was anchored nearby and its crew was raising sail, apparently readying to depart. The men stopped what they were doing and gawked as the battered *Bar Jack* slid by, my crew dirty, weary, grim and proud as only those who have been to the gates of Hell and back can be.

I saw Commodore White on the quarterdeck, his walrus whiskers and rotund build unmistakable. He put his hands on his hips and shook his head. We lowered anchor and eased to a stop.

"Not sure what we do now," Rackham said. "We ain't got a dinghy."

"I suppose we could swim ashore. The water looks pleasant enough," I said.

As it was the *Pyramus*' crew furled the sails and put out a launch. Apparently our arrival was sufficient occasion to postpone her departure. The commodore himself was on the dinghy and I gladly gave him permission to come aboard.

"I'll be goddamned, I didn't expect to see you again, LeRoque," he said.

I introduced him to Rackham, Sydow and Kearny.

"Honor to meet you, Captain Kearny," the commodore said. "I've heard good things but didn't expect you'd take up with a bunch of English girls. Your ship was the *Enterprise*, correct?"

"It was. These women saved our lives, commodore."

"And the *Enterprise* saved ours," Rackham said.

"What the hell happened?"

"We had a bit of a scuffle with a sea monster," I said.

"Ja, it was a lively fight."

* * *

Arrangements were made to debark the *Enterprise*'s crew and find them passage back to the United States, mostly at my expense, though with a promise of remuneration. Commodore White had orders, if any of the *Squirrel*'s crew turned up, to return them to England as soon as possible. When I told him Seymour was the sole survivor and we had fetched a supply of anitite from Volcan Rojo, he decided the *Pyramus* would forego its patrol mission and return to England immediately with Seymour and his precious cargo.

I shook Seymour's hand before he stepped down to the *Pyramus*' launch.

"Remember, don't open that box until you're back in your laboratory," I said.

"Yes, hum, it's in the Pryamus' safe now. I couldn't get to it even if I wanted to."

"Farewell, Paul. I shall see you soon."

"Farewell, James, and, hum, thank you."

* * *

We lingered the better part of a fortnight, mostly staying in tents on the beach while we cut a new sail from our spare cloth and scrounged wood to repair the *Bar Jack*'s aft deck. The *Enterprise*'s crew went out piecemeal on merchant ships heading for the states. I dined with Captain Kearny at the Pelican Inn the evening before he departed.

"I hear you almost came to blows with a British officer," I said.

"The bastard was trying to recruit my men to serve on his ship."

"We are a tad short-handed these days."

"They should recruit your women. By God, they're some of the best sailors I've seen."

"They should, but old habits die hard."

"Aye, they do."

"What will happen when you get back?" I asked.

"Out of job, I bet. I violated standing orders and lost my ship."

"I'd wager more trouble is coming," I said. "They'd be fools to cast aside a fighter like you."

"You don't know the Navy Department," Kearny said. "When I tell them about the *Méduse*, I may get laughed out of Washington, or put in the brig."

“If you need affidavits, I’m happy to supply them. I’ll urge the Admiralty to send letters of commendation to your Navy Department. You should get a medal, not a discharge.”
“I appreciate it, captain.”
“And, if worst comes to worst, I’m sure the Royal Navy could find a place for you.”
“Only over my goddamned dead body.”

* * *

We loaded the *Bar Jack* with barrels of sugar and kegs of rum and set sail for home, cruising northward to catch the westerlies of the North Atlantic. On a particularly pleasant morning, Kitten and Sydow approached me and asked to be married. I was by no means certain I had the authority, but I agreed and performed a joyous, if awkward, ceremony that ended with the couple jumping over Sydow’s saber.
As a wedding present I gave them my dueling pistols. They planned to raise money when they arrived in England then travel to Texas to have a go at breeding horses.
“It might be a bit cramped in Leo’s stateroom,” I said. “I can lend you my cabin for your wedding night if you’d like.”
“Nah, captain, we can manage,” Kitten said.
“I’m sure you can.”
I suspected they had “managed” before.
The North Atlantic was cold and rough and kept us on our toes but, finally, on 7 October, 1819, we entered the wide mouth of the Bristol Channel.

* * *

A small crowd gathered at the pier as the *Bar Jack* settled into her slip. More people accumulated while we tied off and secured the ship, some clapped and cheered, some shouted questions.
“Did you really go into The Radius?”
“Did you see the Red Volcano?”

Our arrival was going to be more taxing than I'd imagined. The gangplank went down but, before I descended, I put my hand on Rackham's shoulder.

"I turn command over to you, Ann. We'll work out a contract later. I don't suppose we can keep the crew from talking but we should avoid mentioning anitite if we can. Pay them double wages; they've more than earned it. Keep the remainder for yourself. Additional money should be forthcoming soon which we'll split with the crew."

"Aye, captain."

"This is hardly goodbye but in case I should forget, please accept my deepest appreciation. I'm certain no one else but you could have carried us through."

We shook hands. Rackham seemed tongue-tied.

"I ... I'm proud to know you, Captain LeRoque."

"The sentiment is mutual, Captain Rackham."

* * *

After fending off well-wishers, questions and persistent entreaties from a local newspaper man, I arrived at the offices of Baxter & Washburn and was presented with a stack of letters. I opened the most recent from Louisa in which she informed me she had taken an apartment in London and was eager that I visit. A letter from my brother posted a few days prior indicated the prime minister wanted to see me at my earliest convenience.

I hired a coach and the next day set out for London with Kitten and Sydow and all of Sydow's specimens. I knew he couldn't wait to see the faces of his former employers at the museum when he showed them the monstrous head of the terror bird. Fortunately no highway men accosted us and the coach safely arrived at the entrance of Boodle's Gentlemen's Club.

"I'd ask you in for lunch but, sadly, women are not permitted," I said.

"Preposterous, kapitan. Kitten is a better man than any of them."

She slugged him for the remark.

"Of that I have no doubt," I said. "I suspect when the museum sees your haul, you'll be asked to join the Royal Society. You'll be a famous naturalist and explorer. Perhaps you won't want to go to Texas."

"We shall see, kapitan."

Kitten, still in her sailor's suit, gave me a hug and drew astonished glances from a party of gentlemen leaving the club.

* * *

I asked the maitre de if my brother was in – he usually took his lunch at the club – and was shown to a private chamber where Archy was conferring with the home secretary.

"I hope I'm not intruding," I said.

"James! Dear God, you're here," Archy said.

The two men stood and Archy introduced me to the secretary as his "little brother." Archy was indeed about a half inch taller than me.

"Bloody good show, LeRoque," the home secretary said. "I've seen Dr. Seymour's report. Astonishing, simply astonishing. I'll leave you two to get reacquainted but I look forward to talking with you soon."

The minister left and Archy looked at the sword on my hip.

"I didn't know you took that with you," he said.

"Oh, pardon me," I said. "I got into the habit of wearing it. I wasn't even thinking."

"That's a family heirloom. You didn't damage it did you?"

"I'm afraid I notched the blade."

"In battle, I presume."

"Yes."

"Then I doubt old Ker would mind. Welcome back."

Archy set aside his appointments for the day and we talked through the afternoon. I learned that Governor Montagu in Jamaica had made a truce with Nashoba and was negotiating a permanent settlement.

"Still not sure if we can get Parliament behind a deal but we shall see," Archy said.

The truce did allow both sides to array all their forces against Kratoka and there was hope he would be defeated.

"There's a rumor making the rounds that the Duke received a package containing the head of some ghastly creature said to be a contrivance of a witch doctor. I don't suppose you know anything about that, Jimmy boy."

"Sorry, Arch, nothing comes to mind," I said, unsuccessfully suppressing a smirk.

I inquired about the incident at Kilve Beach. The home minister sent agents to investigate. A girl was missing, two, in fact, but the townsfolk said they drowned when they strayed too far out on a rowboat.

"We know a coach arrived at the village prior to the incident carrying prominent individuals," Archy said. "But we don't know their identities with any certainty. The agents found no evidence of wrongdoing but grew very suspicious. We've got another man looking into it now, one of the Bow Street Runners. If anyone can get to the bottom of it, he can."

Eventually Archy had to excuse himself to attend a dinner engagement he couldn't put off.

"You know, brother of mine," he said. "This hair-brained adventure of yours has put you on the map, so to speak. The prime minister probably will meet with you tomorrow. He wants to set up a commission to investigate all the queer happenings and try to make some sense of them. I think he has you pegged to be on it, perhaps even lead it."

"I'm honored to be considered but I'm not sure what I want to do. Rest, I think, more than anything," I said.

"Of course, but the minister is not well disposed to taking no for an answer. We'll see you tomorrow, James."

"Before you go, Arch, do you know if Elliot is in town?"

"Darnsby? I should think not. He just made Lieutenant Colonel and was sent to his new battalion."

* * *

Foregoing a cab I walked to the Knightsbridge neighborhood and found my cousin's apartment. It was actually an elegant little row house near Hyde Park. I knocked and a fetching blonde girl opened the door.

"May I help you?" Her eyes were blue and accent Norwegian. Louisa's new maidservant, I was sure. Where did she find these people?

"I'm James LeRoque, Louisa's cousin. Please tell her I'm here."

"Oh, my heavens, it's you ..."

"Yes, perhaps I should let myself in."

She just ogled as I passed into the foyer, took off my hat and unbuckled my sword belt.

"She ... my mistress ... she's in the study ... through the parlor to the right."

I found Louisa sitting at a small table writing a letter. The room had her signature clutter of books and papers. She looked up and was, I believe, momentarily taken aback.

"Hello, Louisa."

"Hello, James."

I went to her and kissed her cheek. We didn't speak for a time.

"Before anything else, I want to apologize," she said.

"Whatever for?"

"Those nights we shared; they were wrong. I blame myself entirely. I was swept away by the possibilities of it all."

"I agree. They were an indulgence, but just as much my error as yours. I doubt in the long run I will look back upon them with much regret. In any case, I believe we were both pawns in Sophie's game."

"She's a sorceress."

"She is, but I love her nonetheless."

"So do I."

"Any news from Juliet?" I asked.

"She's on her way home. She believes she knows where there's a copy of Cossio's book. She wants to make use of the *Bar Jack*."

"That would be up to Ann. It's her ship now."

"God, I want to meet that woman."

"Then I'll summon her here to sign the contract for the ship. You can watch the *Bar Jack* sail up the Thames."

Louisa beamed and clutched my hand.
“I'm glad you're back, James.”

Author's Note:

The goal of the book, beyond telling what I hope is a good story, is to create a world ripe with possibilities for adventure. This is part of an effort to set the stage for a forthcoming role-playing game called *Dark Trails*. Ideally the book will inspire potential players, game-masters or even authors to dream up their own adventures within the world.

Some of the characters who appear in the book are historical: Jean Laffite, who did have unusually white teeth; Jim Bowie, who in his youth laundered contraband slaves for Laffite; Lawrence Kearny, who commanded the original *Enterprise* that ultimately drove Laffite from Galveston.

It's unlikely a young Osceola would have been in Jamaica, but in an altered world where the Seminole Confederacy has gained recognition as an actual nation, who knows? The town of escaped slaves and Seminoles called Angola did exist until Florida became a U.S. territory in 1821. It was then destroyed.

Any errors in the book are my own.

Mark Murphy Harms

markmurphyharms@gmail.com

thepeltast.net

Made in United States
North Haven, CT
10 April 2023

35292459R00150